ROMAN GAMES

Sam could smell Paul's body. In all his many sexual fantasies he had overlooked the sense of smell, and now he realised what had been missing. Paul had a sharp tang; it seemed to hit Sam somewhere inside his brain and his cock at the same time. It made him want the man who was standing so close to him more than he had ever wanted anything or anyone before. His prick pushed against the crotch of the overalls, and the cold brass buttons cutting into his cock's flesh lifted his desire and excitement up another notch.

He was still not sure exactly what Paul was going to do to him but, whatever it was, he knew he would wish it had been done many times before.

ROMAN GAMES

Tasker Dean

First published in Great Britain in 1999 by
Idol
an imprint of Virgin Publishing Ltd
Thames Wharf Studios,
Rainville Road, London W6 9HT

ISBN 0 352 33322 7

Cover photograph by Colin Clarke Photography

Typeset by SetSystems Ltd, Saffron Walden, Essex
Printed and bound in Great Britain by
Mackays of Chatham PLC

SAFER SEX GUIDELINES

These books are sexual fantasies – in real life, everyone needs to think about safe sex.

While there have been major advances in the drug treatments for people with HIV and AIDS, there is still no cure for AIDS or a vaccine against HIV. Safe sex is still the only way of being sure of avoiding HIV sexually.

HIV can only be transmitted through blood, come and vaginal fluids (but no other body fluids) passing from one person (with HIV) into another person's bloodstream. It cannot get through healthy, undamaged skin. The only real risk of HIV is through anal sex without a condom – this accounts for almost all HIV transmissions between men.

Being safe
Even if you don't come inside someone, there is still a risk to both partners from blood (tiny cuts in the arse) and pre-come. Using strong condoms and water-based lubricant greatly reduces the risk of HIV. However, condoms can break or slip off, so:
* Make sure that condoms are stored away from hot or damp places.
* Check the expiry date – condoms have a limited life.
* Gently squeeze the air out of the tip.
* Check the condom is put on the right way up and unroll it down the erect cock.
* Use plenty of water-based lubricant (lube), up the arse and on the condom.
* While fucking, check occasionally to see the condom is still in one piece (you could also add more lube).
* When you withdraw, hold the condom tight to your cock as you pull out.

* Never re-use a condom or use the same condom with more than one person.
* If you're not used to condoms you might practise putting them on.
* Sex toys like dildos and plugs are safe. But if you're sharing them use a new condom each time or wash the toys well.

For the safest sex, make sure you use the strongest condoms, such as Durex Ultra Strong, Mates Super Strong, HT Specials and Rubberstuffers packs. Condoms are free in many STD (Sexually Transmitted Disease) clinics (sometimes called GUM clinics) and from many gay bars. It's also essential to use lots of water-based lube such as KY, Wet Stuff, Slik or Liquid Silk. Never use come as a lubricant.

Oral sex
Compared with fucking, sucking someone's cock is far safer. Swallowing come does not necessarily mean that HIV gets absorbed into the bloodstream. While a tiny fraction of cases of HIV infection have been linked to sucking, we know the risk is minimal. But certain factors increase the risk:
* Letting someone come in your mouth
* Throat infections such as gonorrhoea
* If you have cuts, sores or infections in your mouth and throat

So what is safe?
There are so many things you can do which are absolutely safe: wanking each other; rubbing your cocks against one another; kissing, sucking and licking all over the body; rimming – to name but a few.

If you're finding safe sex difficult, call a helpline or speak to someone you feel you can trust for support. The Terrence Higgins Trust Helpline, which is open from noon to 10pm every day, can be reached on 0171 242 1010.

Or, if you're in the United States, you can ring the Center for Disease Control toll free on 1 800 458 5231.

One

———

Sam looked up into the blue sky. A private plane travelled across it, leaving a white trail which quickly blurred. He gazed at the landscape of sharply rising hills and shimmering lakes. Much of the land was barren and wild. There were many places where almost no one ever came. Sam had often made use of this half-abandoned region. The flat red rocks which tumbled around the sides of many of the lakes and the copses of wood and tangled undergrowth, whose thorns protected him from any unwanted intruder, had been well used for his private games.

Sam slowly lowered his hand to the valley that cut deeply into his broad and powerful chest. Automatically he let his hand tangle with the dense dark brown hairs which massed in swirls around his large nipples. He delayed letting his fingers reach his left nipple. He got such a twinge of pleasure every time his finger tips reached that fleshy peak that he deliberately postponed and intensified the delight just by imagining how good it would be. He allowed two of his fingers to make a gentle scissor movement against his nipple. At the very first contact his whole body tensed and he felt himself harden.

Sam felt two distinct trickles of sweat. One travelled down his back to the triangle of hard bone at the top of his arse and the other zigzagged down the front of his supple, tensed upper body, through a triangle of hairs to his rising cock. Every part of him seemed to throb with sex.

He hesitated. In this region, a remote lakeside farming area, there were, officially at least, no gay men. Although the place was full of farmers who lived alone or with their families, there was no openly gay man or couple. Sam had no personal problem about his sexual desire for other men but he had a social anxiety; a fear of being seen as not one of the *real* men who toiled around him in an austere land where there was no room for any form of weakness or difference.

But Sam had discovered two years ago that beneath the surface of macho bonding there was another hot and secret world where men's virile bodies met in tense moments of pure lust.

Sam had been a kind of apprentice at a small engineering factory. One of the younger apprentices, Paul, who was just twenty, had caught his eye. He was lazy and arrogant but that made him all the more attractive to Sam. Boyish blonds were not normally the type of men who featured in Sam's rich fantasy life but Paul was different. He had the long lazy body of a youth who was becoming a man. Beneath the rough cloth of his revealing overalls Sam had caught tantalising glimpses of how Paul's fleshy areas were hardening into the first glistening muscles of early manhood.

Once, as Paul was changing out of his overalls, Sam had caught sight of the almost adolescent curves of his bottom shimmering with its light cover of blond hair. Sam could see, as Paul straightened himself up, that his arse was already developing new muscular contours.

For the first time in his life, Sam desperately wanted to give up his usual caution. He hesitated, feeling his cock stiffen with desire as it rubbed against the coarse cotton of his overalls. They were loose fitting but not loose enough to hide Sam's uncontrollable hardness.

It was the younger man, Paul, who took the initiative. He stopped, midway through pulling his white underpants up his firm thighs. For a few moments he held his seminakedness immobile. At that moment he seemed to be sexy in a way only a body halfway between youth and manhood could be. Sam could sense the wildness of youth and the virility of early manhood fused together in Paul's slim but firm body. Then, slowly, Paul turned towards Sam. He hadn't said much to Sam before that moment and Sam tensed up, half-expecting Paul to accuse him of looking at his young body like a queer would.

For a moment it seemed as if Sam's worst fears were about to come true. Paul looked at Sam with a hard expression and his blue eyes seemed aggressive and cold. But it was soon clear that Paul had a different kind of aggression in mind. His left hand moved up the side of his thigh past the taut elastic of his half-pulled-up Y-fronts to his cock which was thick and large, even before his hands started to caress it.

As Paul's prick grew harder, his large lips formed into a pouting grin.

'What do you like best, Sam?' he asked in a voice which sounded quite different from the voice Sam normally heard on the factory floor. With his free hand, Paul shut the door which led to the main changing room and placed a can of petrol against it so that no one could come in.

Sam, who was always the sex boss in his own fantasies was now, for the first time in his life, no longer in control.

'What do you mean?' he asked Paul.

'Well,' said Paul, 'do you like the front of me or the back of me most?'

As he said that Paul tugged at his cock more until it was now pointed directly at Sam's crotch area. Then Paul slowly turned and showed Sam his arse with its covering of golden hairs which glistened under the neon lights. Paul used one hand to keep caressing his cock and the other to caress the slopes and crack of his young man's arse.

He turned his head over his muscled shoulder blade and now, openly grinning at Sam, repeated his question. 'So what do you like best, my back or my front?'

Sam was surprised to hear himself respond. 'Both.'

Paul continued to caress himself. 'You can't have both. You have to choose,' he said with a teasing grin which revealed the white flash of his teeth.

Sam suddenly knew exactly what he wanted but he still couldn't speak his desires aloud. Paul, who had all the sharpness of a young man hot for pleasure, sensed Sam's hesitation and knew what was needed to pull Sam into the game.

Paul wriggled his body so that slowly his underpants fell from his thighs to the floor. He then went over to Sam and started to undo the brass buttons of Sam's overalls.

'You've been watching me,' whispered Paul. 'But I've been watching you too. And I'm not the only one here who's noticed how sexy your virgin body is. Under the tractors I've sneaked some looks at your big chest and your big nipples covered with hair. I'm not the only one here who's tried to see how big your cock really is and how firm your arse is under your overalls. And how much you like sliding your arse on the steel bars under the machinery when you think no one is looking.'

Paul moved very close to Sam and allowed his penis to swing loose as he concentrated now on caressing his own tight nipples.

'So,' continued Paul, 'I am going to guess what you need me to do to you before you can do anything to me.'

Paul pulled a tin of machine grease towards him and with one hand he moulded the transparent grease into a ball. With the other he started to unbutton's Sam's overalls.

Now Sam could smell Paul's body. In all his many sexual fantasies he had overlooked the sense of smell. He realised now what he had been missing. Paul had a sharp tang. It seemed to hit Sam somewhere inside his brain and his cock at the same time. It made him want the man who was standing so close to him more than he had ever wanted anything or anyone before. Now his prick was pushing against the brass buttons in the crotch area of the overalls. The cold buttons cutting into his cock's flesh lifted his excitement and desire up another notch.

Sam was still not sure what Paul was going to do to him but he guessed that, whatever he was going to do, he was going to wish it had been done to him years before.

Paul didn't disappoint. He pulled open Sam's overalls and somehow that in itself was a wonderful sexual sensation as if for the first time Sam's nipples were entering a world of other men's lips and hands.

Paul caressed Sam's left nipple with his hand and the right nipple with the expertise of his round lips. Sam felt Paul's saliva drip warmly over the rising point of his nipple. It was better than anything he had fancied when, alone with memories of men he had seen and wanted, he had pleasured himself in the intensity of his imagination. Paul's blue eyes fused with Sam's before the cunning youth smiled at him, urging Sam to do what Paul, silently, was commanding him to do.

Sam, in a blur of pleasure, knew what he must do. Unbuttoning and then loosening and lowering his overalls, he revealed the firmness of his cock and his naturally athletic thighs.

As he lubricated Sam's nipples with the dense grease designed to please machines and not men, Paul whispered to him. 'You know Sam, what makes you so special is that you have the body of a well-built hetero guy. You are such a sexy Mr Average Joe that when someone like me realises that you want cock and arse you start making me really hungry to touch every bit of you.'

It was only then that Sam knew what he wanted more than anything else in his repressed and narcissistic life. He wanted something raw and hungry. As his cotton overalls fell down over his firm and hairy legs he knew that he wanted to gently but firmly push his cock between Paul's thighs.

He pulled Paul towards him so that he could feel Paul's big cock rubbing against his own taut stomach. At the same time, Sam could feel his own larger penis thrusting between Paul's inner thighs and reaching, as if on some automated pilot, the outer edge of the wild and dangerous rosebud of Paul's young arse.

Paul groaned as he felt both Sam's unexpectedly commanding cock and also his own suddenly released cockhead pressing against the rim of the crater of Sam's arse. He tried to stop Sam's assault. 'They all want you,' he pleaded. 'You can have almost anyone you want. You are the prize. Don't settle for me.'

But Sam realised at last what Paul really meant when he begged Sam not to thrust his cock into Paul's warm arse. He guessed Paul wanted to feel a prick as big and gentle and reluctant as Sam's driving into him so far and so deep that Paul could imagine that when Sam came inside him, Sam's wave of spunk would crash against the back of Paul's own golden-haired tits. And that Sam's penis, which started as a pupil between Paul's slim thighs, would end up as a master rod of pain and pleasure – thrusting inside against all of Paul's young-man's slopes.

Sam was barely aware of his actions. He had unconsciously turned Paul around and covered the young man's fleshy silk-haired arse with the machine grease and then he had made Paul bend over so that Sam could only see Paul's arse as he thrust not just his cock but every part of his virile body, his thighs, arse, tits and slapping hands, on to the silky crevice of Paul's submissive backside.

Sam recalled triumphantly riding on top of a body full of electric touches and he gladly massaged Paul's surfaces with his large hands, finding himself addicted to doubling the pleasure of every part of the young man's physique. Paul's commands swung wildly from motions of resistance to pleas urging Sam deeper into him.

It was more than an hour later when Paul turned round. The small factory was in darkness but he felt that the cramped room they were in was lit by the sexual charge between them. He wiped the last cool ribbons of Sam's generous spunk load from the pliable slopes of his arse. He looked with a young gay man's mix of shock and gratitude at Sam's powerful hairy body and whispered through his warm lips something that Sam had never expected to hear.

'If I was a woman I would want you twice a night. You only look average but that's much more than an average weapon you've got there.'

For a few minutes Sam admired Paul's nakedness. He could not believe that he had just collided with such a sexy body. Paul flicked his hands against Sam's cock. Sam watched Paul's slightly curving young cock stiffen and flesh out and Paul spoke again in a low and husky voice.

'Sam, you've also got one of the best arses I've ever seen. And I don't think a cock has been up it yet. But that's what it wants. That's what it needs. Please let me be the one to return the compliment you paid up my arse just now.'

Sam didn't know whether he was ready for that yet. He

looked uncertainly at Paul's long, thick cock with its head swelling like a pink ram's head. Suddenly they could both hear someone pressing against the door.

'Who's in there? What's going on?'

What might have been Sam's greatest pleasure was brought to a sudden halt. For almost a year after that encounter, whenever Sam was alone and horny, he would start to imagine what Paul's youthful cock would have given him that day. He often imagined Paul forcing Sam's virgin arse to face Paul's cock and Paul making Sam cover his longing arse with the dense lubricating mass of machine grease as a prelude to the undulating motions of Paul's slightly curving prick.

Sam started this sexual fantasy again. He had almost reached down beyond his hairy navel to grasp the stiffening warmth of his penis when a voice jolted him out of his favourite afternoon fantasy.

'See that?'

The voice near him was unwanted and Sam had to hide his erection by grabbing an oil cloth from the tractor and pretending to wipe a spring with it.

John Marks, his forty-year-old supervisor, nodded in the direction of the plane in the sky. 'That's Denton's plane.'

Sam didn't understand for a moment.

John came over to him and gave a mildly contemptuous laugh. 'Your young lord and master. Denton James, the Lord of Skate.'

Sam wondered why John always had to lecture and boss him. The other two mechanics he hardly ever spoke to.

'You're a typical lake man, Sam. A bit slow.'

John had been the local middleweight boxing champion and his square face with its battered nose was standard boxer look. As thick and boxerish, thought Sam, as his wide and powerful torso which stretched the blue overalls he habitually wore to their limits.

John inspected the tractor Sam had been working on. 'You've got to get inside the rim to get it right,' he declared aggressively. 'The trouble with you, Sam, is that you think those delicate fingers of yours will always find the trouble spots. With a BMW maybe, but with a tractor never.'

He snatched the oil cloth from Sam. Fortunately Sam's cock was now only just stiff. He felt safe although he thought John looked too quickly down at his crotch area when he snatched the cloth from him.

Sam seriously wondered for the first time if John, despite being divorced and swaggeringly macho, ever had the same feelings which Sam sometimes, against his own will, had about John. Sometimes when he had to support John as he climbed up one of the bigger tractors, Sam felt an unwanted tingle of lust as John's sturdy frame rubbed against his softer, younger body. Sam tried not to think about those moments.

John looked into Sam's blue eyes. 'I sometimes wonder what goes on behind those eyes. There are some secrets there. I can tell.'

For a few oddly tense seconds Sam's blue eyes and John's deep black eyes were locked together. Sam broke away first and John smiled as if he had knocked out some opponent in the ring.

Sam tried to distract John. 'Have you ever met him?' He gestured at the plane which was now quickly descending to the private runway a few miles off.

John gave a strange laugh. He looked suspiciously at Sam and adjusted a few screws on the tractor before answering. 'Yeah, a few times. More than most people. The Lord of Skate is what they call a recluse. He doesn't like seeing anyone if he can help it. I've driven for him sometimes when Bill the regular chauffeur is on holiday. When he is on Skate all the people who work there leave the big house by six. They come back from the island by boat. The only person he has there with him then is some bloke from Turkey.'

Sam was instantly intrigued. He wondered why he'd never asked any questions about his employer before.

The island of Skate was in the middle of the largest lake in the region and Sam's cottage overlooked the island and parts of the big house on it. Some of Sam's best games with his body had been played in sight of that island. Without thinking Sam started to caress his chest in broad circular motions as he watched the plane land. The rhythmic caressing, under his overalls, made him feel intensely satisfied.

'Stop doing that!' snapped John. 'Only girls do that.' He turned away abruptly and walked back into the main machine repair building.

Sam was too startled and embarrassed to say anything. He knew he had to be careful with John. John seemed too keen to know everything about Sam's life in and out of the workshop. Sam knew that whatever was allowed in London, in the lake area he would be taking a huge risk to reveal his true nature.

From an early age Sam had known that it was the male body he was drawn to, like a moth to a flame. He had tried very hard to resist the magnetic pull he felt towards certain types of men he saw in the streets, on the boats and in the pubs. He was sure that none of the men he so casually and randomly wanted would be as good as his perfect man would be. He had to save his warm youth for the right man, the perfect moment. Sam sensed that if he let himself go he might easily become addicted to sex with many men and so he held himself back from any contact, despite the intensity and frequency of his desire.

Sam knew that being a champion swimmer for the lakes had been a perfect alibi for his bachelor lifestyle. Swimmers were well known here for being fanatical about channelling all their energies into their sport. So Sam tried to put at least some of his sex feelings into swimming, running, work and repairing the cottage he had inherited.

He didn't feel his occasional longings for men were bad but he wasn't sure that the gay men in the lake area would be prepared to do the kind of things he thought he wanted them to do. Paul had assured him that he was wrong about that and had told him that at least three of the most macho men in the village where they worked had let him do things to them that Sam hadn't even imagined in his best wanking sessions. Sam remembered again what Paul had said to him before he had left the region himself.

'You have all the makings of a great lover. All you need is the right kind of teachers. I was the first but I know I won't be the last.'

Paul had explained to Sam that it was the very masculine

ordinariness of Sam's body – his deep voice, easy grin and sporting skills – which made him especially sexy for men who wanted sex with other men.

'You're Mr Regular and that's what makes you such a turn-on. I've seen you in your swimming trunks and you look as if your cock would never do anything naughty. What a false impression that is! But for men like me it's a great turn-on. Is he or isn't he? Will he or won't he?'

Paul had been able to have only a few brief sessions with Sam before he moved away. As he told Sam: 'We never got round to the big one. Pity.'

Since Paul had left, Sam had had sex only with himself. Once or twice, especially when he was swimming, he had seen men's eyes sometimes linger a bit too long on his broad swimmer's chest and the teasing combination of his narrow waist and rock-hard arse tightly held by his red trunks. But, although Sam felt a strong attraction to some of the men who looked at him in that way, he held back. It was partly out of social caution and partly because he wanted his first big sexual experience to be something very special and intense. He wanted his body and mind to be blown away.

But sometimes, as had happened today, some thing, some word, some smell, some sight perhaps of a man with a naturally muscular body digging roads, triggered inside him a violent outbreak of desire. Then he knew as soon as he had clocked off that he would have to drive quickly back to his cottage and lock himself into a wild storm of sex with himself. Sam had come to regard these sex sessions as healthy preparations for the day when, by chance, he would meet the right man. The sex fulfiller.

Today he had been aroused by the sight of a dark young man stripped to the waist, delivering oil to the machine repair workshop. Sam took in the firm natural muscles of the man's shoulders and he sneaked a glance at the man's chest, youthfully strong, over which the first down of black hair had appeared. He imagined how equally sexy his lower body would be, although he was so tightly squeezed into his jeans that Sam didn't need much imagination to guess at his vital statistics.

The young man had a typical lakeland face, weathered but

handsome, and he gave Sam a lazy grin as he asked him to sign for the delivery. Sam felt the heat of the young man's body as he turned away from him to allow Sam to sign the docket on his broad shoulders. Sam allowed his hand to rest for a moment on the other's silky skin. A tremor of wanting passed through Sam's own body. He quickly broke his contact and turned away from temptation. After that encounter it was almost a physical agony for him to have to hold himself back until five o'clock.

He entered the main room of his cottage. It contained only two battered armchairs and a wooden bench that was placed against a low window. Through it Sam could see the familiar overgrown garden which led down to the lake. In the distance he could see the small island of Skate. It was bare except for a small, dense wood and a solid stone manor house.

Sam went into the back bedroom. He opened the wardrobe door to reveal a full-length mirror. He stood in front of this and pulled his shirt off over his head. He loved the touch of the rough cotton against his chest. He looked at his long muscular torso in the mirror as he had done so many times before. Dark brown hair emphasised the firm division of his chest into two distinct halves, each having his large fleshy nipples as their natural centre. In one 'quickie' session with Paul, the younger man had just wanted to suck hard on Sam's nipples while he furiously wanked himself off, forcing Sam to plunge his hand into Paul's overalls and smear Paul's stomach with the sticky pool of his spunk.

Paul had taught Sam what a sexual turn-on Sam's large and pointed nipples could be for certain men, and that made them seem sexier now to Sam also as he gazed at them in the mirror. A line of brown body hair, now turning coppery in the light of the late afternoon sunlight, ran down to his navel which he gently circled with one of his fingers.

He pulled down his jeans and watched his thighs and calves emerge, also encased now in a sun blur of hair. He tantalised himself by putting his hands inside the front of his tight Y-fronts and stroking the dense mass of hair above his cock which was stiffening again as he gazed at his sinuous body burnished by the sun.

He pulled down his Y-fronts, turning as he did so. This let him see both the hard chiselled shape of his arse with its deep dimples and his swelling cock which was now rising so fast that it stuck out far ahead of his flat stomach and hairy thighs. He resisted the temptation to simply grab his prick and jerk on it, giving himself instant satisfaction. Instead he pulled down his Y-fronts and lumbered into the bathroom, unchanged for forty years. From a flaking wooden cupboard he took a stone jar of machine oil. His experiences with Paul had made him find machine oil the sexiest lubricant of all.

He tipped the jar gently towards the deep cleft in his chest and allowed a few drops to trickle down through that private valley, down over his hard, tensed stomach and then slide through his navel to the stem of his cock where the liquid parted and seeped over both of his heavy balls.

He poured a few drops of the oil on to both his nipples where the liquid fell with explosive force making his whole upper torso stretch back towards the ceramic bath. He then poured another thin trickle of the oil down between his well-defined shoulder blades. As always, he loved the way the liquid shot down his spine towards the hairy triangle of bone at the top of his crack. Again the liquid parted and he could feel it travel more slowly over both of his buttocks where two lines of hair delayed its progress towards the back of his thighs. The oil smelt to him of pure man-sex.

Sam moved quickly into the main room now burning scarlet with the setting sun and stretched himself along the wooden bench. Even flat out he could see the island of Skate and the wind-lashed waters of the lake churning around it.

He felt his cock was begging him to grab it but he remembered that pleasure delayed was pleasure increased. So, instead he caressed his chest again in broad swirling motions making his hands and sensitive fingers get closer and closer to his rigid nipples. Finally he grabbed firmly hold of both nipples and squeezed them hard and brutally. As he did so he conjured up his current favourite fantasy. It was based on Dino, an Italian swimmer he'd shared a shower cubicle with in the swimming competition last year.

Sam visualised Dino again. He had the compact size and understated muscularity of a swimmer. He had a good playful Italian face and nose with hazel eyes and a sexy smile. His upper body had a precise T-shape of coarse black hair on it and his stocky legs supported what Sam guessed, before he even glimpsed them, was a hairy arse and a large teasing penis.

Dino was in the room with him now wearing his patriotic green, red and white swimming trunks. Dino had been macho and very nationalistic. But now in the room with Sam he looked provocatively at Sam's gaze and watched intently as Sam's larger naked body moved towards him. He was giving Sam the come-on with half-closed eyes, dense with desire. He wanted hot sex.

Sam allowed his erect cockhead to brush lightly against Dino's belly and the thick line of hair above it. Dino's entire compact body shuddered repeatedly. Sam put his hands on Dino's hips touching the taut silkiness of Dino's swimming trunks.

Dino leant forward and pressed the tip of his tongue to Sam's left nipple. Sam felt a quake of lust at the wet, delicate caress of Dino's tongue. He saw Dino's cock struggling against its owner's restricting trunks and, lowering his hands, Sam started to pull Dino's trunks down. In the mirror behind them Sam could see Dino's young arse appear and the head of Dino's cock emerged above the line of his trunks. Breaking free of Dino's tongue, Sam bent down, brushing his hair against the Italian's dark torso and gently taking his cock in his mouth. It tasted of bitter honey and filled Sam's mouth like a dome.

Dino groaned. 'I'm going to come deeper and deeper down your throat. I'm going to fill you with my cockhead and stem. Can you feel me going to go all the way down you? I'm going to make my cock go down your throat until it feels as though it's at the top of your arse.'

Sam sucked on the head and stem of Dino so vigorously that it felt as if he were sucking Dino's spunk out of him. Suddenly Dino whispered something in Italian and Sam, guessing what it was, quickly pulled Dino's trunks down until they were held tautly halfway down his thighs.

Sam turned Dino round so that Dino's dark, well-defined body and throbbing cock were revealed to both of them in the mirror. At the same time Sam, wrapping his arms tightly around Dino's torso, pulled Dino's arse towards his cock. Gently at first he rubbed his hard penis against Dino's crack. Dino arched his head back so that Sam could press his mouth against the Italian's waiting lips. Sam felt Dino's tongue again, this time electrifying him with the circling of tongue around tongue.

Sam's cock was now rigid and insistent. Dino whispered in English this time. 'Ride up me. Ride up me.'

Sam excited Dino even more by slowly sheathing his cock in taut rubber which gave the stem of his cock a silky shell to his hungry hardness. Then he eased his throbbing cock up the silky textured ridges inside Dino. He saw Dino in the mirror groaning and pushing his own sturdy prick through the funnel of his clenched hands.

Sam reached for some oil and poured it first down Dino's arching torso then down the narrow space between his own stomach and Dino's back. He felt the oil trickling into Dino, who was now rhythmically pulling Sam's cock deeper and higher into him.

'Lift your cock right up inside me. Ride it up me. Higher. Higher,' he moaned.

Sam felt his cock growing larger and larger inside Dino. He was giving the young Italian something he had always wanted and imagined but had never dared have before. Dino's eyes were now dazed with pleasure and his upper body was arched back over Sam's broad shoulders.

Sam could feel every part of his own body, his cock, his dimpled arse, his sunlight-dappled torso and his thighs, crashing against Dino's. He knew that Dino was aware of every inch of Sam too as he felt all Dino's hairy surfaces shaking with Sam's possession of him.

He squeezed Dino's small but erect nipples ever harder as he felt his cock press higher and higher inside him. Dino had now stopped speaking and was only groaning as wave after wave of pleasure soared through him.

'You never knew how good this could be, did you?' whispered Sam before he kissed Dino's full lips again. The bitter honey taste of the other man gave a final boost to Sam's desire to possess and liberate the sturdy body. Almost losing control of himself, Sam lifted Dino off the floor with his last compulsive climax.

Dino slumped lifelessly against Sam's larger, masterful body while Sam, still dazed, contented himself with coming down by rubbing his come-soaked hands over the compact hairy chest of the Italian who, he knew, he had taken to paradise and back.

As Sam felt the gluey liquid of his pleasure harden on his torso and thighs, the image of Dino faded and Sam found himself looking at his own sweat-soaked face and come-drenched body in the wall mirror. He turned his satisfied nakedness towards the sea and the island of Skate. He was startled by what he thought was a flash of light coming from one of the upper windows of the manor house. He looked again and saw only the blank shine of the windows. He guessed he must have seen some last reflected ray of sunlight.

He slumped his young body in an armchair. The setting sun was now making all the clouds on the horizon look like tongues of fire. He wondered why in his fantasies he habitually played the part of the 'liberator' and 'possessor' of another man. Yet in real life, when he was attracted to another man, it was he who wanted to be liberated and possessed. What did he really want sexually? Could he really know that just by fantasising?

He looked at the cracked oil painting on the wall. It showed slaves being whipped by Egyptian overseers. Even their coarse naked bodies excited him sometimes. But on this island he just couldn't risk acting out his sexual dreams. In reality he had only snatched a few furtive glances at the real Dino and when, once, the real Dino had let his lovely hazel eyes rest on Sam's, it had been Sam who had broken away and pretended not to see, not to understand.

Would he ever engage in real sex again and what would he

actually want to do to others and have others do to him? He knew Paul had not taught him everything. He'd left too soon. Much too soon. For a second he smelt Paul's tang again; it always turned him on. Sam was convinced that he had to wait for the man who would be his sexual equal and then he would find out what he was truly missing.

He washed the sex and sweat off himself and carefully placed the stone jar of oil back in the old cupboard. It was time to prepare himself for a 'normal' night of beer drinking with his workmates.

John's raw and battered boxer's face was already red with drink when Sam sprung lightly into the pub. Ralph, the other young mechanic in the estate's machine repair shop, looked with relief at his friend's entrance.

John gave Sam a caustic gaze. 'What have you been doing that's made you so late?'

Sam bought them both beers before answering. 'I didn't think you needed to clock in for the pub,' he replied aggressively.

John seemed to be giving off a sexual predatory aura tonight. His open shirt revealed an unruly mat of black hair which reached right up to his thick neck. The man's big fists clenched round the glass of beer.

Sam deliberately held John's look. He half suspected that the older man could somehow sense what Sam had been doing to his body just a few minutes before. Part of Sam wanted John to know. He wanted to know how John would react. But caution pulled him back and he talked to Ralph, a fresh-faced blond man in his mid-twenties. Although he was a little older than Sam was, Sam thought of him as younger. Perhaps it was because Ralph was so open and simple. He had a pretty wife and a nice kid. He liked Sam and the two men worked well together although they had no deep contact.

All the while Sam was talking to Ralph, he was aware of John's eyes watching him as if waiting for Sam's mask to slip. Ralph was praising Sam's performance in the last swimming competition. For an instant Dino's compact body and what he had done to it in his imagination flashed before Sam's eyes. The next time Dino would feature in his fantasy, Dino would be more resistant to Sam's advances. They would struggle. Sam might have to bind Dino's hands together to give Dino an excuse for allowing himself to be so totally possessed by Sam. As if on cue John suddenly interrupted Ralph and in an aggressive tone addressed Sam.

'Yeah, you seem very popular with all the men swimmers. But you don't seem very interested in the women ones.'

'I'm not in competition with them,' replied Sam defensively.

John gave Sam a cunning look. 'Do you remember that Italian one? What was his name?'

'I don't remember,' lied Sam.

'He was very good-looking, if a bit small,' continued John watching Sam's reactions closely. Sam pretended that he was uninterested.

'Dino was his name,' said Ralph. 'He was a great swimmer. And the girls loved him. My Kate wanted me to introduce her. I said hell would freeze over first.'

John ignored Ralph. 'I meant his body was small,' continued John. And then in a half-whisper which was aimed at Sam he added, 'Everything else about him was very big.'

John's harsh black eyes tried to engage Sam's but Sam refused to look at him. Ralph started to chat again about Sam's talent for diving. Sam wondered what Ralph would think of him if he knew what he really wanted to do with some of his fellow male swimmers.

John suddenly took hold of Sam's wrist. It was almost like an electric contact. Sam could feel the brute force of John's hands and through them he could feel the force of John's solid punished body. He reeked of masculinity and yet Sam could no longer ignore the fact that John seemed drawn obsessively to him.

'My turn,' said John giving Sam's wrist a slow burn with his hands.

Sam fought against a purely chemical sexual excitement he felt in the older man's grip. He turned his lithe body slightly towards the wooden bar to hide his stiffening cock. He hated the man and yet was drawn to him. It was as if one of his sex fantasies had been taken over by someone else.

Ralph noticed nothing and Sam knew that both he and John were communicating with one another at a level Ralph would never sense. Ralph stood between them talking and smiling. But the two other men knew he was only a buffer between them. Sam could now smell John's distinctive body odour. It both repelled and titillated him. It had a strange foxy quality.

By the fourth pint John's eyes and face seemed more attractive to Sam. He saw underneath the squashed boxer's nose and the weary eyes how appealing John must have looked when he was the same age as Sam was now. And gradually, through the drifting words and cigarette smoke, Sam found a sexual potency in John's battle-torn and knowing face. He knew about boxing and giving pain but Sam also thought that he would know about rough sex and the taking and giving of pleasure.

Sam had just started to imagine what John's thick square body would look like naked when the call came for last orders. Ralph insisted on a final pint and, while he was ordering, John leaned across him and spoke to Sam.

'I have to go to Skate island to repair the generator. Do you want to come?'

Sam hesitated. He had an intuition that the invitation meant something more than fixing generators. Could this be his chance to actually possess and be possessed by another man, to really walk in the earthly paradise garden and to wake up with another body? Another act of flesh instead of illusions in a broken mirror.

Sam nodded back at John as if afraid that Ralph would see his agreement and understand its true meaning. John's black eyes flashed triumphantly and he pressed his two fists together.

'Good,' said John with a harsh laugh. 'You need the experience.'

Ralph handed them their last beers. 'Denton and that Turkish bloke. That's a strange pair,' declared the young blond innocently. 'Why import a Turk when there are a lot of willing blokes on the islands who need a good job? And it's odd to lock yourself away with someone who comes from such a foreign place.'

'What do you mean lock himself away?' asked Sam.

'Well there's no one else on that island most of the time.

That's strange. And there are no girlfriends or women ever seen there . . . except the cleaners.'

John gave Sam a long silent stare.

John dropped Ralph off home first then drove on to Sam's more remote cottage. His foxy body odour seemed to fill the Land Rover's interior. It was suffocatingly strong and Sam wound the window down. There was an almost full moon shining brightly in the star-dotted sky.

John drew to a stop at the top of the path that led down to Sam's cottage and the two men sat in silence for a few moments.

'You've got to fight for what you really want,' said John in a tone of voice Sam had never heard before.

Sam said, 'It's always been easy for me.'

'Then we should start to make it harder shouldn't we?'

Sam was now more keenly aware than ever that John was dangerously sexy; his punished body seemed more tempting than it had ever seemed before.

John pointed to Skate Island. 'That's an island that's very different for certain special people.'

'What do you mean?' asked Sam.

'You'll find out if you really want to,' replied John. 'They do things the Roman way there,' he added.

Sam said goodnight and got out of the car. He started to walk down his path when he was suddenly aware of that foxy aroma behind him. He did not turn round until he felt powerful arms grab him and turn him round. He smelt John's lips before he tasted them and felt John's rough skin rasp against his younger yielding flesh. He felt the solid torso of the other pressing against him and his whole body ignited with desire. He wanted John to force himself on him, to compel him to do whatever the older man wanted. His whole body shook with the urgency of this strange new desire to be squeezed between John's arms which Sam knew were well used to grappling with boxers. Now he wanted to be grappled with and there came into his mind the vividest image of what he would like John to do to him. He imagined John's thick vibrating cock between the rocks of his thighs.

Then suddenly John was gone. The Land Rover drove off

leaving only a fading foxy scent lingering in the moonlit air. Sam felt his body shudder and tremble and he might have thought it had been just another of his fantasies except for the rough feeling that still lingered on his lips and the burn on his shoulders where John had held him in a bear hug.

He undid his shirt to let the night air cool him down. He looked towards the Island of Skate and wondered what John's hints about the island meant. The Lord of Skate and the Turk.

Two

_____

The motorboat cut through the green waves. Even with the breeze the day was hot, especially since both John and Sam were wearing their thick mechanic's overalls. A large metal case containing tools sat in the centre of the boat.

As John bent down to make some adjustment to the outboard motor, Sam glimpsed part of John's solid chest through his unbuttoned overalls. It was covered with a thick mass of black hairs and was the body of a man who could still pack a dangerous punch. As he stretched down Sam could see how thick his thighs were. For a second or two Sam found himself wondering what it would be like to have such a physique pressing against him, pressing down on him. He glanced away, afraid to allow his attraction to show itself in any obvious physical way. John had not spoken about what had passed between them three days ago and, even in the workshop, he had only addressed a few curt words to Sam.

The spray made by the boat lashed across Sam's boyish face. He longed to strip off his clothes and plunge into the lake and feel the water course over every curve of his lean and well-honed body. It was when he was swimming in the sea that Sam often felt most sexy. Sometimes when his long arms were cutting into the water ahead of him and his buttocks were rising and falling, thrusting his entire body forward, his cock would stiffen so that every time his lower body plunged back into the water it would smack against the watery surface as if he were fucking the ocean.

The only safe way of approaching the island was from the eastern part which was on the opposite side of the island to the manor house. The boat pulled in against a small jetty and Sam nimbly jumped off and secured the ropes to the jetty's iron stake. Nearby there was a boat house where they found a wooden trolley. John and Sam carried the metal box of tools to the trolley and John ordered Sam to pull it along a path that led through the woods that faced them above the empty beach.

'Is the house far?' asked Sam.

'Far from anything you've known,' answered John, a sly smile crossing the broken features of his face.

The wood consisted mainly of conifer trees packed densely together and soon the lake completely disappeared from view. Although it was a bright day it became darker the deeper they travelled into the wood.

'Come on lad, harder,' shouted John and gave Sam an unexpected slap on his backside.

Sam felt the blow travel through his entire body. It was a new sensation, one he had not felt before, and he was surprised to realise that he would like to feel it again.

Sam was very aware of John's foxy body smell and his stocky figure behind him. He half wanted John to grab him from behind as he had done before and bear hug him, pressing him against the commanding firmness of his boxer's physique. Perhaps John would rip open his overalls and caress his torso with one firm hand. Maybe he would lower his other hand down the silky line of Sam's body hair over his navel and down towards his rising cock.

Sam felt an erection rising at these thoughts. But John attempted nothing.

Just then they came to a clearing in the wood in the middle of which stood a life-size sculpture depicting two Roman wrestlers. The older, bearded wrestler had the younger wrestler in a fierce hold and had forced the younger wrestler to his knees.

The older wrestler's body was pressing hard against the younger man's back and his bearded face reared above the younger man's defiant yet almost defeated face.

John looked for a long time at the statue and said nothing. He looked for a few moments at Sam. 'What do you think?' he asked in a low voice.

'I've never done any wrestling,' said Sam glancing across at John. Their eyes met. John's seemed to be glowing and teasing.

'I used to wrestle as well as box,' replied John. He casually put his hand inside his overalls and started to caress one side of his chest. 'It's not like swimming. In wrestling both men have to want to completely and totally dominate the other. In real wrestling like these two blokes are doing only one man can end up on top and in control.'

As John said this he continued to caress his chest and undid two more of his overall buttons revealing a portion of his hairy upper stomach. His black eyes were once again fixed on Sam.

Sam could feel his body tingle with mounting excitement and he felt his arse tighten and the curving dimples he had there deepen. John started to undo more of his buttons until Sam could clearly see his large navel around which swirled patterns of black curly hairs. Then, just as Sam felt his cock stiffen, John started to do up his buttons again. Soon only his thick neck was exposed.

John smiled at Sam. 'What you have to wait for you appreciate more,' he announced. He looked down at Sam's crotch where the outline of his cock could clearly be seen stiffening against the taut material. 'And it looks to me as if you might be full of the right kind of appreciation.'

He went over to Sam and roughly grabbed the younger man's cock, cupping his balls with a fierce grip that sent shudders of pain and pleasure through Sam's young flesh. He pushed his face close to Sam's. 'You don't know what you want yet but you are going to get it. Be patient. It will be better than you ever imagined.' He brushed his broken nose against Sam's. 'You can't imagine the pleasure you are going to feel from bodies that know what you need.'

John broke away from him and he gestured to Sam to pick up

the metal box of tools. They continued walking through the wood.

Sam felt dazed. John's words had aroused him to such a pitch that he was almost tempted to unbutton his overalls and grasp his cock. He wanted to rub his foreskin over his cockhead faster and faster until his warm spunk splattered over the dark orange tree trunks which now looked to him like the stems of giants' penises.

Without any warning the wood came to an end and directly ahead was the sturdy square of the island's manor house, saving Sam from his temptations. The house was a mass of slate-grey stone except for a cream-coloured portico flanked by Greek-style pillars. There were four windows at each side of the portico on three floors and Sam realised how big the house was. From the mainland it had seemed smaller. Closed wooden shutters pressed against every window as if the house was waiting to withstand some attack.

'We don't enter by the main door,' explained John and led Sam round to one side of the house where a massive wooden back door was hidden. He rang a brass bell.

As they waited for the door to open, he turned back to Sam. He put his hand inside his clothing and started to play with the rounded slopes of his chest again.

'Do you know what I'm thinking?'

Sam shook his head.

'I'm thinking what I could do to you. How I could make you really happy.'

Sam frowned. 'I'll decide what I want.'

John gave him a sex-soaked grin. 'Maybe. And maybe not.'

The door opened and John stood to one side so that Sam would have an uninterrupted view of whoever was about to appear. In the darkness Sam could make out the shape of a very tall and muscular man, so brown that he would have been almost invisible if he hadn't been wearing a white T-shirt. The man had extremely broad shoulders and a steel-hard chest. His torso tapered to his lower stomach where his muscles protruded in geometric shapes through the crisp white cotton. His waist was slim and below that he filled out again with massive thighs. He was over six feet tall.

He stepped out into the sunlight so that his face was visible for the first time. Sam was shocked at his physical beauty. His skin was olive coloured, smooth and silky. He combined that Eastern colouring with a face that could have come straight off one of the statues of the young Roman wrestlers Sam had just seen. His eyes looked pitch-black but were subtly flecked with dashes of brown. He smiled warmly at Sam, revealing dazzling white teeth.

'You must be hot in those clothes,' the man said in a voice so deep that Sam felt it almost vibrate inside him.

'We're all very hot,' declared John. 'Sam, this is Arif. He runs this house for the Lord of Skate.'

'Leave the tools there. I'll take you to the generator in a minute. Come and have a beer first.'

They went down a long dark corridor to a huge kitchen dominated by a wooden table that could seat twenty people and a stove which looked as if it could cook for the same number.

Arif went to the refrigerator and took out some jugs of beer. As he did so, Sam found himself unable to draw his eyes away from his bottom. It was very firm but also broad and inviting. Sam felt drops of sweat fall from his chin on to his chest hair which was showing through his mechanic's clothes.

Arif poured out the beer and Sam could feel him glancing at his chest through the loose-fitting overalls. It pleased him to know that Arif was admiring his slim, firm body with its down of burnished body hair.

'How is the boss?' asked John.

Arif grinned back at Sam. His teeth gleamed like snow against the smooth perfection of his olive-coloured skin. Arif's eyes caught Sam's and Sam felt dazzled by the light which seemed to shine from them. As Arif explained the problem with the generator, Sam was aware of his distinctive aroma. It was a musky coffee smell. Of all the smells of other men's bodies which had excited him before none had made him tremble like he was trembling now. Sam clenched his chilled tankard of beer to try to cool his body down.

Sam looked at Arif's classic profile and guessed that he was in his late twenties. His body showed that he was at the peak of his physical prowess. Sam hoped he would get the chance to let Arif see how his own body, although less big and less densely muscular than Arif's, was also in perfect condition; a taut and lean swimmer's physique. Sam could see himself diving into the sea with Arif diving after him. Gaining on him. Grabbing Sam's legs and subduing them, pulling Sam's body towards his. Sam wondered if Arif's cock was as large as the rest of him. Sam imagined sliding his body in the sea under Arif's and pressing his cock against Arif's. Suspended in the waves both men's cocks would grow hard against each other's.

Before he got too excited, John ordered Sam to the outhouse where the broken generator was kept. Sam tried to stop thinking about sex altogether and, under John's instructions, threw himself into the complicated repair job they had to carry out before sunset. They were working in a stone building with only one small window so they used oil lamps and torches for light. They worked hard and soon Sam could smell his own sweat and John's. But he did not want to undo his overall because he knew that if he stripped to the waist he would not be able to control his sex fantasies. And maybe he would not be able to stop John from taking him.

Sam suspected that a naked John would reveal a square mass of hairy chest. Sam wasn't sure that he would be able to resist grabbing the other man and forcing him to take his cock in his mouth, sucking his gluey spunk out of it.

'There'll be no light tonight either,' said John blocking Sam's thoughts. 'This is going to take at least another six hours. We'd better warn Arif.'

The two men stepped out into the late afternoon sunlight. The lake was navy blue. They walked through an apple orchard back to the house and Sam noticed some wooden bee hives dotted amongst the trees.

John saw where he was looking. 'They could do wicked things to a man's naked arse.'

Sam gave him a puzzled look but John didn't offer to explain his remark. 'I could do with a shower. Do you think there's any hot water?' he asked.

John grabbed Sam by his shoulder. 'Don't shower here until you're ordered to.'

'What do you mean?'

John stopped Sam and looked hard into his eyes.

'You are going to find out. Nothing bad is going to happen to you unless you think it's bad to get what you have really wanted all your life.' John nuzzled himself against Sam's chest. 'Don't wash your sweat off yet. They like a young man's sweat on this island. It's treated like a local delicacy.'

Arif took the news about the generator with a wry grin. 'Well we have a thousand and one candles,' he said winking at Sam.

Sam felt so attracted to Arif that every word he said to him seemed sexually provocative. Sam leant his body against the warmth of the Aga cooker. He remembered that Paul, in one of their quickie sessions at the tractor factory, had once rubbed his hands in the sweat from under Sam's arms and then rubbed that sweat around his blond balls. Sam had followed this up by rubbing his hands in the sweat of Paul's armpits and then rubbing it around his own large nipples. The sight of him doing that made Paul's curved cock shoot right up and force itself between Sam's thighs. Sam had then clenched his thighs together, squeezing Paul's cock and holding it immobile while Sam had complete freedom to thrust his stiff member against Paul's deep navel. Sam remembered how much he had enjoyed the sensation of coming and pouring all his spunk into the blond crater of that belly while at the same time Paul had come between Sam's thighs and his hot young spunk had trickled down his legs.

Sam's reverie was interrupted by Arif. 'I think Denton would like to say hello to you both.'

Sam thought he detected a hint of a laugh in Arif's low seductive voice.

'How is the Lord of Skate?' asked John.

Sam watched the way John's black eyes and the blackish brown eyes of Arif played with one another as they spoke. Sam sensed the sexual tension between their two very different but equally virile and powerful bodies. Sam had never doubted his own virility, his own pure masculine sexiness, but he had never before been in a room with two men who seemed to him to reek of so much more sexual knowledge.

Suddenly Paul seemed very much like a prelude to something much closer to what Sam really needed. He was ready to be taught more now. And being on the island had the effect of making him feel far less cautious than on the mainland. It was as if the island had an atmosphere all its own. Sam sensed that different rules applied here. Here desires like his didn't have to be disguised and kept in small secret places. He was sure that here desires like his could be out in the open. Everything about the island felt sexy.

'The Lord,' Arif replied to John's question with a flash of his teeth, 'has been practising some of the moves you taught him.'

John again put his hand inside his overalls and Sam could see how his hand was moving down from his chest towards his hairy stomach and navel. It seemed as if John had to touch himself now in some of the sexiest parts of his solid, experienced body. As if he was recalling some deep, deep pleasure.

'Good to hear it,' commented John. 'I think he could be a natural, a champion.'

Arif crossed his powerful and muscular arms over the broad expanse of his chest. Sam imagined the handsome Turk's arm muscles rubbing against his chest and the yielding softness and expectancy of his nipples. Sam wondered whether they were the centre of as many sensations as his own, and if they were as big. As Paul used to tell him, 'I can come just thinking about your swimmer's chest and those giant nipples. Squeeze my arse between them again.'

Arif glanced at Sam who immediately cut off his memories of Paul. Sam felt certain that the other man was guessing at the contours of his body under his stained work clothes.

A phone on the wall started ringing and Arif answered it immediately. 'Yes. I think so,' was all he said. 'The Lord of Skate would like to meet you Sam.'

Arif's pronouncement was deep and measured; his voice felt simultaneously like a command and a caress. Sam saw John and Arif exchange knowing glances and, catching a reflection of himself in the kitchen window, asked, 'Shouldn't I clean myself up?' He had machine grease smeared across the top of his overalls and a slash of grease diagonally crossing his face.

Arif shook his head. 'Oh no. Not at all,' he replied. 'You are just right the way you are.'

Sam felt Arif's bright eyes on him again. To avoid Arif noticing his puppy-dog admiration Sam looked down to Arif's mouth. His lips curved a bit too perfectly for Sam's taste. They were lighter than the rest of his skin and seemed now voluptuous and moist.

'Come on, my Sam,' said Arif spreading out his arms in a gesture of welcome. 'Follow me. He is waiting for you.'

John and Arif led Sam through a series of corridors that got wider and grander as they moved through them. Sam couldn't help but notice the shape of the arses of the two men in front of him. John's arse was the typical arse of a middleweight boxer, square, solid, an arse you could grapple with. Arif's was quite different. Although he was a very tall and broad man, almost a giant, his buttocks seemed bigger and more prominent than even his unusual size would have suggested. His bottom flowed out from the base of his muscled back like a shelf of hard, promising flesh. It was as precisely muscled as the rest of him. Sam could see that through the tightly clinging jeans which also revealed Arif's confident swaying walk. Sam had heard that Turks were very sophisticated lovers, coming from a civilisation where male sensuality was encouraged and not repressed.

Sam was stimulated by that thought. He tried to imagine how the two men's cocks differed too. Sam guessed that John's would be squat and bullying, Arif's long and seductive. His penis would be like his voice, a command and a caress. A long deep caress. Sam wondered if the two men had done it together and, if so, who had done exactly what. He started to conjure up a few possibilities but all of them made it difficult for him to keep his cock from rising again.

They were now walking down a wide corridor towards tall double doors. In the four niches in the corridor were life-size statues of Roman emperors. It occured to Sam that there was a touch of the Roman about Arif's own face, although it was softer and more sensual as if honey had poured over the classically square features. Arif opened the tall doors and gestured for Sam and John to go in. The room was so full of the setting sun shining directly in their faces that for a few moments Sam couldn't make out anything very clearly. As his eyes adjusted he was aware of a vast clay model of some very old city which covered what he guessed had once been a billiard table. He recognised the round arena of the Roman Colosseum and he knew the clay model city laid out in intricate detail in front of him was ancient Rome.

But what held his eye even more than the superb model was the very Roman figure of the man who was standing at the far end of the model and who now nodded a greeting at them. Denton, Lord of Skate, Sam guessed, was in his late twenties and to Sam he looked almost identical to some of the sterner faces he had just walked by. His face was almost too handsome to be attractive to Sam. It was almost too perfect with piercing blue eyes and dark blond hair that tightly curled over his forehead. His blue denim shirt and jeans revealed an athletic physique with unusually big shoulders. The only flaw in his Roman look was that his nose looked as if it once had been hit with some force. It was bent very slightly to the right and that was the flaw that transformed him from being too perfect into being very sexy indeed.

Sam thought that in many ways Denton was the blond twin of the dark olive-skinned Arif. Arif was larger and fleshier of course but they both shared this strangely attractive Roman look.

'Hello, John, and welcome back. And you must be Sam, the machinery man. Welcome to my island.'

Denton gestured them to sit down on a vast sofa which was covered in red velvet. Sam glanced nervously at his oil-stained overalls and Denton laughed. 'Don't worry Sam, this is a working sofa.'

John and Sam sat down and Denton sat opposite them on a chair which looked like a gilded throne. With the sun behind him Sam could now see Denton much more clearly. His square face was softened by a large sensual mouth and two deep dimples in his cheeks when he smiled. Sam also noticed how muscular Denton's thighs were through his tight jeans.

'You smell as if you've been working hard.'

'We have, sir,' answered John. 'And I'm guessing we are going to have to work even harder tonight.'

Sam thought John said that with a mocking tone and Denton half-grinned back. 'We'll have to see about that.'

Arif brought in a stone jug of beer and handed them larger than pint-size tankards. He filled them full and Sam nervously took a swig. He almost choked. It was obviously home-made and much stronger than any brew he'd had before.

Denton watched Sam closely. 'Be careful Sam. That's quite strong stuff. You've got to take strong things carefully.'

Arif joined them on the sofa and Sam was instantly aware of his musky coffee smell. It excited him and he thought of Denton and Arif making love together. What did their spunk smell like when it mixed together? Would Sam ever smell that?

'So we have no light tonight?' Denton asked, pulling his hands through his tight hair.

'None,' replied John looking intently at Denton.

'It will have to be early to bed then,' said Denton with a twinkle in his eye. There aren't many things you can do without light.'

John briefly explained what more needed to be done to the generator and Denton seemed quite pleased. 'So both of you may have to stay on the island for a couple of days then?'

The large model of Rome had become bright red, illuminated by the setting sun, and Sam thought it looked very beautiful. To ease his tension, he told Denton so. Denton gestured for him to come and look closer at the details and Sam was thankful of the excuse to get closer to him.

Denton took him round the model, pointing out to him some of the main buildings. 'That was the Senate House,' he indicated. 'And that was the Forum.'

He quite casually put his hand on Sam's shoulder and Sam had to force himself not to jump back. He tried to concentrate on what Denton was telling him.

'That's where the slave athletes were trained. I know you swim but do you wrestle?'

'I've never tried it.'

'It's a great sport for men when it's done like the Romans did it.'

'Do you wrestle?' Sam asked, glancing across to Denton's piercing blue eyes. Sam sensed they were full of secrets he wanted to share in.

Denton nodded. 'It's almost my greatest pleasure,' he said stroking Sam's neck absently. 'I like the necks of swimmers. They remind me of wrestlers' necks.'

Sam could see at the collar of the open-necked denim shirt that Denton's chest was covered with a silky down of dark golden hair. Sam had a sudden urge to stroke it.

'And that's the Circus Maximus where the chariot races were held,' Denton continued. As he spoke to Sam he lowered his hand from Sam's shoulder and started to undo the top buttons of his overalls.

Sam could feel the other man's hand starting to caress the left side of his chest, his fingers slowly moving towards Sam's large and very sensitive nipple which was now tense and waiting. Denton expertly held the nipple in a firm grip.

'I see you have some very special features, Sam. We appreciate them on this island. As you will soon find out.' Denton's hand was now circling Sam's nipple as if drawing its circumference on Sam's chest. 'A very special feature, Sam,' he whispered, as if he didn't want the others to hear him. 'You should guard features like that. Only let them be known and explored by those who know what they are doing.'

'Are you one of those people?' asked Sam, hoping his rising phallus wasn't too obvious.

Denton's reply was to move one of his fingers to the top of Sam's nipple and to gently draw on it a miniature circle. The sensation Denton created travelled first to Sam's other nipple which became instantly just as hard and then down like an electric current to the tip of his now semi-erect penis. Sam had never felt so many sensations from just one touch. He knew at once that he was in the hands of someone who would lead him further sexually than he could ever have gone in his solitary fantasies or in his sessions with Paul. Sam could now smell the honey musk of Denton's body and it seemed to make all his flesh tingle. He moved towards Denton who slowly withdrew first his finger and then his hand, as if he was testing Sam.

'In Roman wrestling,' said Denton, 'you have to take control of many parts of your opponent's body. But everything you do is geared to one end – to make the other man utterly submit to you.' As Denton excited Sam further by these words, he perversely started to button up Sam's overalls. 'Total submission leads to total pleasure,' he whispered into Sam's ear. 'That is my first Roman lesson for you, Mr Machine Man. Maybe you should take a shower now?'

Sam was still slightly dazed and disappointed when Arif took him to what looked like a football club–sized communal shower room. The tiles on the walls and the floor were all gleaming red.

'What's this used for?'

'We sometimes have amateur wrestling matches here. So this shower room was built three years ago.' Arif handed Sam a bar of soap and an immaculate white towel. 'You will find a clean T-shirt and jeans your size hanging up in the cupboard in the corridor outside. After you've showered there'll be supper ready for you in the kitchen.' Arif quickly turned on one of the showers and went out.

Sam went over to a wooden bench and started to undo the buttons of his overalls. As he did so he remembered the way Denton had unbuttoned him and caressed him. Closing his eyes Sam imitated what Denton had done to him, squeezing his left nipple so hard that Sam felt his cock stiffen and the purple head squeeze out of its yielding foreskin to hit the resistance of his uniform's rough cotton.

Quickly Sam undid the rest of his overall buttons, allowing his penis to break free as the clothing fell around his feet. He walked quickly to the shower and started to caress his body with the soap. The hot water seemed to instantly locate those parts of his body which gave him so many different kinds of erotic sensations and pleasures. He felt it tickling his large, golden-haired balls and the thick down that flanked the crack of his arse. He felt the water splashing against and bouncing off his nipples, as usual, sites for him of many intense sensations. But these already seemed dimmed by the memory of what Denton had been able to do to

33

him just now with just one naked finger. Sam knew he was not going to be able to match that but still he caressed his torso in broad circular motions, fingering his tummy button and his teats which gave him small surges of pleasure while he turned his other hand into a tunnel of bony flesh. He pushed his large cock through his soapy hand, allowing it to travel up and down, faster and faster, until he felt his come race from his balls through his thick stem to shoot in a spurt of warm virility across the shower room. He could not stop one loud shout of pleasure as he released all the sexual tension in that one fountain burst.

As he traced a small circle of his spunk round his nipples, he had a sudden sense of being watched. He looked around the shower room at the row of wooden lockers and the gleaming red-tiled walls. Sam wondered if he just wanted to be watched. There didn't seem to be any spy holes or anything like that in the room. Maybe Arif had put something there without Denton knowing? He turned off the hot water tap and cooled his excitement down with a thick splash of icy-cold water. It reminded him of some of his best sea swims.

Quickly he dried himself and found a white T-shirt in the cupboard and a pair of white denim jeans that did indeed fit him perfectly. He looked at himself in a long mirror. Now he looked exactly as Paul had once described him: 'Mr Ordinary', 'Mr Regular'. He was the swimmer, the mechanic, the easy-to-get-on-with guy you could have a few cold beers with and some jokes. And part of Sam wanted to be just that; he didn't want his sexual nature to make him so different from others. But it was not just being gay which made him different. He knew that what really made him different was the tug he felt towards a kind of wild sexual adventuring and pleasuring which maybe was too extreme. Perhaps he had expectations that could never be met in reality or certainly not in the lake region.

Darkness was falling when Sam returned to the kitchen. On the wooden table there was a plate of cold ham and salad. Arif was standing there looking even more immense and sensual, lit by a candelabra of six candles. His eyes played over Sam's body and Sam allowed himself to enjoy the caress of his eyes.

'Aren't the others eating?' Sam asked.

Arif poured him another large tankard of beer. 'No. They have other things to do. But John said you should go to bed after your supper because he wants you up at six tomorrow morning.'

Sam wondered what he was being excluded from and why. Had he failed some test? Did he not respond enough to Denton's touch? He certainly wanted to. Despite his recent release just the sight of Arif's body, defined so well by his taut T-shirt, was making him feel hot again. 'What are they doing?' he asked tensely.

Arif turned his large face to Sam and gave him a sexy wink. Then he shrugged. 'Sporting stuff.'

After Sam had finished supper and was feeling slightly woozy with beer, Arif took him to a small bedroom on the upper floor. Arif lit a candle for him and left him alone, leaving behind just the musky scent of his body.

Sam undressed and got into bed. He could hear the lapping of the lake all around him but it didn't soothe him. He was too aroused to sleep. He knew he didn't want to play sex memory games with Paul or Dino; it was time to touch and know real bodies. If he was so desired why was he being left alone? He lay in bed trying to guess what was going on in the rest of the house. Was Denton with John? Was Arif with both of them? He tossed and turned then made a snap decision and got out of bed. He blew the candle out, pulled on the white T-shirt only and quietly stepped out into the dark corridor. He stepped cautiously down the back stairs that led to the kitchen. It was dark in there too. Cautiously he glided along the corridor which led to the room where he had met Denton. Very slowly he opened one of the double doors. The room was now bathed in lunar light and the model of ancient Rome looked very realistic with all its buildings silvered by the cool shimmer of the full moon.

Sam recalled the touch of Denton's finger on the tip of his nipple and what that had done to the rest of his body. He turned sharply as he heard a noise. It sounded like shuffling and heavy breathing but it didn't come from inside the room. Sam patrolled around the model trying to discover where the mysterious noise was coming from. Then he noticed a small door next to the heavy curtains by the open window. He went up to it. He could see a crack of light and was sure that the shuffling and breathing noises were coming from the room behind the door. Sam found the handle and very, very slowly turned it. He opened the door a fraction so that he could see just a small part of the room. It seemed to be lit only by moonlight and a few candles and he could see what looked like a section of a boxing ring.

Arif came abruptly into view. The sight of him shocked and excited Sam for Arif was naked except for what looked like a loincloth, consisting of a thong belt with a loose front and back flap. His skin glistened with oil and his body was everything Sam had guessed it would be and more. His chest was massive and lightly covered with curly black hair. A line of hair ran down past his powerful upper torso to his flat stomach and navel. The loincloth revealed enough of his arse to show that it was even more firm and inviting than Sam had imagined it to be, with double dimples on each side of his fleshy rump. Like his belly, it was covered in a down of jet-black curly hair, as were his heavily muscled thighs and legs.

Arif was half-crouching. Then John came into Sam's restricted line of vision and started to grapple violently with the Turk. John's body too went beyond Sam's fantasies about it. It was square and absolutely solid muscle covered with a thick mass of tangled black hair. John was forcing the larger Arif against the ropes with the sheer force of his chest and groin and, although Arif had youth and suppleness on his side, John had a body forged into iron and was now using his skill and solid power against the younger man. He managed to force Arif around and then, arm locking him, irresistibly bent Arif's entire body close to the floor of the ring. Arif tried to grab John's crotch but John fended him off and then forced his head and chest to the canvas surface of the ring. Sam could feel his penis turn into a cold steel rod as Arif's generous bottom was now sticking high in the air and facing his direction. Only the loose flap of his loincloth prevented Sam from seeing what he now desperately wanted to see – Arif's naked arse.

'Submit slave,' shouted John. 'What you did to the blond boys I'm going to have to do to you now.'

Arif struggled to kick out at John but John merely grabbed the younger man's leg with his trained hand and forced Arif's leg back to the canvas.

'Submit slave,' shouted John again.

'Never,' shouted Arif back at him and tried to escape John's arm lock by swerving his giant body away from John's solid mass, but he couldn't break free of John's armhold. Arif grimaced.

Sam was holding his own erection now between his hands and was pulling his foreskin back and forth over the smooth throbbing dome of his cockhead. 'Show me his arse!' Sam whispered urgently to himself.

As if answering Sam's command Arif shouted, 'I submit!' And John, looking towards someone Sam could not see, started to lift up the back flap of Arif's loincloth to reveal his oil-covered buttocks. Sam could see, for the first time, the two lines of curly black hair that ran down both sides of Arif's crack. They seemed to be protecting the rosebud that Sam now wanted to see and thrust into with his hungry cockhead.

'Prepare him for me,' commanded Denton's voice.

With his free hand, John started to slap the wide expanse of Arif's firm arse. He started to slap first the left and then the right side. His alternating blows got faster and faster until sweat was pouring down John's own boxlike chest and stomach towards where his thick cock was struggling to break through his loincloth.

Sam was now thrusting his lean body back and forth against the door, its wooden surface pressing hard against his nipples, chest, cock and thighs. He imagined that he was in the ring with his fully erect penis sticking out below the waistline of his white T-shirt. He imagined advancing towards the inviting darkness of Arif's submissive backside. Arif's arse was now being slapped at a furious rate by John and Sam saw it open out to reveal a bright pink rosebud with a dark hole in its centre. Arif was groaning loudly.

'He's ready now for his master,' said Denton in a low whisper. He was hiding a leather whip against his golden thigh.

John turned Arif's body in Denton's direction. 'Lift your arse up higher for your master,' yelled John, now pouring with sweat as he punished the young giant under his control.

Arif lifted his buttocks even higher in the air. To his delight, Sam could just see the top of a cockhead coming into his line of vision and he watched it moving closer to Arif's punished arse. The large pink phallus touched the centre of Arif's arse and he shuddered violently. Then Arif moved himself hungrily up and seemed to pull the penis into his dark depths.

Then, out of the candlelit shadows, Sam saw Denton raising something he couldn't quite make out. He heard the smack of leather on flesh.

'Wait for your master to decide when you get cockhead, slave boy.'

Sam saw John at this point use his free hand to grab one of Arif's large reddish nipples and twist it violently so that Arif grimaced and groaned again in a burst of pain and pleasure. The ex-boxer then took Denton's thick and expert cock in his hand and capped it with a strange-looking protective sheath down which were ridges marked out in black leather.

'Yes! Yes!' groaned Arif as Denton tantalised him by using his large cock to slap first the left and then the right side of Arif's bottom.

Sam was desperate to see more of Denton's body but only his leather-sheathed cock was in view. Denton had now grabbed John's member through his loincloth and was rubbing his hand up and down against the only semi-visible thick stem which could be seen through the cotton cloth. John's head leant back as he started to climax.

Unexpectedly Denton stopped his slapping motion and started to slide his prick deeper and deeper into Arif's arse until Sam could see Denton's down-covered balls squeezing against the Turk's musk-scented slope.

'Accept your master's leather cock,' shouted Denton, and

once again Sam became aware of a strange swishing noise and the smack of ribbons of leather on yielding flesh. Sam heard Denton shouting with ecstasy as John too started to shoot his come inside his loincloth.

'I'm your total slave now,' cried Arif. 'I can sense your hot juice squirting inside your leather cock. Your cock must be swimming with your come.' And then Arif's front flap was thrust aside by his huge cock as it too started to pump its sticky fluids over the canvas floor of the ring.

Sam couldn't control his own pleasure-hungry cock any more and it started to shoot come against the unyielding plank of the wooden door. Sam covered his mouth to stifle his own shout of total gratification. His whole body seemed to be exploding in star burst after star burst, lifted out of himself by the wild sexual sensations that were racing through him. He quickly recovered himself and ran back through the room and up to his bedroom.

He was shaken by how much he had wanted to join the three men and how little he knew. He was not even sure whether he most wanted to be the slave or the master.

The next day Sam was to discover that John and Arif had enjoyed new levels of sexual pleasure too. They had seen his perfect body reflected in the mirrors of that room and watched him observing them.

Sam himself had not realised he was being viewed or what he had done to them until Denton came to his room that evening. 'I've seen you on a video from the shower room and know how much you want to join us. That alone earns you the right to be initiated in our secret brotherhood here. Tomorrow you will begin to be trained up and you will start to find out how much we know here about men and pleasure. When I decide you are ready for our real Roman games then I will come and fetch you. Until then, obey.'

Three

Sam woke up slowly. His body felt lazy and voluptuous. He rubbed his hands across the golden down of his firm thighs and listened sleepily to the sound of the lake lapping against the rocky shores of the island. He only half remembered the promises Denton had made to him the previous night. Sam drowsily remembered the words 'initiation' and the promise of some ultimate 'Roman game'. His cock stiffened at these fleeting suggestive recollections and, under the fresh-smelling white cotton sheets, he laid his hand protectively across the taut contours of his torso tugging at the large nipples around which circles of tangled dark blond hair swirled.

He heard the sound of motorboats bringing over the people who worked in the house and on the farm during the day. Sam guessed that they had nothing to do with, and no knowledge of, the secret life of Skate – the life which started the moment their boats left the island.

But what really happened here? Sam surmised that he had only just touched on the outer edge of this hidden world created by Denton. All he knew for sure was that after so many years of self-repression he was ready to finally lose all the inhibitions and restraints which he, as much as society, had imposed on himself. He felt certain that, on this island, he was at last going to find the pleasure and maybe even the person he had so often conjured up in his mind.

He arched his youthful body in the bed and sensed the vigour and hunger of his limbs. He felt he was now in a state of perfect readiness and fitness for his destiny and, whatever form it took, Sam knew the great moments of his erotic life were growing close.

His thoughts were broken by a sudden knock on the door. He pulled the sheet to his chin. 'Come in.'

Arif entered wearing a white shirt and black jeans. He was carrying a tray on which was a cup of milky coffee and a large slice of bread dripping with honey.

Sam was immediately aware of the pungent masculinity of Arif's physique and the subtle tang his body gave off. He sat up and Arif, creasing his broad face with a scintillating smile, placed the tray on Sam's lap and half-aroused cock.

Arif went to the window and opened the shutters. Sam could see a bright blue sky and just the tops of some of the trees in the pine woods. The Turk turned his large body back to the bed and leant against the window ledge with an easy seductive grace. His eyes travelled quickly and appreciatively over Sam's exposed chest.

'Ah good,' he said laughing. 'It's not just starlight and candle-light which makes your body look so fine. They were debating it at breakfast.'

'Who are "they"?' asked Sam.

Arif looked evasive. 'Young men with great talent who you will meet soon, I hope. If you pass all the tests.'

'I'm not a second-hand car,' replied Sam with a provocative grin.

Arif smiled, revealing a flash of snow-white teeth. 'Sam, everyone who stays overnight on this island is road-tested.'

'I thought I was road-tested last night.'

Arif shook his head and pulled his hand through the dense mass of his black curls. 'That was just your registration.'

The sound of farm workers rose from the orchards in the front of the house. Arif glanced down at them and then looked back at Sam. 'I'm here to tell you some of our basic laws. We live like most people until the boats leave at four o'clock every day. After that our own laws rule this island and they are more severe than the law on the mainland. You will find out more as your training proceeds. From ten until four you will work like you did before. We have a lot of machinery that needs maintenance and we need a lot of electricity. You will discover why quite soon. After four you will place yourself in the hands of your trainer who you must completely obey. If you don't you will have to leave the island and you will never be allowed to return. Who your trainer is will be revealed to you at four o'clock today. You have to accept him, you have no choice. Do you understand?'

Sam nodded, trying to control his physical excitement at the prospect of such arbitrary and total submission.

Arif continued speaking as he walked towards Sam's bed. 'The food you eat is also chosen for you and you must eat and drink everything you are given. Do you understand?'

Sam nodded.

'Do you accept?'

Sam nodded again.

Arif beamed at him. 'I'm very pleased, Sam. We have about three new initiates a year and I don't always feel interested in them. But I feel differently about you.' Arif knelt by the side of the bed and gestured for Sam to eat his honey-covered bread.

Sam did so. The honey was obviously from the hives he had seen on the island and tasted of wild flowers. Some of the honey dribbled from Sam's mouth down to the sharp curve of his chin. Arif leant forward and with one dark finger scooped some of the honey from Sam's unshaven chin. He held the honey in the air for a few moments and watched as the sharp morning sunlight made the translucent honey shimmer. Arif glanced at Sam and then glanced at the buttons on his white shirt.

Sam did not need any further instruction. He gently undid the four top buttons of the shirt and allowed Arif's powerful muscled chest to appear. The broad torso of the Turk was covered with a light but sexy layer of densely curled black hair which reminded Sam that the Turks had once mixed long ago with the last of the Romans in Byzantium. That thought made Sam glance up at the chiselled features of Arif's face which would have made him as complete a Roman as Denton except that Arif had almond-shaped eyes too large and sensual even for a Southern Italian. Sam saw in the blackness of Arif's pupils the entrance to pleasure domes he had not even begun to imagine yet.

And, as if to confirm Sam's thoughts, Arif brought his honey-drenched finger to his left nipple and rhythmically tapped the finger first against the dark outer circle and then against his nipple's sharp peak. Sam could see and sense that this drumming beat was making Arif's eyes roll. His head stretched back revealing the taut sinews of his neck.

Sam could no longer control himself. Already his slim long cock was pressing hard against the wooden tray on his lap. Sam leant forward towards Arif's exposed and sweetened nipple. The steamy ribbons of coffee rising from Sam's tray mixed with the musky scent of Arif's flesh as Sam approached the nipple. He started to blow hard on its hairy outer circle and, each time he blew, Arif arched his head further back with pleasure he wanted to disguise but increasingly could not.

Sam, for his part, felt like an astronaut growing closer and closer to an alien planet the nearer he got to Arif's nipples. The great dark mass of the Turk's flesh gave way to the smooth darker pink areola and then in the centre the final duskiness of the nipple peak.

Sam, acting now entirely from instinct, landed his generous mouth around the outer circle of Arif's little bud, soaking it with the clear juice of his spittle. The hot red cave of Sam's mouth teased the as-yet untouched peak of Arif's nipple. He felt it with his lips and wanted to force his tongue down on it, circling and possessing it. But, remembering Denton's words, he held his tongue back resisting as hard as he could the honey-covered tit.

Arif was now swaying in his anxiety for Sam to complete his act of piracy and seize the golden-coated peak.

'Pleasure delayed is pleasure increased,' whispered Sam, who never realised before that he had it in him to be such an assured sexual tease.

Arif shook his powerful, trembling head from side to side as if commanding Sam to stop encasing his nipple in the hot winds of his mouth and instead to suck on it with all the combined force of his tongue and throat.

Still Sam delayed, almost waiting for the cup of coffee which was between them to cool before he would release Arif from his longing to be sucked by him. Then Sam knew the right moment had arrived. He closed his lips tighter around Arif's nipple and bringing his tongue from the moist depths of his throat he started to caress the puckered outer circles of it with his tongue's wet tip.

At the very first contact with Sam's tongue Arif's entire generously built body shuddered. Then, all Arif could feel through the honey-scented daze of his body was the great sucking power of Sam's long tunnel of a mouthpiece.

'You are making my whole body swim inside your throat,' whispered Arif, as Sam gently pulled him towards the Venus trap of his now compelling mouth, tongue and throat.

When he went into Sam's room to prepare Sam for his stay and initiation, Arif hadn't expected that it would be he, the famously seductive Arif, who would find himself the sexual captive of such an ordinary Mr Average recruit. They had all agreed that Sam had a nice, classical swimmer's body but none of them had realised the full extent of Sam's erotic power which was also, guessed Arif now, largely unknown himself.

Arif had to use all his willpower to tear his torso away from the licking bliss of Sam's combined lips, tongue, and throat actions. It was just because Arif felt that he wanted to stay trapped inside Sam's mouth for hours and hours that he forced himself to break away.

As he buttoned up his shirt, Arif was aware that Sam had started to take him to several places it was dangerous for him to go. Sam was the first initiate who had shown he had the kind of power Denton had warned Arif about.

Arif stood with his back to the window, and the cool lake breeze, and tried to forget the way Sam's saliva had dissolved the honey around his nipple and had replaced it with circles of touching and kneading sensations so wonderful that Arif could have bound his entire body then and there. The remnants of the honey gluing his shirt to his chest reminded Arif that Sam had just made his body dance and burn and shudder like no other man had ever done before; not even Denton his official trainer and lord.

Still trembling, he looked at the young man in the bed who, when they had viewed him in the showers on video, they had classified as nice Mr Average swimmer – to be placed in grade B of the wrestling circle. For the first time Arif wondered whether it was not an apprentice but a master whose pale blue eyes he was now trying to escape.

'Work with John until four o'clock in the main generator room,' said Arif in a voice still thick with desire. 'At that time we will reveal to you who your trainer will be. Remember you have to give him absolute obedience.'

The word trainer obviously excited Sam. 'Who will he be?'

'That you will find out at four,' said Arif, and left the room quickly.

Sam wolfed down the rest of the bread and honey. He got out of bed, put on his white boxer shorts and went to the window.

His bedroom was at the back of the house and he could see men and women picking apples off the trees and working in the greenhouses plucking ripe tomatoes from the vines. They were all lakeland people. Some were known to Sam and he wondered if any of them had any idea about what went on here when they left in the afternoon. Denton was obviously very adept at keeping his secrets.

For the first time Sam noticed, beyond the orchards, a large circular brick structure with no roof. It looked like a scaled-down version of one of the buildings he had seen in Denton's model of ancient Rome. It was sealed off from the orchards and glasshouses by a ten-foot-high brick wall. Then he sensed, rather than saw, out of the corner of his field of vision, a flash of flesh.

He stared at the dense undergrowth which ringed the brick structure. There it was again. Sam had twenty-twenty vision and he was sure he had glimpsed two naked young men wearing some kind of leather loincloth and shoulder straps. He peered again. There was a violent rustling amongst the bushes and, gazing in that direction, Sam was sure he saw naked thighs racing towards the brick building. Then there was the sound of a wooden door banging shut.

Sam dressed quickly and was going to investigate further but then he remembered Arif's instructions. He did not want to get thrown off the island for disobedience before he had found out at least some of its secrets. He hoped what he had just done to Arif, which had rather surprised him with its intensity, was enough to ensure that Arif at least had a good reason to keep Sam here.

Sam walked through the empty house past the long corridor filled with marble busts of Roman emperors and went out through the large kitchen towards the generator house. When he went inside he saw that John was hard at work replacing one of the main electrical circuits. John's black eyes flashed at Sam and there was just a hint of a smile before his boss assumed a business-as-usual expression.

'Morning. Sleep well?'

'Yes.'

'Good. A lot of work to do.'

John explained what he wanted Sam to do. It was an easy but messy job and soon both men had faces and arms blackened by machine grease. Sam was very aware of John's sturdy masculinity so close to him. He remembered how he had performed last night and had a brief recollection of John's hard, knotted, muscular body, a square box of raw power. But Sam shook those thoughts away. It was too dangerous to work around generators with a hard-on!

The morning passed quickly with Sam determined not to think of sex or the secrets of the island and particularly not to think about the older man who he was working alongside.

One of the apple pickers, a slim young man with bright blue eyes, brought them a lunch tray. On it was bread, cheese, walnuts and apples. There was also a large jug of fresh apple juice. The young man smiled at Sam and John as if he knew more than they thought. He walked away without saying a word.

'You have to eat everything,' commanded John. 'It's one of the rules. The food and drink is specially chosen for us.'

'Why?' asked Sam.

'Builds muscle and gives energy. You will need both here.' John's square face was crossed with a hard look.

'Who is my trainer going to be?'

'That's a secret. You will know at four when the boats leave the island for the day.'

'What will he do to me?'

'You'll find out soon enough.'

'Will I enjoy it?'

John wiped some grease from his fleshy lips so that he could eat his lunch. 'Remember last night?'

Sam nodded and worked hard to repress his memory of it. They finished their lunch quickly and in silence, each man lost in his own thoughts and anticipations of what was to come.

For Sam the afternoon seemed interminable. He kept as far from John's body as he could because by now, in the heat of the day and working so hard, John's body was reeking of that foxy sweat which Sam found too much of a turn-on to get too close to. Nor did he glance at John's hairy torso which from time to time was revealed through his workmate's half-open overalls. And Sam kept his own overalls fully buttoned up despite the heat. He also resisted slipping his hand through the lower pockets and touching his cock. That would be too dangerous. Normally he would have found a quiet place and brought himself to a climax, maybe imagining John roughly taking him, but today, he decided not to take that risk.

He would indeed be, as he had promised the superb Arif, 'obedient'.

Sam heard the large clock over the main greenhouse chime two o'clock, then three and then three-thirty. As the time inched closer to four Sam found his thoughts wandering away from his engineering tasks to what was now going to happen to him. Would he meet Denton and Arif again today? Would he be allowed to watch another wrestling match? Would he be allowed to wrestle? Who would his trainer be? Younger or older? Would it be one of the fit young men he had seen running through the bushes that morning?

Sam found it hard, the closer it got to four, not to use the machine grease to slip his cock through the rubbing circle of his fist. But he did resist. Then finally, just when he thought the moment would never arrive, the clock chimed four.

Both John and Sam stopped work and heard the sound of people getting on the motorboats and leaving the island. Soon their voices and motors faded into the distance. All that could be heard were the songs of the many birds who found refuge on the island and the rustling of the wind in the trees.

John took Sam's tools from him and placed them neatly in a metal cupboard. He turned to Sam and spoke in a new low tone. 'OK, here are your instructions. You are not to wash. You are to go exactly as you are through the back apple orchard to a wooden gate in the wall there. You will knock on the gate three times.'

Sam stood waiting for John to continue but John just gestured for him to go. He didn't need any more encouragement. He raced out of the generator room and, skirting around the house, ran through the now-deserted apple orchards kicking fallen apples to one side as if they were tiny footballs. In his haste Sam found himself facing an expanse of sheer brick wall. He could not see a wooden door anywhere.

Then he noticed some bee hives around which tiny groups of bees seemed to be dancing in the air. Next to it, he realised, was the door. It was cunningly painted to look like part of the brick wall. Obviously this was another security precaution to keep unwanted visitors out. Sam sprinted towards the gate, steering clear of the bee hives. After his session with Arif this morning he didn't want the supply of honey to be disturbed in any shape or form.

Breathing heavily, and now with machine grease trickling down his body, he reached the disguised gate. He took a deep breath and then knocked three times against the wooden surface. There was silence for a while and then Sam heard the sound of someone clearing his throat.

'Who is there?' asked a voice that was young and thick with the local lilting accent.

'Sam.'

'Are you ready to obey your trainer?'

'Yes,' replied Sam instantly.

'Whatever he asks you to do?'

'Yes,' repeated Sam, putting extra conviction into his voice.

'When you go through this gate you must be prepared to accept two rules. I will tell you each rule and then you will say "I accept". Do you understand?'

'Yes,' said Sam trying to hide his impatience to discover what was on the other side of the gate.

'First you will never tell anyone what you see and do behind this gate. Do you accept?'

'I accept.'

'Second, once you reach the next stage you cannot stop. You are part of a competition you will not be allowed to leave. Do you accept?'

'I accept.'

The door was unbolted and Sam was instantly aroused by the sight of the young man who greeted him. He was thickset and muscular with dark, tanned skin. But what made him so exciting to Sam was the way his sturdy body was shown off to the sexiest effect by the strange outfit he was wearing. He was naked except for a thick leather belt around his waist, and leather flaps covering his penis and buttocks, which could be tantalisingly glimpsed as he walked ahead of Sam. One half of his upper torso was sheathed in a tight leather vest which seemed to emphasise the sexiness of his semiexposed chest with its circles of curling ginger hair. Around his thick neck he wore a leather collar and on his head was another tight band of leather which was dotted with copper studs.

The man was obviously very fit and Sam wondered what exercise it was that could make a body so manly and virile. Sam's eyes had been glued to the swaying cheeks of the young man's hard arse so it was with a shock that he realised he had been led to a large circular brick building. The young man gestured at a door that had painted on it the Roman numerals XI.

'The trainer of team eleven is to be your trainer, apprentice. Remember you must obey everything he says.'

The handsome young man strode away leaving Sam with only a fleeting impression of a smiling, dangerous freckled face. Sam hoped that he would have the chance to encounter his guide in a more intimate way in the very near future. Cautiously, and with some trepidation about what was waiting for him behind the heavy green door, he pulled the door open and stepped inside.

He found himself in a circular room with faded brick walls and a sand floor. The room was dark but for a circle of light which came from a round window above the door. Sam closed the door behind him and allowed his eyes to adjust to the gloom. He could just make out a wooden beam that stretched from wall to wall at chest height and, dangling from the ceiling above the beam, two metal chains a few feet apart which held two metal circles. These swung a few feet above the beam.

It was then that Sam became aware of another figure in the room besides himself. It was a man dressed as his guide had been, only this time the leather outfit was on a more muscular, boxy shaped and very hairy body with thick thighs and a powerful chest. It was an older man, maybe in his late thirties. Sam felt his tits harden with excitement at what that body might do to him.

Then the figure spoke. 'I am your trainer, you are my apprentice.'

Sam recognised John's voice and was even more aroused by the prospect of being trained by a man he had always felt an intense but repressed attraction to.

'Why didn't you tell me?' asked Sam smiling.

John's response startled Sam. He angrily hit the wall with a short leather-bound stick he carried. 'Silence, apprentice boy,' he snapped, and hit the wall again with the stick. 'Inside the school you are not allowed to speak unless instructed to. And do you understand that you must do everything I tell you to?'

Sam was amazed at how much more powerful and commanding John's voice now seemed in this strange secret compound than in the generating room just a short while ago. It was as if, in this space, John had been given an extra force. Sam wondered expectantly whether this new forcefulness also extended to sex.

'Yes, I understand,' Sam replied.

'Now, unbutton the top of your overalls and strip to your waist.'

Sam did what he was told, carefully stopping his unbuttoning just below his navel. He was aware that he was standing in the centre of the circle of light and guessed that his upper body was glistening with sweat.

'Now,' commanded John, 'caress your upper chest and tits with your hands. Rub that engine grease into them.'

Slowly Sam crossed his hands across his chest and started to rub in a circular motion. The engine grease blended into the chest hairs and he moved his fingers towards his large nipples, which were already hardening as his fingers slid around and then over his pink peaks. Sam could feel his cock stiffening at the pleasure he was giving himself. It was a pleasure intensified by the thought that John was watching him and, Sam hoped, getting excited himself at the sight of Sam's indulgent caresses.

Sam could not quite see John, who was standing outside the circle of sunlight, but he could tell that John was rubbing some part of his body as Sam increased the speed and excitement with which he stroked himself. He felt an irresistible urge to lower one of his hands down the thin trail of hair that led to his navel and to his cock, which was now pressing hard against the rough cotton of his overalls. But just as his hand started to slide downwards, John shouted at him.

'No. Not yet. Strip naked.'

Sam's torso was now criss-crossed with lines of engine grease that looked like black whiplashes on his fair skin. He slid off his overalls, took off his socks and shoes and then removed his white boxer shorts. John handed him a leather belt with a leather front and back flap attached to it.

'Put that round your waist,' he said curtly.

Sam did as he was ordered. John then handed him a leather vest to put on. As Sam pulled it down over his body he realised that it did not quite reach his belly, so his midriff was left exposed. He also became aware that the leather vest had two detachable patches around the area of his nipples. Sam tingled at the thought of how they were going to be used.

'Now,' said John, 'you are going to do some of the first basic tests and exercises to see if you can indeed become a player in the Roman games. Get on to that beam and then, using the metal rings, see if you can lift your entire body in the air, wrapping your legs around the chains.'

Sam sprang up on to the beam. He put his hands into the metal circles and then used them to lift his body up towards the chains, around which he wrapped his legs, so that he was suspended almost upside down.

'Good,' said John. 'There are some that can't even do that. They have to go. We only have the best here. Wait in that position.'

John left the room through a door Sam had not noticed. He caught a glimpse of a darkened corridor and what seemed to be the light of flickering flames playing on the red brick wall.

Sam felt his body swaying back and forth above the beam and the sand floor. He felt the leather belt around his waist catching the sweat that trickled from his long powerful swimmer's thighs. And he could also sense the grease-stained sweat trickling from his chest to his throat and the nape of his neck where it concentrated in small streams eventually running over his face too. Sam realised that he must now look quite sexy, as only a handsome young man stained with a war paint of engine grease and sweat can. Sam, remembering his leather flaps as well, wondered if his new 'Apache' look would have extra appeal for John.

Just then he heard the sound of naked feet shuffling through sand. The inner door opened and John entered. He was followed by two men dressed exactly as Sam was. One of the men was a stocky blond with a severe crew cut. The other was lithe and long bodied with a light covering of hair over his entire body which gave the impression of a fur coating. Both men had hard faces and bright, snapping eyes.

As if obeying orders the two men did not look up at Sam hovering above them. John slapped both men on their shoulders with his leather stick and ordered them to jump up on the beam and sit back to back. The two men did so. When they were both in this position Sam's face was suspended close to theirs but still neither man looked at him or in any way seemed to acknowledge his presence. John placed his stick between the necks of the men who were now pressed back to back.

'Exercise seventeen. You both know the rules. You have to try to wrestle the other man off the beam remaining seated and back to back. Start now.'

The stocky blond immediately tried to wrap his solid arms around the exposed waist of the leaner, darker man. The darker man, in turn, lifted his hands up and grabbing the hard, square face of the blond tried to bend his head back towards him. This movement forced the blond to abandon his waist lock on the other man and to grab the darker man's thin but strong arms. It was soon obvious to Sam that, although the blond man was much stockier and more muscled, the darker wrestler had a wiry strength which was now resisting all efforts by the blond to free himself from the iron grip on his head.

The blond wrestler changed tactics and, lifting up his legs, wrapped them around the darker wrestler's thighs and started to tip him off the wooden beam. The darker wrestler had to let go of the other man's head and use his arms to secure himself on the beam. This defensive gesture allowed the stocky blond to wrap his arms and hands together in a body lock around the darker man's exposed midriff and to twist him off the beam. But the darker man's strong long legs now came back into play and secured him firmly back on the beam.

Sam could see that both men were sweating profusely now and were starting to realise that, despite appearances, they were so equally matched that neither one was likely to topple the other off the beam.

Sam could smell the distinctive aroma of both men. The stocky blond was sweet like burnt honey, the furry darker man was more musky sour. Both scents excited Sam.

John spoke. 'OK, break that. Now just try some friendly wrist wrestling.'

Still back to back, both men grabbed each other's wrists over their shoulders and were trying to force their rival's wrists down on their shoulders.

John spoke to Sam. 'I think these wrestlers deserve a little reward for their efforts from that apprentice who's hanging uselessly there. Go on apprentice – give some pleasure to these men. They might be your team members soon.'

Sam did not need any more encouragement than that from his trainer. He swayed forward towards the stocky blond who still did not look directly at him. Sam liked that. It made him feel he could do anything to him. He swayed forward again, close to the golden stubble on the square jaw of the wrestler's chin, then touched the stubble with the tip of his tongue. The blond wrestler, still not looking at Sam, shuddered a little and Sam could see his penis starting to stiffen under his leather flap.

Sam gently and expertly moved the tip of his tongue up from the chin to the man's lips. There were drops of sweat on the wrestler's upper lip which trickled down to land on Sam's tongue. They splashed there and Sam instantly felt the acrid taste of the man's flesh. He prised the wrestler's lips apart and forced the tip of his tongue into his mouth. The wrestler resisted with a wall of teeth but Sam persisted, lashing the teeth with his tongue until the teeth were lifted and Sam's tongue continued its silky, moist journey into the other's mouth. Sam's tongue cruised over the blond man's tongue sensing, even before he made contact with its hot, rough surface, that the stocky wrestler had been working hard to hide his attraction for Sam's grease-stained swimmer's body, which had been swaying so provocatively alongside him.

The moment their tongues met Sam felt the blond wrestler's hand reach for and encircle Sam's cock, which was now almost fully erect. The wrestler used the engine grease that had trickled over Sam's penis as his lubricant as he rhythmically gathered up the flesh around Sam's stem and forced it towards Sam's now fully exposed cockhead. Sam guessed, as his own cock flesh was rubbing against his purple knob, that the wrestler was starting to teach him how to use his own body in a new way to pleasure himself.

Sam decided to reward the wrestler and, swaying over the big blond, took hold of one of the leather flaps over the man's left chest and lifted it up, revealing a large swelling nipple. Sam slowly extracted his tongue from the wrestler's mouth and moved it quickly over the surface of the leather vest to the exposed nipple. Sam knew that one of the things he did best was sucking off another man's large and yearning dugs. He gently placed the circumference of his open mouth around the outer circle of the wrestler's nipple. Sam felt the wrestler shudder again. By now Sam guessed that the wrestler knew that Sam's hot tongue was poised above the tip of his nipple and then Sam darted his tongue down to the nipple's peak with the accuracy and speed of an adder. At the very first flick of Sam's tongue the stocky wrestler's entire frame shook with delight and, almost as a reflex action he squeezed Sam's rigid phallus.

Sam sensed the darker wrestler's crystalline blue eyes on him and then he felt the other man's firm hand starting to rhythmically smack first the left and then the right cheek of his exposed arse. The force of this smacking swayed Sam's entire body back and forth so that the blond wrestler's hand became a tunnel of flesh that Sam's cock was now riding up and down, lubricated by the engine grease. Sam felt ripples of pleasure spreading out both from his punished arse and his rubbed prick.

Sam released one of his hands from the metal circle and putting it inside the slimmer man's leather vest, just below his neck, slid it down towards his furry chest and his left nipple. He pulled up the furry flesh around the nipple and used that flesh to rub and pull hard. The lithe dark man gave out a moan of pleasure and he started to smack Sam's arse harder and harder until the room was filled with the unmistakable sound of flesh hitting flesh. Sam now sucked deep on the nipple of the blond wrestler while, simultaneously, he allowed his hand to travel down the slim, lightly muscled contours of the darker wrestler until he reached the furry bowl of his navel. Sam gently pushed a finger into the very centre of the man's soft and yielding flesh. Deep from inside the man's throat Sam heard a muffled growl of satisfaction. Sam moved his hand on, travelling over the barrier of the wide leather belt and reaching under the leather flap beneath finally arriving at the tangled mass of hair which marked the beginning of the man's pubic area. The penis itself, Sam could see, was rising fast. The cockhead was beginning to squeeze out of its protective covering of skin which encouraged Sam to use just two fingers along the stem of the wrestler's cock, stopping just below the head. There, forming a finger ring around the entire circumference of his cock, Sam started to rock his fingers back and forth, keeping to the same rhythm as the dark wrestler's smacking of Sam's arse and the blond wrestler's loosening and tightening grip of Sam's cock.

Sam then saw that the darker wrestler had used his spare hand to get under the blond's leather flap and was now rubbing up and down the blond wrestler's large, thick member whose purple head had quickly become a steaming red.

All three men were now locked in the same rhythmic beat and each of them could feel the sensations of the others in their nipples, cocks and arses so that each felt his own sensations were being tripled in intensity.

Sam confirmed this impression by noting the almost dreamy gaze in the wrestlers' blue eyes, half-hooded by their eyelids which were also quivering with the sensations which darted between all three of them. Sam felt he was close to coming. He could feel inside his firmly gripped cock a surge of his spunk and he could sense that inside the dark wrestler's now rigid rod, his hot sperm was also desperate to gush out. The blond wrestler too, though a bigger man than the others and in need of even more stimulation, was also on the edge of consummating his pleasure. The double impact of Sam's hard sucking on his nipple and the darker wrestler's rubbing clench around his thick cock was obviously all he could stand.

Sam was desperate to shoot his spunk through the air and over them both but the other two men seemed to be fighting to control and delay their climaxes. For a second Sam was baffled as to why they were doing this. Then he saw them both glancing down at John beneath them. John had a huge erection too, but was manfully resisting touching it or any other part of his body. Instead he had his leather stick raised in the air and Sam realised that both wrestlers were waiting for John's command to come.

Sam felt instinctively that he, as an apprentice, should also try to control himself and delay his climax but, as the smacking on his arse got pleasurably harder and harder, and as his cock moved faster and faster up and down the squeezing tunnel of flesh created by the blond wrestler's large hand, he was finding it more and more difficult to control his entire body's desire to squirt the bounty of his sperm over them all.

Almost desperate now, Sam could feel that his body was close to overwhelming his mind and his will, and giving itself the release it now so urgently needed. Luckily, just at the very second Sam knew he could no longer keep back the consuming wave of his desire and spunk, he glimpsed John below bring his leather stick down through the air; a gesture of final release.

Instantly the blond and the dark wrestler, clearly more advanced in their training than Sam, let their desires take their natural course. Now the effect of damming in their need to climax became obvious as warm white semen shot out of both their cocks in a series of shuddering bursts. At the same time Sam felt his own sperm shoot up the long tunnel of his cock and travel far across the room. A second wave Sam directed at the entwined necks of the two wrestlers. Both of them smiled for the first time as they felt Sam's grateful fluids travel like hot lava down their spines.

Sam was pleased to see that he had helped produce large quantities of spunk from both of the other men. The darker wrestler's furry body, well above his navel, was now a mass of gleaming white liquid while the blond wrestler's large and heavily muscled upper thighs were covered with his creamier juice.

After a few moments John ordered them down. Sam watched them as they stood beneath him, obediently lined up in front of John who used his stick to trace outlines round the main sites of drying come on their bodies.

'That was your reward for the day. No more today for either of you. Get to the pool and then the room of the Master of the School.'

Both men exchanged a brief glance. Sam could not make out whether it was one of fear or pleasure or, as he was coming to expect, a strangely satisfying mixture of the two. He noticed that as the wrestlers left the room neither of them even tried to look up at him or to make any gesture at all.

Sam was suddenly aware that the position he had been in for some time now was causing him to ache in his arms and legs. He was used to swimming of course but this suspending of his body in the air with the chains was making many more demands on his muscles than any form of swimming. As he swayed there he prayed that John would order him down soon. His mind returned to its thoughts about pain and pleasure. He was beginning to see and to feel directly how the right mix of pain with pleasure actually did increase the range and depth of even favourite sensations. He started to realise that his relationship with John had been perhaps the first taste of what he now was finding increasingly desirable and pleasurable. He had always wanted something different sexually with John who was far from being his normal type. Certainly John was much older than the men he was usually excited by. But it was precisely this difference in his desire for John which had made John so magnetic and had, perversely, made Sam so determined to resist him. Now he wondered if his resistance was not simply an act of teasing delay on the very good grounds that 'pleasure delayed is pleasure increased'.

Sam was roused from his thoughts by a growing awareness in the silent room of the fading aroma of the two wrestlers and the rising foxy scent of John below him. Sam had always found the particular smell of other men the first thing which aroused him. He could tell from how he reacted at a purely animal level to such body odours how much he was going to enjoy sex even with someone he had only just met. And there was something about John's foxy aroma that Sam knew was a certain guarantee that sex with John, whatever form it took, was going to be very, very special.

John broke into Sam's speculations with a harsh command. 'Get down. Back on to the ground.'

Sam didn't need to be told a second time. His limbs seemed to be thanking him themselves as he unwound his legs from the chains and first lowered his body to the beam and then leapt from there down to the sandy floor.

John handed him a glass of water which Sam drank carefully. He stole a glance down John's hairy body to the area below the wide leather belt. To Sam's disappointment the flat black flap indicated that John no longer sported the interesting bulge he had when the three apprentices were pleasuring one another above his shaven head.

'Well you've proved you've got some stamina. But there's a long way to go. And as I've got to bear the burden of training you, the Master of the School has wisely made it a rule that once a day, for one hour, a trainer is allowed a private session with each of his apprentices. This is an hour set aside for the trainer's pleasure, not the apprentice's, although he may get some. But that is not important. Do you understand?'

Sam had to work hard to hide the excitement he felt at John's words. 'I do.'

He glanced again at John's classic ex-boxer physique. Solid and firm with a well-developed powerful chest covered in a dense mass of wiry tangled hair which ran in a straight line down to his rock-hard stomach and precise, deep navel. Beneath that, the thick leather belt marked the line that guarded what Sam could see and desire from what he could not see but guessed he would desire most of all if he could.

Sam remembered how he had accidentally witnessed the sex-wrestling scene between Arif, Denton and John, and how Denton had skilfully put his hand under John's loincloth and taken what Sam had guessed was a thick and willing stem. Sam remembered how John's big head had arched back to climax at the same time as Denton had thrust deeper and deeper with his leather-sheathed cock into Arif's large and sensual arse. It seemed to Sam that the sex of all those men was now distilled into John.

John took the glass of water from Sam's hand. In the excitement of his sexual reverie, Sam had forgotten he was still holding it. John's harsh weather-beaten face with its slightly flattened and thickened nose drew close to Sam's youthful features. Sam absorbed eagerly not only the older man's battered signs of virile manhood but also the flashing brown of his cunning eyes and the dank foxy smell which rose from the many tempting contours of his body.

'You must learn to concentrate,' John whispered roughly.

'Maybe I need to be taught that first,' replied Sam. He was trying to conceal how much he wanted John to teach him anything which would involve deep physical contact between the two of them, especially here in the austere circular brick room which seemed to Sam to be almost like a prison cell.

John smiled, his dimples cutting into his rough and stubbly cheeks. 'But this is my private hour of pleasure, apprentice, and you are my newest recruit. Do you understand the rules?'

Sam nodded almost too eagerly. He realised almost at once that to reach the zone of deep pleasure he wanted so badly he would have to hide just how much pleasure he hoped to get from John. Sam tried to put on a more reluctant and wary expression.

John, however, had guessed that Sam wanted anything and everything that John would do to him. But that didn't worry John because he knew that he was going to torment Sam in a way that Sam was still too raw a recruit to guess at. John was going to do to Sam as he had done to so many of his very best apprentices in the past. He was going to torment with pleasure. He was going to take Sam to a peak of pleasure and then to show him the next highest peak and then, he would withdraw, leaving Sam longing for precisely that which would be denied, until the next time, the next private hour.

'Get back up on the beam,' he commanded.

John watched as Sam's agile body effortlessly leapt up to the beam and sat sprawled on it with all the arrogant and foolish beauty of an active and handsome young gay man in the first and best of his encounters.

John remembered the broad and powerful swimmer's chest Sam had hidden now under the leather apprentice vest. He recalled Sam's unusually large nipples and the circles of dark blond hair that framed their tempting peaks. John had often stolen a look at the classic mix of swimmer's taut stomach and thin waist leading out to a well-fleshed but firm bottom and a large willing cock. John revelled in the sight of Sam's perfectly proportioned and well-muscled thighs and legs with their down of dark blond hair, shining now in the circle of sunlight which framed him.

Denton, who was an expert on bodies and desire, had told John after he had first met Sam, that what made Sam so desirable was that he looked so average 'Mr Nice Guy'. Denton had told John that someone like Sam would always need a darker, controlling figure who could reveal to him intensities and games which Sam would never discover on his own.

What John had not added to Denton's shrewd analysis was John's own certainty that Sam contained within himself a great capacity for erotic intensity, indeed a great capacity for Roman games, but that he needed the right, forceful and more experienced man to lead him to the hidden side of his nature. As John watched Sam sitting on the beam trying to hide from him how much he wanted John to force him into new pleasures, John knew more than ever before that it was his destiny to break this young man who had led such a charmed and easy life into pleasures that only someone like John, whose life had often been a struggle and a fight, had been forced to discover. John gazed at Sam and knew Sam was trying to guess his thoughts and intentions. But John was too skilful. Sam would not know until John was ready to reveal to him the full extent of what he could do for Sam.

John had been to caves deeper and darker than any Sam could even imagine and he had come back with the sensual equivalent of gold. Sam was going to be shown that gold. He was going to know and feel it. But John was determined that Sam would earn that knowledge. He was not going to hand it him on a plate. With these thoughts in mind John advanced closer to his apprentice.

'Put your ankles in the chains and lie back on the beam with your shoulders and head tipping down to the floor over the other side of the beam.'

Sam looked puzzled but, as John had anticipated, he did precisely what he was ordered to. John surveyed his apprentice. His thighs rose in straight lines to his lower legs which bent towards the metal circles where his feet hung suspended by his ankles. John enjoyed looking at Sam's large feet and toes. John thought to himself that Sam had no idea yet how much pleasure those toes were going to give and receive and he certainly had no idea how John was going to achieve that.

Sam's leather flap had naturally fallen down over the beam revealing to John all of Sam's fleshy but firm arse. But John noted with a brief grin that Sam had clenched his cheeks tight together as if determined to hide from him what Denton had called 'the sacred circle of the apprentice and the forbidden tunnel beyond'.

John was amused that Sam, like so many of the apprentices that had come to this island, certain that they knew precisely what they wanted, did not yet know himself. They did not know what they really needed, what their own sexual master, buried inside each of them, was trying to lead them to. That was the purpose of this island's Roman games, to bring them to the ultimate truths about their own pleasures.

John deliberately did not move or speak for a long while. He wanted Sam to build up in his own imagination fantasies about what John was going to do with him and what he might be allowed to do with John. John wanted Sam to heat himself up. That was the perfect way to start their games.

He watched Sam's handsome full face, with his remarkable eyes, steal quizzical glances at him. He watched Sam's eyes graze his ex-boxer's face and his ex-boxer's torso. He saw Sam dare, now and again, to steal a look at the state of his protective leather flap. John knew that Sam also longed to see the exact shape of his well-hidden arse. John knew that Sam could correctly guess that it was firm and hairy but he could not guess at how sexily boxlike it was or how the crevasse in the centre of his arse was so provocatively protected by a dense mass of almost metallically resistant black hair.

To increase what John accurately guessed was Sam's already rapidly rising temperature, John placed his hands behind his back at the base of his spine and started to smooth his hands over the hidden shape and texture of his buttocks. It gave John considerable pleasure to feel the hairy boxlike shape and dense muscled hardness of his own bottom. It made him hot too when he slipped his hands deep into the hairy ravine that so deeply divided the two mounds of his arse. But John didn't allow his thoughts to wander in the direction of how Sam, with his swimmer's shape and vigour and sharply rising desire, might add to the delights of that zone of his body. That, John had decided, would come later, much later, in their training sessions and would, in all probability, also involve Arif and Denton. They too were certain Sam had the potential to join their innermost circle.

John could see that his self-caressing had indeed achieved the effect he had intended. Under the lose protection of his frontal leather flap, Sam's large cock was rising in a series of swift shuddering motions. Soon, as John could plainly see, the leather flap was taut and creased as Sam's potent rod tried to burst through that barrier.

John was now satisfied that Sam was ready for some real attention. He pretended for a few moments that he was going to focus his attention on Sam's arse and he deliberately moved, with a not entirely false gleam in his eye, towards where the amply haired and fleshy backside was exposed like some large peach ready to be bitten into. John was more than satisfied to see that, as he got closer to that prize, Sam defensively clenched his buttocks together like a spoilt and overprotected child.

John waited until the last possible moment before he veered away from this tantalising labyrinth of pleasure. He registered the barely concealed disappointment in Sam's bright eyes as he, with teasing, deliberate casualness, sauntered away from what he had pretended was his hot and immediate target. Instead now, John moved to where Sam's head and shoulders lolled back off the beam and into space.

John placed his face close to Sam's and brought the thin military line of his lips close to Sam's fresh, puckered mouth. John could smell Sam. He smelt to John of lake water and youth and desire. It was an aroma that passed like an electric current down from John's nostrils to every part of his body. He brought his mouth ever closer to Sam's in a series of tiny advances through the space between them which was both a physical space and the special electrified space of desire between two men destined for one another.

John was experienced enough to be able to tell from the flare he saw in Sam's nostrils that his raw, invasive foxy tang was now pouring over the younger man and sharpening his animal need for anything and everything that John might deign to give him. But John denied his apprentice any easy or instant pleasure. John was saving up pleasure for himself. This really was *his* hour and Sam would have to learn that sometimes youth had to yield to man; easy innocence to hard-earned knowledge. All of Sam's young man's vigour and urgency of wanting was now spread out before John. And John was determined to make the most of the time Denton had allotted him of total power.

Defying Sam's desire to touch the fire tip of his tongue with John's rough one, John pulled his tempting half-open mouth away from Sam's yearning lips. He ignored the silent plea in Sam's large eyes for John's mouth and tongue to return close to Sam's youth-flecked face. Instead, John lifted up his leather baton and started to roll it at an almost imperceptible speed down Sam's leather-cased torso. Starting at the naked neck, he allowed the leather stick to roll over the button flaps which covered what John knew to be one of Sam's most distinctive features – the large swelling nipples that crowned his unusually broad and well-defined chest. He allowed the stick to rest on the nipple area and gently rolled the stick up and down so that even through the leather John knew Sam was feeling the teasing, testing rigidity of his tool of absolute command. John knew his tactic was working when he sensed how hard Sam was trying to suppress his spontaneous sigh of deep sensual enjoyment.

John lingered there for a while watching Sam's eyes silently plead with him to unbutton the nipple flaps and make direct contact between his fingers or tongue or even, most desired, John's dense manly cock and Sam's naked flaring pink nipples. But John was a true expert at Roman games and he knew the pleasure of delay. He denied the plea in Sam's eyes and let his leather baton roll down beyond Sam's chest to the exposed taut fitness of Sam's stomach and navel. There three circles of dark blond hairs seemed to form protective rings around Sam's deep navel.

John locked his harsh autumn eyes on to Sam's, forcing Sam

to realise that it was John who would decide where and when and how their bodies met. He turned his rod vertically and used its tip to trace around Sam's third and outermost circle of dark blond hair. Sam tried to reach for John's cock but John denied him that too easy satisfaction with a smart rap of his leather stick. Sam winced but said nothing and John knew that his blow had given Sam as much pleasure as pain.

John began circling his stick round Sam's pleasingly large and sensitive nipple without ever quite touching it. He could hear Sam's breathing get faster with excitement as he undid the second nipple flap and there repeated his circling gesture around the nipple's peak but this time with the rough surface of his finger. Still John only patrolled around the outer rim of the nipple denying it direct contact. He saw in Sam's strong blue eyes the young man pleading with him to directly touch his nipple but John merely whispered, 'Pleasure delayed is pleasure increased.'

John now ran his stick over the firm well-exercised stomach and navel, which was gleaming gold in the burning rays of the late afternoon sunlight. John's stick then reached the thick leather belt. Still circling Sam's right nipple with his finger, John allowed the stick to roll gently over the leather flap towards the mound in the centre of it which he knew marked the spot where Sam's cock was aching against the leather; aching to be gripped by John's rough, broad hand.

John gently rolled the leather stick up the flap towards Sam's hidden cock, then expertly guided the stick so that it rolled up and over the taut mound and then back again. He saw Sam close his eyes and John guessed at how much Sam was enjoying the feeling of that stiff rod caressing what by now must be his fully exposed cockhead rubbing against the rough surface of his costume.

Almost imperceptibly, John started to change their basic physical relationship with one another. John had decided that Sam had been the pretty swimmer tease for too long. Now it was John's turn to see if Sam lived up to his many obvious promises. John moved alongside Sam, still moving his finger in teasing circular motions around Sam's hungry teat until he had glided down to where Sam's legs were suspended from the metal circles. He pulled his hand away from Sam's nipple conscious that he had never given it the satisfaction it was crying out for. That was another lesson pretty boys like Sam should learn. Blue eyes and Tarzan's torso did not buy you automatic rights in the more serious and rougher game of sex.

John took hold of the lower part of Sam's thighs. He squeezed their discreet muscles and ruffled the silky down of dark blond hair. He pulled them further apart and using all his strength dragged Sam towards him and lifted his entire body backwards, pulling Sam's arsehole up to his mouth. Sam was still vainly attempting to hide his secret place by clutching the two cheeks of his arse tight.

John grinned. He had beaten much stronger resistance than this. Before John launched himself he took a moment to enjoy the peachy firmness of Sam's bottom as it was now completely exposed to him. Then suddenly he pressed the lower side of his large tongue against the very centre of Sam's rosebud. Expertly he used his lips to force his tongue against his target which was as sweet and as hot and as initially resisting as John had hoped it would be. Sam was a pleasure worth waiting for. A catch worth even more than John had expected.

Sam was still resisting so John curled the tip of his tongue backwards so that it started to touch the very top of Sam's anus where there was a tiny ridge of flesh. John, with almost imperceptible movements, let his tongue slide up and down and over this ridge which he guessed was the key to opening up Sam's arsehole for his use.

John could feel that Sam was now arching back and he guessed that Sam's desire to be pleasured was fighting hard against his fear of how much John might take control of him. John knew that in sex the full force of his nature suddenly blazed forth making him dangerously desirable, especially to men like Sam, who had not yet fully learnt the unique excitement that could be attained from total surrender.

John now eased his well-practised tongue around the halo of golden down round Sam's rosebud. At first John's motions were very slow with only the tip of his tongue running around the taut and sweet-tasting textures of Sam's flesh. But gradually John increased the speed with which he patrolled the inner frontiers of Sam's puckered skin. He also now pressed more of his tongue down hard against Sam's defiantly withheld arse.

He then added to the pressure on Sam by putting two of his fingers around each of Sam's large nipples and did to them exactly what his tongue was doing to Sam's arse. As John had guessed, Sam could not resist this double assault. Sam lifted up his entire lower body towards John's mouth and let his bottom open up to John's insisting tongue.

Sam was feeling new highs of excitement as he surveyed the burly ex-boxer's hairy torso half-hidden by his leather trainer's outfit pressing hard against his thighs and legs now held high in the air. Sam felt his muscled shoulders straining to lift his lower body up ever higher towards that stern square face and that powerful mouth and tongue.

Sam watched with disbelief as John undid his own leather nipple flaps and brought out his raw exposed left nipple towards Sam's expectant rosebud. Slowly Sam could feel the hot peak approaching him. Then John rammed the nipple hard into Sam.

Sam almost screamed with sensation. It felt as if John's teat had penetrated like a giant prick inside his arse. All the ridges and valleys of his anus seemed to be rubbed by John's unyielding peak. Sam felt his arse opening wider to let more nipple flesh in.

John slowly withdrew his left tit. Then through his clenched mouth he leant over Sam's naked torso and whispered, 'My right one is even bigger and will ride you even harder.'

As John said this he squeezed Sam's own right nipple between his two fingers until it too become a steely peak from which John was now drawing, with his fingertips, almost electric currents of desire.

Sam looked down between the swelling slopes of his swimmer's chest and saw John lowering his torso and exposed right nipple and directing it towards his arsehole. Sam saw, with a delight he did not now disguise, that John's right nipple was indeed almost twice the size of his left. Sam was learning that John, as a trainer, kept all his promises.

Once again Sam felt first the animal heat of the hard peak of the nipple as it travelled over his golden down and then plunged into his arse filling it with a wonderful rush of rough flesh and tangled hair. John now was rocking gently back and forth so that his nipple plunged in and out of Sam's rosebud making the entire entrance to Sam's normally well-protected arse vibrate.

Then, to Sam's surprise, John deftly lowered his mouth over the top of Sam's cock and squeezed his lips against its smooth circumference. Just as John's nipple was invading Sam's inner regions so now John clenched and unclenched his mouth alternately pulling into and then releasing Sam's cockhead inside his mouth. Sam could feel the spittle in John's mouth drip on to his foreskin which was now tightening as every drop fell, forcing Sam's inflamed glans to emerge, as Sam guessed John had intended.

As soon as it emerged John closed his hot mouth around it. Using spittle as lubricant John started to twist Sam's cockhead from side to side just as John's nipple was twisting Sam's inner rosebud from side to side. Sam felt suddenly that the two most sensitive parts of his body were linked together by John's double action. In a daze of sex-saturated sensations, Sam was aware that sometimes John would be making his prick and arsehole twist in the same direction at the same time. Sometimes he would twist them in different directions at the same time and two quite distinct sets of delight shot to Sam's brain or whatever part of him was the receiver of this new total system of pleasure.

Then, sometimes, John would break into a certain roughness. His nipple would be twisting violently against Sam's anus and his mouth would be rubbing his cockhead almost raw then he would alternate this with a much lighter and more tender touch, allowing his teat almost to be guided by the gently rocking motions of Sam's arse and his mouth would seem just to be hovering over the surface of Sam's cockhead just sufficiently in contact with it for it to feel as if a silky condom was being pulled over it.

Sam did not know how long John continued with these exercises. Time seemed to be lost in a labyrinth of sensations that Sam wanted never to end. Then he was aware of John withdrawing both his nipple and his mouth. John stood full square in front of him. Sam could see that John's own cock was now striving hard against the front leather flap. Sam could also see how pointed his nipples were through the opened nipple flaps in his leather vest.

John started to undo the buckle of his broad leather belt. His square face with its boxer's semi-flattened nose seemed sexier than ever to Sam. As John was unbuckling his belt he looked straight into Sam's eyes. 'No, apprentice. I've earned my right to fully ride you for my pleasure and my pleasure alone. If you get any pleasure, that's incidental. This last part of my private hour is for me and my needs. Your body is at my service. Do you understand that?'

Sam nodded with a slight hint of anxiety at what John might have in store for him and which, if Sam was to stay on the island and enjoy the Roman games, he would have to submit to without resistance.

John's buckle was finally undone and he let the belt and the leather flaps fall to the ground revealing his cock. It was as large and long as Sam had guessed it would be with two thick blue veins down either side. John ran a fingertip along each one of the blue veins.

'Those are my ridges of ultimate pleasure,' he said proudly. 'But you will have to pass many more tests and win some real matches before you will be allowed to get anywhere near to finding out where they can take a real wrestling man.'

Sam nodded and became instantly determined that he would do whatever he must to reach the point where he would come to know what those twin ridges could do.

'Put your legs down for a minute, apprentice boy. They will have to go back in the air in a moment.' John turned to a wooden box on the wall. He opened it and took a leather sheath from it which seemed to have hundreds of miniature balls stitched to its surface. He placed the device into a glass box which appeared to be some kind of steamer. He pressed a button and a jet of hot steam passed over the leather sheath. He glanced at Sam with a knowing grin. 'In this school we have constant scalding hot steam for reasons you will find out if you are accepted. You won't be disappointed.'

John took the leather sheath out of the steamer and strode back over to Sam. 'Those long legs have had enough of a rest now. I want them raised high in the air.'

Sam obeyed instantly. His legs were lit by the last of the sunlight which poured through the circular window. John seemed to like that.

'The sunlight is catching your downy hair. It makes you look as if you are covered with a thick layer of blond fur. I like that.'

Sam watched fascinated as John deftly pulled the leather sheath over his large phallus. It stretched tight over his hard flesh and John laced it firmly at the base of his stem just above his heavy-looking balls. Then John lovingly poured some lubricating jelly over his massive organ. His dark black eyes locked on to Sam's blinking blue ones.

'At last I've got the golden swimmer where I want him. I've been reserving this moment for a long time, ever since I first saw you and knew that you were going to join our Roman games. Well this is part of the ritual of the games and, one day, you will be able to do to some raw apprentice what I am going to do to you now.'

As the larger and older man started to approach him, Sam felt apprehensive for the first time. Maybe the pleasure he had had so far from his encounter with his trainer had been as much as Sam could take or needed. Maybe what John was going to do to him now would cause him more pain than pleasure.

John seemed to read his thoughts. With both hands he rubbed his cock up and down. 'Don't worry lad. Although it's not my main concern, I don't think you'll want to miss what I am going to do to you. Now obey. Obey.'

Sam felt his whole body tense up as if already he had passed sufficiently far into the world of Roman games that he automatically responded to a trainer's commands and instantly put himself and his body under orders.

'First command,' said John as he brought his staunchly erect cock closer and closer to Sam's exposed and defenceless arse. 'I want to see you using those large and powerful hands of yours to pleasure your fine swimmer's chest and the giant-size nipples that nature has given you to enjoy. I'll teach you to enjoy them much more than you think you can. We've seen, remember. I am going to show you how, when you combine what you do to them with what I am going to do to your virgin arse, you will find out what real nipple pleasure really means. That's a bonus for you apprentice boy. Start caressing.'

Sam did not need another order from John to start moving the palms of his hands over the firmly fleshy contours of his powerful chest. He knew those contours very well just as he knew how they led inexorably to the high peaks of his nipples. But now, Sam guessed, he was going to feel something new and even more satisfying. What new sensations was John going to superimpose on Sam's usual techniques of bliss?

Sam let the palms of his hands touch his chest for just a second before lifting them to hover above his skin for a few seconds. Then he returned them for one more brief encounter between the rough flesh of his hands and the softer hairier surface of his chest. He set up a rhythm that was almost like a drum beat on his chest and he was very careful at this point to avoid any premature contact with his large nipples.

John seemed to sense that Sam was going to go into his routine with his chest and nipples and that John would cunningly incorporate that into his own plans for the beautiful swimmer's submission below him.

The first thing Sam was aware of, and which he had never anticipated, was John wrapping his fingers around Sam's long cockstem and slowly gripping it in his fighter's clench leaving only the very top of his cock free of this tough control. Then John, leaning his large square body forward, pushed Sam's penis against the thick line of wiry, tumbling black hair that ran from John's deep navel to the stem of his prick like an overgrown trail.

John had released his vicelike grip on Sam's phallus and was now only holding the top of Sam's cock with his bare palm. This he was using to push Sam's member against the hair line from John's navel to the base of his cockstem.

The back of Sam's cock first met ticklish outer hairs and then John forced Sam's tool to rub deep into the dense and wiry hair which exactly matched the length of Sam's cock. Sam could feel

71

the firm but yielding flesh of John's stomach under the hair and the muscles which formed two hard flanks to its softer centre.

John started moving his stomach up and down very slightly so that Sam's cock was beginning to wank that pleasing surface of dense hair and softer flesh itself. Sam gradually grew aware of what John was aiming for. As Sam got more and more excited by the way his cock had been trapped between John's hand and stomach and was now being rubbed up and down there, so the tip of Sam's liberated cockhead was now touching the outer rim of John's deep hairy navel.

Sam suddenly felt an unexpected desire to enter that large and unusually deep navel. Sam realised that John must have guessed how he could manipulate Sam's desires so precisely because he now whispered revealingly to Sam.

'That's my small arsehole and you can fuck it raw.'

The words passed like an electric charge up Sam's spine and up the length of his cock too which grew instantly more rigid as it now unambiguously spilled into the waiting well of John's navel. Its ring of wiry hair was already creating a teasing circle around Sam's prick.

Sam was about to find out how good John's timing and combining of mutual pleasures was. At the precise moment that Sam was starting to enter John's navel with his cockhead, John laid his leather-sheathed penis against the bottom of Sam's peachy arse. At the same moment as the very top of Sam's raw glans was pressing itself against the entire outer hairy circle of John's navel, the tip of John's sheathed cock was making first tentative contact with the base of Sam's spine where a triangle of golden hair pointed down to the crevice of darker hair which protected Sam's rosebud. The touch of leather was light at first, like a feather brushing tantalisingly against Sam's hair and ruffling it delicately. But then Sam became aware of the swelling weight of John's erection pressing against the leather casing. Just as Sam's cock seemed to be magnetically drawn to John's deep navel so John's prick seemed to want, of its own accord, to thrust up from the base of Sam's spine towards his semiexposed anus.

Now Sam could feel inches of the back of the leather-sheathed cock rubbing gently but firmly against the opening crack of his arse. He allowed his hands now to cup both sides of his chest and pull at the flesh around his nipples. His cock was plunging deeper into John's hairy navel which seemed to be the cue John was waiting for to roughly encircle Sam's thighs with his boxer's hands and prise them apart revealing both more of Sam's peachy arse and more of his still-clenched arsehole.

'I'm coming in and you're not stopping me,' said John, his voice now dense with lust.

Instantly, Sam could feel the leather-bound penis forcing open his still-fighting rosebud but suddenly Sam knew he wanted to feel John inside him. He wanted him so much that even his own cock thrusting into John's submitting navel and his swelling nipples seemed to crave the vital sensation of John's sheathed cock riding deep inside him.

Sam had already imagined the pleasure he would get from John's entry into him but he had not anticipated how special it was going to be. The first surprise Sam got was that the leather was thin enough for Sam to feel every detail of John's bone-hard member underneath. The floor of the tunnel of his arse felt at once the two ridges of John's prick which curved up to form a V shape. These two ridges perfectly matched and swayed against two ridges which formed a circular frame inside Sam's arse. As these ridges met, both John and Sam felt spasms of pleasure spin through their bodies. It was as if the pleasure from one man ricocheted from one to the other; as if the rim of pleasure in Sam's arse spun into John's cock and raced down the full length of its stem and into John's own as yet untouched arse.

Sam longed to move his hands, that were still cupping and rubbing his pecs, upwards so he could close his fingers tightly round his large nipples. But John seemed to sense that and shouted at him.

'Leave those giant tits alone until I command you to squeeze them, oh slave boy!'

Sam soon realised why John was making him delay that delight. Now that John's sheathed cockhead had soaked Sam's rosebud with pleasure, Sam allowed his defences to fall and the muscles of his buttocks began to relax. John was quick to take advantage of what, Sam later realised, he must have known was the hypnotising effect of the first round of delighting sensations on Sam's normally unrelenting vigilance.

Before Sam could do anything about it John's prick was sliding well past Sam's puckered entrance and deep into his inner arse with John's stem now thrusting up further than anyone else had ever been; inside the potentially generous and largely unexplored cavern of Sam's arse.

But more than that Sam was now feeling the effect of the hundreds of tiny leather balls which covered the stem of John's leather sheath. Suddenly it seemed to Sam that every small ridge, every tiny valley, every miniature sphere of flesh that lined the tunnel of his arse was now being pleasured by these tiny balls which rolled everywhere inside him as John, using Sam's thighs as his thrust supports, was now plunging his large cock up into Sam in an assault as sudden as it was total.

Sam could feel both the thousand mini-sensations that the tiny leather balls were making all over the rubbed hot surfaces of his arse and at the same time the big satisfying pleasure of feeling the entire swollen rod of John's big phallus thrusting deeper and deeper inside. First, thrusting like a piston at the back of his arse, now thrusting up at the front of him as if John's cock was rubbing just beneath the surface of Sam's navel and taut stomach wall. All the positions which John's penis found inside Sam gave both Sam and John larger and larger shocks of pure sexual satisfaction until each thrust became a small orgasm of sensation for the two men, now bound together, and transmitting quakes of pleasure one to the other. John's increasingly rough and complete possession of Sam was intensified by the pleasure Sam was getting from thrusting his own virile member at least an inch deep inside John's large hairy navel which, in Sam's imagination, was indeed now John's small arse and one he was loving to thrust into as John's wiry black hair made his cock's thrusting just that bit more pleasantly difficult and abrasive. Sam wanted his cock to be made raw by John's matted black hair.

Sam could see that John's entire square face was by now locked into the pleasure he was taking from the younger man's obvious total submission to him. His concentrating black eyes were locked on to Sam's blue gaze.

'Slave boy – squeeze your nipples hard and then push them towards that mouth of yours which I'll deal with later.'

Sam was obedient as he was learning so fast to be and started to use his hands to push his erect nipples towards his mouth. His swimmer's neck was agile and flexible enough to make the demanded contact between lips and nipples possible as well as desirable.

Then, in his rough boxer's style, seizing the initiative, John let go of Sam's thighs which were now bent almost as far back as Sam's chest, and took control himself of Sam's large excited nipples, bending both of their erect points towards his lips.

John did not need to hold Sam's thighs back against Sam's torso any more because at that moment John decided to thrust the last hidden and largest third of his swollen cockstem into the hidden depths of Sam's arse.

Sam felt for the first time that an entire man was inside him. John's already large penis seemed at that instant to grow immense inside Sam. John's cock seemed to be rubbing against his spine and his stomach and he felt that John's cockhead was reaching almost as high as his chest.

'All of the cock inside me,' groaned Sam.

'Still more to come,' yelled a triumphant John whose square-built hairy body was now thrusting deeply into the younger man's almost perfect swimmer's torso.

Sam felt, as his nipples were about to touch his mouth, the full force of John's excited conquering glans and stem. Even John's large spunk-filled hairy balls were now pressing insistently against Sam's peachy arsehole.

'Don't come!' commanded John urgently.

But, although Sam wanted to obey his trainer more than ever before, the closeness of his hot nipples to his moist mouth, the size and racing thrust of John's cock in his wide-open arse and the sensation of his own vigorous cock plunging now against the final hairy wall of John's navel made it impossible for Sam to control himself.

His spunk shot into John's deep belly; load after load of grateful scalding liquid pumping uncontrollably into John. It was pouring out of his navel, running down, as burst after burst erupted into John's tangled black hair line, oozing to the stem of his still-thrusting cock, now plunging at its highest possible speed into the dark depths of Sam's submitting arsehole.

Just a split second after Sam started to come in rich lards again and again, he felt John's leather cock-sheath fill out with a torrent of liquid which Sam knew could only be John's huge sex-load pouring out of the beautiful hole of his cock. Sam felt then the last extra, undreamt of pleasure, which came from John's cock swelling even more inside him, where wild waves of viscous fluid, red-hot, even behind the protective leather barrier, expanded the outer limits of the leather sheath and brought a contact between cock and arse to Sam's inner cave that arched his entire body and seemed to send it spiralling upward towards the sky beyond their fused and yelling bodies.

'Take my come! Take my come!' yelled John at the top of his voice.

Sam could only respond with one last rich gush of spunk which poured over John's stomach like a white spreading stain of bliss.

It felt to Sam that every part of his body, inside and out, was being possessed by John's sheathed cock and its seething surface of pleasuring tiny leather balls. It seemed to Sam at the moment of his maximum physical ecstasy that John's sheathed cockhead was even inside both Sam's large nipples filling them with John's climax.

He could only start to think of these pleasures when he started to come down from the heights John's rough-hewn but knowing body had taken him to. At the peak of John's possession of him Sam lost touch with all his thoughts and was only aware of wave after wave of pleasure breaking over him. There was one moment when Sam felt he was actually rising towards the circle of red sunset sky which filled the window and which reminded him of how he used to give himself so much pleasure in his cottage at sunset. It seemed an age ago that Sam had almost despaired of finding other men who were prepared and able to go as far as he did in his fantasies.

In a daze Sam felt the slow withdrawal of John's cock from inside him. He wanted to grab John's hairy thighs and force him to push his cock in again but he knew that he had to obey his trainer. Sam passed into a half-dream. There his body felt sudden memories of the pleasure he had just been given and shuddered appreciatively. He wondered as he started to emerge from his dreamy state, whether he had given satisfaction to John. He did not have to wait long for an answer.

'Get off the beam, apprentice. Rest on the sand.'

Sam let his body fall on to the sandy floor and lay in a pool of scarlet light which picked up the mix of youthful fleshiness and hard swimmer's muscular definition which he had always guessed other men might find appealing.

Sam opened his eyes to see John buckling on his leather belt and flaps again. Sam inhaled the older man's compelling foxy sweat as it trickled from out of his leather top down his exposed hairy stomach. John looked at Sam with a dark flash in his eyes.

'You did not disappoint your trainer . . . for a beginner that is.'

Sam closed his eyes. He was pleased to think that what they had just done together might be only a beginning.

The hissing sound of the steamer and the distant sound of another young man apparently giving his best to a trainer in the next-door room, merged to form the kind of memory which Sam knew he would be able to use later when, alone, he could please his own body. His reverie was interrupted by John's voice.

'Now, apprentice, a more gentle end to your first formal session. Stand up.'

Sam obeyed. John advanced towards him and closed the leather flaps on Sam's nipples.

'Let's keep those hidden for special occasions,' said John. 'And special masters.'

'Who?' Sam started to ask, but John clapped his hand over Sam's mouth.

'You will find out at the right time and if you have the right talents.' John pressed the palm of one hand against the leather flap that protected Sam's arse whilst putting one finger slowly into Sam's navel. He pressed his sexy virile face with its classic boxer's square roughness against Sam's softer cheek. 'There are a lot of other things I want to do to you in my private hours.'

Sam almost trembled with pleasure at the thought of what those things might be. Then, out of the blue, John gave Sam's arse a hard smack. Then another and then another. A flash of red light seemed to go through all the pleasure zones in Sam's brain. Then the blows stopped.

John lowered his voice. 'That is a taste of what might come your way.' Sam started to reply when John gave Sam's mouth a light slap. 'No. You stay silent. Remember? I'm not interested in what pleases you.'

Sam gave a curt nod. Even John's denying disciplines gave him a little thud of pleasure.

John spoke again. 'There are more rules here which you must remember. Before I take you to your next training session you must remember that you must not speak at all unless a trainer asks you a question. Trainers you will know because they are the ones with these wide leather belts. Apprentices have narrow belts like yours. You must not speak to another apprentice even if he speaks to you. He will be punished for that. Don't try to be clever and seek out 'punishments' because you think they might be fun. We know how to give punishments that no one could consider fun. You will not have sex or any physical contact with another apprentice unless you are ordered to do so by a trainer or a master.'

'How will I recognise a master?' asked Sam.

John gave a broken grin and was about to smack Sam's arse again when he stopped himself. 'You will not need to be told that,' responded John. He opened the inner door of the room and gestured for Sam to follow him.

Sam found himself in a brick-walled curving corridor, lit by flame torches in metal caskets on the walls. There were many small wooden doors to Sam's left. But to Sam's right there were far fewer doors and they were much larger. These doors were made of metal with handles of circular wrought iron.

Passing one of the smaller wooden doors which was ajar, Sam caught a glimpse of a very tall and lithe blond man in his mid-twenties being arm locked from behind by a handsome black man who was also tall and slender. The agile black man's sensual lips were brushing against the ear of the blond almost as if he were whispering to him, but you could tell by his eyes that he had a trainer's command. The blond man was trying to resist the arm lock on him and, for one second, Sam caught a glimpse of the blond man's eyes. Their bright blueness was swimming with what Sam guessed was his knowledge of what his powerful trainer was going to do in the next few seconds.

'Don't look,' shouted John with a sharp slap on Sam's thigh. 'You'll see enough when we are ready to let you see.'

A few moments later John halted Sam in front of one of the larger metal doors. He pressed his face against Sam's shoulder. 'This is circle two of the four circles of the school. Now listen to me very carefully because if you make a mistake it makes me as your trainer look bad. You wouldn't want that, would you?' Sam shook his head. 'Inside this door you will find two more doors. One blue and one red. You take the blue first. Just stand there. You don't have to do anything. Then you will be led to the red door. That will be your next test.'

John opened the metal door and Sam stepped inside. The door slammed behind him. Sam was confronted by the two doors John had described and Sam knew that he was about to enter the next phase of his initiation into the Roman games.

At the thought of it, against his will, Sam's body trembled with desire.

Four

The blue door swayed open and Sam entered. It was a circular room again. But it had no window. It was covered from floor to ceiling in dark blue tiles. In the middle of the room was what seemed to be an empty large circular bath although Sam could not see any taps.

Sam was grabbed from behind by two compact but muscular bodies. He started to struggle with them but almost immediately one of them whispered something in a thick accent that Sam guessed might be from Thailand. The other man replied in what Sam was sure was an accent from the north of England. The combination seemed potentially exciting to him.

'Your master says don't resist,' said the man with the Thai accent. He spoke with a firmness which Sam recognised should not be argued with and Sam nodded.

With a few quick, painless movements Sam was blindfolded. He felt skilful and sensual hands first undo his belt letting his leather flaps fall to the floor. Then he was aware of his leather vest and leather boots being removed. All this was done with perfect precision. There was, so far, almost nothing sexual in the contact Sam had with these two deft and fast-moving strangers. As he thought this he could hear the sound of water pouring from high above into the empty sunken bath. Very soon it seemed that the cascading water was filling the bath he had seen.

Now that he was naked except for his blindfold the attitude of his two unseen minders seemed to subtly change. One of them started to caress his chest.

'A hard-working chest,' said the voice with an accent Sam now recognised as Yorkshire. 'I know such things. I was a coal miner.'

The other man, with a lighter and more silky touch, half-encircled Sam's lower back resting his arm on the ledge of Sam's dimpled arse.

'You must be cleansed,' said the other voice, unmistakably gentle, seductive and Thai. 'We are here to relax and cleanse you, apprentice.'

Sam was going to speak directly to them but then he had a flash memory of John's battered face saying, 'If you make a mistake it makes your trainer look bad.' Sam didn't want anything bad to get back to John. Sam had to be with John again. He had already started to guess what John was going to do with him next and he was determined not to miss one of those strokes.

The Thai man led him to the edge of the bath and with a completely unexpected physical strength lifted Sam in his arms and carried him to the water. Sam was instantly aware of the concentrated, smooth muscularity of the Thai's upper body, as the left side of Sam's torso now pressed against it. Sam deliberately leant his neck against the shoulders of his carrier which felt as densely muscular and as perfectly carved as Sam had imagined. He was sorry to find himself being detached from the man as he was eased into the bath as, in just the few, bare moments of their physical contact, Sam had felt the compelling and seamless combination of the other's strength and tenderness.

But, before Sam could feel the full impact of this regret, he was aware that he was already passing into the sensual orbit of his other unseen helper. As the Thai laid him gently on a ceramic shelf inside the bath, Sam's shoulders were suddenly grabbed and held in a vicelike grip by his other unseen aide. Sam knew now, of course, that the other man was an ex-miner from the tough county of Yorkshire, but Sam had not really taken in what this meant until he was, literally, in his hands.

The man, Sam guessed from the way both of them had pressed themselves against him, was no taller than his Thai helper but, whereas the Thai exuded a virility which needed no crude proving through subtle and inventive physical grace, the Yorkshire miner gave off the vibrations of a man who had to fist-fight his way to acceptance. Now, he had to prove himself again as he massaged Sam's well-exercised swimmer's shoulder with an aggressive kneading motion which seemed to involve lifting up almost the whole of Sam's upper back. As the Yorkshireman did this Sam became aware of the other man's vigorous breathing. Above the noise of the still-cascading water Sam struggled to identify from his increasingly heavy breathing the exact position of the ex-miner's mouth.

Sam could feel desire returning and surging again through the inexhaustible youth and hardness of his body and this time he was going to ignore the commands of his trainer, of Arif and of Denton, and act on the wild impulse which had just possessed him. Sam waited for another few gruelling minutes of the other man's almost assaulting massage and then, when he was almost certain of the position of his masseur's mouth, he abruptly leant back and grabbed what he guessed rightly was the solid flesh of the back of the man's neck. He pulled the invisible Yorkshire-man's hard-breathing mouth to his full fleshy lips with an action so sudden and so fast that the other man had no warning and could take no precaution.

Suddenly Sam's sweet-tasting and playful lips had closed on the other man's harsh and suspicious mouth. Before the York-shireman realised what was happening to him he was feeling Sam's tongue plunging deep into his mouth, twisting round his ambushed tongue like a hungry cobra. The usually wary frontiers of his lips were overwhelmed by Sam's generous and sweet mouth and he had no time to think of resisting.

That was not the end of Sam's generosity. At the same moment as he made his assault on the Yorkshireman's unseen mouth, Sam had taken one of the man's hands and, gliding it down his long swanlike neck, had guided it over the upper firmness of his chest to the swelling peak of his large nipple which was now almost submerged by the rising waters of the bath.

As Sam suspected, the Yorkshireman had not expected anything like Sam's entrapment and, as Sam had also hoped, he had no defence against it. Sam was just starting to learn the powers he had and had not yet used.

The ex-miner clamped his hand as hard against Sam's nipple as Sam's mouth was clamped against the man's almost virginal lips. The violence of their embrace forced the man's compact body to ride against Sam's broad shoulders where Sam could feel the precise contours of the man's body. His muscles were sculpted in the way muscles can be only when they have been formed by years of unremitting, authentic physical labour. The cleft in the man's chest which Sam explored by tensing his own swimmer's shoulder blades was the kind that could only be achieved by daily toil. Sam now wanted to know the shape of his caresser's stomach and cock.

Sam's seduction of his unseen helper had not gone unobserved or unappreciated by the Thai man. Sam felt his arse being deftly caressed under the churning water and then, as he plunged his tongue deeper into the Yorkshireman's ambushed but willing throat, Sam was aware of a strange pressure against his lower stomach.

At first, still blindfolded, Sam, thought it was the Thai's face rubbing against him. But then he realised that what was massaging him was in fact the smooth, firm contoured flesh of the Thai's arse. The perfect circle of his arse was being adroitly aligned to kiss Sam's navel.

Sam said aloud, 'Yeah, arse circle against navel circle, the new perfect fuck.'

The Thai responded to this with a groan. And the Yorkshireman obviously glancing down from his deep embrace with Sam was also excited by what he saw because Sam could now, for the very first time, feel the other man's cock rising stiffly and pressing with a throbbing, rhythmic insistence into Sam's lower back.

As Sam's navel and the Thai man's bottom pressed tighter together, the Yorkshireman's small but perfectly chiselled body slipped into the bath. The unseen pleasure giver forced his way under Sam's half-floating body in the warm water and suddenly Sam felt the full force of the man's thick-cut cock rubbing up and down the clenched crack of his arse. The Thai man, clearly responding to the other man's movements, now slid his baby-smooth arse down from Sam's navel to Sam's rising, seeking penis. Sam was delighted to feel the firmness of his cock rubbing gently up and down the taut smoothness of the Thai man's arse whilst simultaneously feeling the naked force of the ex-miner's thick prick half-lifting from beneath as that cock moved up and down and swayed back and forth across the sealed valley of his arse.

Sam felt that all of them knew that they were not, this time, going to go all the way but it was good enough for all of them, for the moment. They could relish their threesome contact as a taster for an encounter which Sam knew they were destined to have again and which would, then, lead on to that complete consummation which all of them desired.

Gradually, the Thai man and the ex-miner floated their bodies away from Sam and he guessed that both of them did this extremely reluctantly and under orders. Soon all that was left of their touch was their hands as they soaped Sam's entire body in the hot water. Sam loved the touch of their four soapy hands sliding so easily and firmly over every part of him. Then the two men, still unseen, made Sam stand directly under where the water was pouring from the ceiling.

This seemed to be a signal for the two men to break from him but as they did so the Yorkshireman snatched a whisper. 'I want to fuck with you so bad it's hurting me. I'll find a way. Screw the rules.'

Then they were both gone.

Sam stood for a moment under the hot gushing avalanche of water. Without any warning it turned icy cold and Sam's whole body went into a state of shock. He panicked and ripped off his blindfold as he leapt away from the icy cascade.

Almost instantly the water stopped. Sam saw that once again he was alone in the blue-tiled room. He saw that his leather flaps had been left for him by the door and he guessed he had to put them on. This he did still chattering with cold. He was used to the ice-cold water of the lake and unheated winter pools but icy water so soon after being hotted up by two unseen virile men was a shock he was not used to.

The blue door was open and he went out of it. The red door confronted him and he went boldly to it. He opened it and stepped inside.

Sam found himself in a large room. Over half the room's space was taken up by a raised wrestling ring. There was a skylight in the roof but most of the light did not come from what was now, Sam guessed, early evening but, instead, came from two powerful lamps suspended from the ceiling and focused on the wrestling ring.

The brick walls had large red banners hanging from them which stretched from roof to floor. Some of these banners were rippling with currents of air maybe from other doors hidden behind them. Sam kept glancing around him as first one ripple of movement and then another made him suspect that there was someone else in the room. He had a sense of someone watching him and waiting. But waiting for what?

Then, in one of the corners of the wrestling ring, Sam saw a strange kind of leather glove much smaller than a normal boxing glove. Sam recalled pictures of old-fashioned wrestling where such gloves had been worn. He guessed at once that this glove was for him.

He leapt up on to the canvas floor of the wrestling ring and walked over to the glove and put it on. It covered half his fist leaving his knuckles and upper fingers exposed. He tied the two leather straps which kept the glove on, tightly around his wrist. He kept dancing around the ring glancing at various parts of the room where one or other of the red banners would ripple out towards him. Then it seemed as if a large door had been opened because all the red banners started to billow out. Sam danced in a complete circle around the ring certain that someone else was in the room.

He spun round and was confronted with Arif standing impos-ingly before the swaying red cloth. The colour emphasised the rich darkness of Arif's skin. But what struck Sam like a blow was the oddly fleshy muscularity of Arif's body. His body seemed both virile and sensual, half-yielding and half-commanding. Sam had forgotten how massive Arif's chest was, how finely chiselled and with a thin black carpet of hair sprawled across it. The line of black hair travelled over his well-defined stomach down to his navel where Sam now saw the large leather belt of a master.

Arif's eyes locked on to Sam's and seemed to forbid Sam to look any lower than that belt. Then he leapt into the ring with a loud thud on the canvas. He was already wearing the same kind of glove that Sam had put on and without any delay he jumped at Sam.

Sam was caught off his guard. For a split second all that he was aware of was a mass of flesh and muscle hurling him against the ropes. Then Sam felt one of Arif's massive arms holding the back of his neck in a vicelike grip and bending his entire body to the floor of the ring.

Before Sam could mount any resistance to this assault he felt his left wrist being gripped and his left arm being bent up behind his back. Arif had in a few seconds completely immobilised Sam.

'Submit,' commanded Arif.

'I submit,' said Sam aware that in their first encounter he had been routed in seconds.

Arif instantly released Sam and jumped up and away from his defeated opponent. Sam staggered to his feet and turned to face Arif. Once again, before Sam had a chance to take in and enjoy the glistening massive physique of his opponent, Arif leapt towards Sam and circled round him moving at a swift predatory speed. Sam soon felt he was just spinning round in a hopeless attempt to anticipate Arif's next attack.

He did not even see Arif coming for him. The next thing he was aware of was that Arif had grabbed him from behind and was lifting his entire body off the canvas. Sam bent his arms back around Arif's neck trying to force his master's head to one side and the two men's cheeks rubbed against each other. Sam was excited by the roughness of Arif's bristles as they rasped against his softer skin and also by the musky scent of the other man, a scent he remembered from their very first encounter.

But much more exciting to Sam was to find the entire back

of his body being squeezed against Arif's sweating torso. Sam's shoulders were pressed against Arif's hairy chest and the needle-like points of Arif's nipples, almost as large as Sam's, were sticking enticingly into Sam's flesh. Sam could also feel Arif's cock straining against its leather flap. Sam knew by now how tempting his swimmer's firm but ample arse was to trainers and masters alike. He also guessed that Arif's present, obvious state of excitement was against the rules because he could feel Arif trying to deflect his desire for Sam into their wrestling lesson. It was now obvious to both men that their desire for one another's bodies was getting stronger and stronger especially as Arif was lifting Sam's exposed arse up and down with increasing speed against his hungry cock, still separated from Sam's willing flesh by a strip of leather.

Then, when Sam was least expecting it, Arif dropped Sam's body completely and, kicking Sam's legs from under him while grabbing his upper torso, flipped him back on to the canvas floor of the ring. In a whirlwind of movement Sam found Arif towering over him, his knees forcing each of Sam's shoulders to the ground.

Arif counted to ten, his musk-flavoured sweat dripping off his massive torso on to Sam's panting face. Before Sam could fully savour the pleasure of this total domination Arif leapt to his feet.

'You have a lot to learn about defending yourself,' Arif declared, wiping the sweat from his broad forehead.

'Sometimes I don't feel like defending myself,' replied Sam teasingly, caressing his hot chest with one hand.

Arif looked sternly down at him. 'You must obey your master inside the school at all times. And I insist that in future you defend yourself properly.'

Arif touched the front of his flap at the exact point where his penis had been thrusting towards Sam's naked buttocks. 'You will find, apprentice, that only by following orders will you discover the pleasures that you can't even guess at now.'

'I will follow orders from now on,' said Sam.

Arif extended his large hand to Sam. Sam took it and Arif lifted him from the canvas floor with the power of his arm.

'You are bigger and stronger than I am,' suggested Sam looking into the sultry darkness of Arif's hooded eyes.

'Strength can be built up like pleasure. In this place the two go together as you will discover if you stay the course. Many do not. Many lack the stamina and the will. The Roman will. Are you a real Roman apprentice?' Arif allowed himself another gesture which Sam guessed was also taboo. With the back of his hand he stroked Sam's cheek which was still glistening with the sweat of his recent exertions.

'I think I could be,' replied Sam giving Arif one of his sunny boyish half-smiles which he knew added a little extra to his sexiness.

Arif brought his handsome face closer to Sam's. 'This master would like it very much if you made it to our Inner Circle.' Arif turned his caress into a slight pinching of Sam's cheek. 'If you don't make it you will miss things that you and your body wouldn't want to miss. I know that.'

Arif broke from Sam and resumed his colder tone of voice. 'I will teach you some basic steps tomorrow. Now it is your duty to massage me. Follow me.'

Sam had to disguise his delight at the prospect of having yet more direct physical contact with this Turkish giant.

Arif led them out of the room back into the flame-lit corridor. They walked past a few more of the larger inner doors on their right and, from behind some of them, Sam thought he could hear the thumping and grunting noises of wrestling matches in progress. Sometimes the noises seemed to be more sexual than athletic but Sam realised that it was another taboo to open any of those doors.

Eventually they reached a large blood-red coloured metal door which Arif swung open. Sam followed him into a spacious semi-circular room dominated by five large marble slabs. Two of these slabs were occupied by men who, Sam saw by the large belts that they both still wore, were other masters. Both men were being massaged. Sam recognised at once that the two masseurs were the stocky blond man and the muscular Yorkshireman he had encountered earlier that day. They both glanced at him and gave him brief nods of acknowledgement.

Sam then turned his attention to the masters on the slabs. One was the very handsome man he had glimpsed earlier. He, like Arif, had classical Roman features, a finely honed body and face and his black flesh seemed to gleam with flecks of light. His large eyes opened briefly to take in Sam and then closed again as if Sam was not yet worthy of his attention.

The other master was even more interesting to Sam. He was, Sam guessed, in his mid-thirties, with a shaved head and strong, square features. Sam saw in a second the well-defined pectorals covered with dark brown hair, the rock-hard, flat stomach and, flanked by two thick, hirsute thighs, a prick which, even at rest, was bigger than any Sam had ever encountered. Sam quickly glanced away as that master gave him a fierce appraising look. Sam was aware that he was being sized up, especially his upper body and what could be glimpsed of his dimpled backside as he strode across the room after Arif. But Sam did not want to give that master the satisfaction of a return glance for a little while. Sam was playing a role he normally despised, the role of the pretty-boy flirt but, in this case, he thought the brutal nakedness of the man's appraisal of him deserved that kind of response.

Arif showed Sam a marble side table on which were placed many different types of oil. Arif picked up a glass bottle filled with a light blue liquid.

'This, apprentice boy, is the oil I like best to be rubbed into my flesh. You will soap me in the shower and then use this on me. How good is your massaging?'

'You won't be disappointed,' replied Sam with cool confidence. He was sure Arif was in for a very pleasant surprise. Sam knew he could massage a man into Heaven and back again.

Sam followed Arif to an adjoining room where there were three shower cubicles all lined with black and white marble. Arif removed his leather boots and flaps but not his belt.

'You will wear your apprentice flaps,' commanded Arif.

Sam was glad because he felt that complete physical contact between him and Arif would result in Sam not being able to control his desire. He now belatedly recognised that this was a wish to be totally dominated and possessed by Arif in a way he had wanted from no other man, not even, to this degree, from his trainer, John.

Arif turned on the shower. The hot water which poured over the massive Turk as he turned slowly round and round in the cubicle further emphasised for Sam the extreme sexiness of the Turkish man's body. Below the big Roman head came the rippling, potent shoulders, a real wrestler's pair of shoulders; broad and granite-hard, rippling with potential power. Then came the raw expanse of chest covered with a tangled mass of black hair. Then the well-defined stomach, slightly fleshy and flanked by lumps of hard side muscles. Sam was almost afraid to glance below the dark circle of the navel to the black jungle of hairs which led down to Arif's cock. Of course, it perfectly corresponded to every one of his body's other giant proportions.

Sam did allow himself to absorb and enjoy the bulk of Arif's hairy black thighs and muscular lower legs which had almost the exaggerated muscularity of a Roman statue.

Sam entered the steaming amphitheatre of marble and started to soap Arif's huge shoulders. Arif had his back to Sam and, lifting up his arms, pressed them into the knotted muscles of his broad neck. This movement revealed to Sam just how many perfectly formed muscles there were in Arif's shoulders and upper back. Now Sam let his soapy hands travel lightly over the complicated surfaces of all these muscles, which seemed to be jostling against one another, as if they had the power and skill to pleasure each other before turning their potent attention to another body – an apprentice's body perhaps.

Then Sam allowed his hands to travel down Arif's spine which was marked by an almost invisible line of furry black hair to his tapered waist. Sam now circled it with his hands, soaping vigorously all the time, feeling a new thrill in holding the centre of Arif's body between his hands. This was Arif's narrowest point. Above, the Turk's body flared and expanded to reach the broad expanse of his solid and massive chest and, below, Arif's body blossomed out, in the rear, into his generous but firm arse with so-tempting double dimples in each hairy cheek. At the front of the body Arif's waist led down to the sexy mound of his fleshy stomach and, below, an even fleshier cock, the full force and length of which Sam had still been denied direct access to.

Sam soaped quickly over Arif's compelling double dimples, knowing that he was going to focus on them in the massaging session which was about to follow, and which Sam was already preparing a good apprentice's strategy for. What he slowed down for was Arif's cock, which he approached from behind, running one of his hands between Arif's thighs as he lightly pressed his entire body against the Turk. He let his other hand move down from the tangled circle of hair around Arif's belly over Arif's stomach through the denser, resisting hairs above Arif's cock to the phallus itself.

Now one of Sam's hands was soaping the back of the Turk's prick, while his other hand slid through the pubic hair and rolled like a silky wave over the front, running down its length towards where the cockhead lay, still hidden under the fleshy tent of protective foreskin. Sam had the additional pleasure of wedging his entire left arm between Arif's granite cliffs of thighs. Arif pressed his thighs together squeezing Sam's arm between their hairy surfaces but his cock could not resist this double assault and, within moments, started to stiffen as Sam watched the black planets of Arif's eyes grow dreamy and hooded. For a minute the two men began to mount a new plane of pleasure, then Arif seemed to realise that once again Sam was taking him too deep, too fast. He reached out for the shower taps and both men immediately found themselves under a cascade of chilling, icy water. Sam leapt back but Arif merely grinned and let the cold water pour over his body as if demonstrating to Sam that his body could take any form of the extreme and still triumph. He emerged from the shower looking more than ever as if he could absorb much more than Sam could throw at him before succumbing or, indeed, even noticing Sam's pleasure tricks.

But Sam too was learning fast. The cold shower only made him more determined to make Arif feel what it was like to be at the receiving end of his seductive powers in full throttle. Arif's pleasure peaks were now a challenge to Sam. Sam had vowed to himself, as he clad his Turkish master in a white towel, that Arif would succumb. Arif would bend his back and roll his eyes and beg Sam not to stop whatever he was doing. Sam was determined to master his master and that process, he had decided, would begin with this early evening massage.

Sam walked a little way behind Arif as he went back into the massage room. Arif's backside swayed from side to side in front of Sam's downcast eyes like a giant, tempting piece of ripe fruit which Sam wanted to grab and bite into.

As the two men re-entered the massage room Sam was instantly aware of the rapacious attention of the shaven-headed master. Sam had the feeling that this man felt an instant and overwhelming attraction to him and that Sam was going to have difficulty in resisting whatever assault this dark master was already planning. He had piercing blue eyes, which Sam resisted looking into again, even though a part of him also wanted to enter into some kind of bonding with this attentive stranger. Sam felt this even more strongly because he had noticed the way the master's apprentice, Sam's ex-miner from Yorkshire, had looked at the master he had been assigned to. Sam had already had a small taste of the raw sexual power of that man and knew that he was not the type who would be easily satisfied. So, when Sam saw in the Yorkshireman's eyes a glint of lust appeased, and noted that this ex-miner was attending his master with special devotion, Sam knew at once that he was a master worth waiting for.

The apprentice wanted new lessons and he wanted them now. Sam decided that he was going to do everything he could to gain access to such a master.

Arif seemed to sense that Sam was momentarily distracted from him and it was not something he was prepared to tolerate. The first Sam knew of Arif's displeasure was when he felt a stick smacking hard against his arse, stinging him, even through the protective strip of black leather.

Sam winced and through his pain saw Arif's dark Roman face flared with anger. He saw that Arif had grabbed a wooden stick with black leather strips tightly wound around it, a silver handle at the top and a small noose of black leather at the tip. Sam instinctively rubbed his buttock with his left palm.

Angrily, Arif grabbed hold of Sam's arm and pulled it away

from his arse and, to Sam's surprise, Arif brought down his punishment stick again against Sam's already stinging flesh.

Sam let out an involuntary gasp of pain and was aware that the four other men in the room, the two apprentices and the two masters, were all staring at Sam and Arif. Although Sam tried to resist the feeling, he knew that their keen attention combined with the mild stinging pain on his rump was actually a combination which excited him. In a sudden, unpredictable flash of anticipation he imagined how it would feel if Arif gave him a really good and deserved thrashing in front of those particular four men. To his surprise, Sam found such a prospect very exciting; it planted the germ of a quite novel sensation of pleasure in him. He felt his body quake with many tiny tremors of joy at the very idea of being in such a plight. He felt his cock start to thicken and it took Sam all his willpower to stop his never-failing cock muscles from throbbing into life again.

'No. No. Not now,' he whispered hoarsely to himself. He had an intuition that if he let this fantasy break out now he would be risking it becoming a reality with these five men scattered around him. So, Sam almost welcomed Arif's third and hardest blow, and his severe reprimand. Sam saw that as Arif delivered the blow his black eyes flashed in a way which, so Sam guessed, meant that Arif took more pleasure in punishing Sam than he wanted to admit even to himself.

'Apprentice, you are here to give me attention and pleasure, not to sway your arse like a pretty boy whore at every master with a rival big cock. Do you want to be sent back on the boat tomorrow?'

Sam was aware, although he could not see, that everyone else in the room had stopped what they were doing and were keenly awaiting Sam's response. Sam himself knew that his strong swimmer's body and his broad, ordinary face were features that none of the other four men wanted to see removed from the island and their own very detailed plans for him.

Sam realised that he had to appease Arif's sudden flare of jealousy. He took a secret satisfaction from guessing that Arif had broken yet another rule of the Roman games by revealing his new possessiveness, but knew he needed to stay and learn more.

'I am here only to obey you, master,' whispered Sam. 'If I do anything else I want you to punish me as hard as you can.'

'You can be certain of that,' responded Arif. 'But not in a way that will give you unearned pleasure.' And, with that warning, Arif stretched himself out on his stomach on the marble slab and gestured for Sam to begin massaging him.

The stocky blond apprentice handed Sam a large bottle of clear massaging oil. They avoided looking into each other's eyes. Sam stood in front of Arif's outstretched body and started to massage his broad shoulders in gentle pressing circles. Sam could feel with his fingertips that Arif was tense. Sam was determined to show that he had a magic touch for massage and he deftly increased the pressure in the palms of his hands so that Arif would soon feel the tension being squeezed out of his shoulder blades. After a few minutes of Sam's firm but comforting manipulation, Arif gave out an involuntary sigh signalling to Sam that he was indeed feeling the soothing effect of Sam's ministrations.

Sam started to push his hands down Arif's long back moving in and out of the deep ravine of his spine. Sam had not fully realised before how pleasing Arif's body was to caress. The basic muscular firmness was overlaid with just sufficient fleshiness to enable Sam to knead Arif's body in many different directions. Over the wide, dark plain of Arif's back, gleaming with pools of oil, Sam's fingers travelled with growing authority, kneading muscle against muscle, forcing tension out of every part of his master's surface. Sam was excited too by the fact that under his leather flaps his cock was now rubbing rhythmically up and down against the dome of Arif's head. Sam used his hands and arms to reach down to the very base of Arif's spine, to the point at which the white towel still covered Arif's arse. Sam was uncertain how far he was allowed to go. He glanced over to the others for guidance and the Yorkshire apprentice nodded at Sam and removed the towel from his master. Then he knelt on the marble slab behind him gradually lowering his massaging down to his master's arse where swirls of black hair surrounded that man's excitingly large hole. Sam knew that his eyes were on forbidden flesh and quickly looked away. Then he started to remove the towel from his own master's arse. Arif made no protest so Sam, following the Yorkshire apprentice, climbed on to the marble slab and knelt behind his master. Arif opened his legs out so that Sam could position himself comfortably between his thighs. Sam was now able to really focus on that part of his master's body which had attracted him from his very first glimpse the night before.

Sam started by massaging Arif's lower spine and sides with the flat of his hands, ironing the big man's dark surfaces with all the considerable pressure which his upper body and powerful shoulders and arms were able to bring to bear to the task. Sam could feel Arif's body relaxing deeply and he could see on the one half of Arif's face that was visible all signs of tension fading. His eyes were already half-closed. But, although Sam was concentrating all his muscle power on his massaging, his eyes were fixed on Arif's arse.

Its entire surface was covered with a fuzz of deep hair. It sloped up sharply out of Arif's lower back and, at the very base of Arif's arse, a triangle of dense hair pointed to the crack. This hidden valley was clearly marked by two frontiers of matted hair more lush than the black fuzz which covered everywhere else.

What attracted Sam most of all were the two dimples on either side of his crack which, when Arif tensed up even a little, developed a second, smaller dimple. Sam was already imagining how much he was going to enjoy swirling inside them, first with his hands and then, maybe, with even more exciting parts of his body.

Sam's massaging had now loosened up Arif's entire back and Sam decided the time had come for him to complete his work there and to bring his magic touch to the sexiest part of Arif's body. As a prelude to this arse massage, Sam bent forward over his master's body and, using all the force of his swimmer's upper torso, kneaded Arif's shoulder muscles together until Arif groaned under Sam's relentless manipulation. When Sam had finished conquering Arif's shoulders, he turned his hands into flatirons again and pressed with all his might on the two sides of Arif's back, forcing the muscles and flesh there in towards the crevice of his spine. Sam concentrated especially on this and enjoyed it most of all because, for Sam, this was a practice run for precisely the kind of massaging he was planning for Arif's arse and which, the apprentice guessed by now, Arif was also beginning to anticipate with pleasure.

Slowly Sam began to lower his massaging hands towards the base of Arif's spine. His wrists started to rub against the point at which Arif's arse started to slope up from the prairie of his back. Sam gently pulled his wrists closer together so that they both started to touch the triangle of hair at the top of Arif's crack. Arif gave a small shudder at this first contact which made Sam even more certain that he was going to conquer, with his very special style of massaging, his master's arse. Sam's suspicion that this was another rule of the Roman games he would be breaking made him even more enthusiastic for the task. And, if he had to be punished then let him be punished; maybe for such a severe offence it would be Denton himself who meted out the punishment.

Encouraged by such thoughts Sam placed his hands in their flatiron position on Arif's flanks. He started to move his hands clockwise against his Master's furry fleshiness there and then, very gently, he started to press both his hands up the side slopes of Arif's arse. As he did so he could feel the man under him tense and, as Sam had hoped, the two inner dimples appeared. But Sam was saving them up for his planned final assault on Arif's hairy crack and arsehole, his ultimate target.

For the time being, Sam eased his hands to the rim of the crater of Arif's main outer dimples and turning both hands flat-up started to use just the side of his hand and little finger to rub very delicately at the rim of the dimples. Sam could sense Arif's flesh tingle at his light touch and, after a few moments, Sam decided that it was time to move on to the next stage of his seduction.

Next, Sam put the palms of his hands inside the dimples and rubbed in a circular motion. Sam saw Arif's lips quiver at this. There was no doubt now in Sam's mind that Arif was not going to be able to resist the next phases of Sam's massage attack. Sam increased the pressure he was putting inside the dimples whilst, simultaneously, he started to push the fleshy inner part of both dimples towards each other and Arif's crack.

What Sam wanted now most of all was for the smaller second dimples to appear so that he could also force them towards each other and start them rubbing against the dark crevice of Arif's crack. But Arif, realising that his apprentice was planning something that went beyond massaging was starting to resist. It was as if he was willing his small second dimples not to appear at all.

Sam, sensing this resistance, was now equally determined to overcome it. He placed his strong hands firmly at the base of Arif's buttocks just where they sloped down into the Turk's thick thighs and started to knead and push up Arif's entire arse so that Arif's hairy balls, which Sam could see, and his cock, which Sam could not, would be rubbing up and down against the white towel under him. Sam also bent over his master and with the tip of his tongue traced the outline of the triangle of hair which pointed down to Arif's crack. The effect of this was exactly as Sam had intended. His master, defying his apprentice, clenched his arse hard trying to deny Sam any access to his hairy crevice. But in doing that Arif had tensed into existence his two smaller inner dimples. Sam placed his down-covered cheek in the left one and felt Arif's entire arse tremble at this unexpected contact. Sam rubbed his cheek gently against the furry surface, his tongue tasting the musky tang of the other man's flesh. He then used his cheek to force the flesh of Arif's dimple towards where Arif was still trying to hide and protect his crack, hiding the two frontiers of dense black hair. But Sam was now using his two thumbs to trace circles on the bottom of Arif's hairy balls. He then prised them into Arif's clenched arse forcing them into the tangle of hair which protected Arif's inner secrets. At the same moment Sam laid the side of his cheek into Arif's right inner dimple and started to push the fleshy side of that towards Arif's partly hidden crack. While he was doing all this Sam never let up the way he was forcing Arif's entire arse up and down which was also compelling Arif's cock to rub against both the towel and his taut stomach. Sam felt his master's penis stiffening.

At last Arif stopped clenching his arse. He let the hairy lines on each side of his crack appear and then the crack itself. Sam took instant advantage of this and, while keeping up his rhythmic kneading, bent down and used the tip of his tongue to run down

Arif's crack from top to bottom. Sam's open lips touched against the wiry tangle of Arif's protective hairiness on each side of his slit.

As he was beginning to approach his central goal Sam was also becoming more and more charged up. He felt his hands growing clammy and he was aware of his own cock stiffening quickly under his leather flap. He wondered if the four other men in the room were looking at him and his master. He hoped so. To Sam's surprise he found that this thought further increased his excitement. He could feel his cockhead breaking itself free of its surrounding foreskin at the very idea of those four men themselves perhaps getting hard with the spectacle they were witnessing. But Sam steeled himself not to look at them to see what they were doing because he did not want any distraction from his task.

Sam firmly parted the halves of Arif's backside to finally reveal his large anus. It shone at the centre of a mass of fierce black hair and Sam knew the moment he saw it so close that it was the entrance to new zones of sensation for both apprentice and master.

Arif was trying to pull his rosebud in so that Sam would be denied any glimpse of its rich inner surfaces and textures but Sam knew how to put a stop to that. He moved his firm young mouth as close as he could to the other man's hole without actually touching it. As gently as he could, he took a deep breath in and then breathed out. His breath ruffled the other's protective circle of black hairs but, much more vitally, shot a sudden gust of air into the very centre of the secret regions and beyond. As Sam had guessed, Arif was so excited by the sensations created by Sam's breath alone that they acted as an irresistible foretaste of what was to come. Arif stopped the desperate clenching and hiding of his rosebud and released it in all its full glory. Sam estimated that the exposed circumference would perfectly match his half-opened mouth. Tenderly at first Sam placed his mouth against Arif's arsehole. For Sam this was the most bonding and thrilling kiss he had ever exchanged with another man.

It seemed to him at the moment of contact that he was instantly connected and in control of every part of his Turkish master, from his massive shoulders to his teasing cock, from the immensity of his hairy chest to the as-yet unknown maze of pleasure which began at the very circle of flesh that Sam was now pressing more insistently against with the moist contours of his lips.

Sam knew that Arif too wanted to feel Sam in every part of him. Only the Turk's inner arse was still a mystery, still withdrawn from the skill of Sam's hands and tongue. And Sam was determined to change that.

Sam sucked hard with his powerful lips, forcing Arif's rosebud deep inside his mouth. He heard Arif moan with pleasure and knew instinctively that Arif was waiting for Sam's tongue to finally make contact with the labyrinth of miniature ridges inside Arif's arse that would take his Turkish master to new heights of sexual bliss. For that very reason Sam withheld the touch of his long moist tongue. He curled it back and held it at bay.

In response to this delay Arif tried to push his bud further into the sucking mouth of his youthful apprentice. Sam used his hands, which now held Arif's backside in a tight grip, to resist the hairy mass of Arif's back-thrusting arse. He felt the handsome man shake with all the desperate intensity of longing denied. That pleased Sam. The apprentice was now playing out the role of the master and the master was learning what it was like to be taken almost to the peak of pleasure and then held back from the last few motions that would take him to the final peak of ecstasy.

Yet Sam, although enjoying Arif's now quite obvious frustration at being denied Sam's lizard tongue, could not for much longer resist giving himself the physical delight that he knew would come from allowing his tongue to roll into the very centre of Arif's rounded cheeks.

Sam gave one final suck which pulled a bit more of Arif's willing orifice into his wide-open mouth so that he could feel the ridges and valleys of Arif's outer rosebud in his soaking cave. Now there was nothing protecting Arif from Sam's tongue, poised to invade that inner sanctum which, Sam guessed, only Denton and John had been able to penetrate before him. The apprentice who had, until yesterday, been thought to be just an

Average Joe, a minor player in their Roman games, was now going to show just how good he was at giving pleasure.

Sam slowly started to unroll his long tongue towards the dark purple ridges of Arif's inner areas. Arif shuddered twice and the edges of Sam's rough but caressing tongue started to flow like an irresistible wave of pink flesh over the dense labyrinth of the generous cave that was Arif's inner arse.

But Sam tauntingly only unfurled a part of his tongue. He wanted Arif to feel the contrasting sensations created by Sam's lips and mouth touching the outer rosebud, now securely imprisoned inside Sam's sucking mouth, with delicate trickles of saliva. And also, the more punitive sensations of the rough sandpaper sides of his tongue inching forward inside Arif's arse. Sam held his rough tongue still for a few moments. He wanted Arif to beg for more of this tongue treatment not in words but by trying one of the oldest tricks of all by pulling in Sam's tongue by contracting his arse. Sam did not have to wait more than a few seconds before Arif indeed started to try to force Sam's tongue deeper inside him. Sam concentrated all his youthful energy into his tongue, and held it rigid and immobile as Arif tried, using his powerful contracting muscles, to pull Sam deeper into his rear. Sam waited a second and wondered if either Arif, or one of the other sexy masters, who Sam was almost sure must be gazing on his forbidden seduction, would command Sam to unleash his tongue and give his master the pleasure he was shaking for. But no such verbal command came. Instead, and much more effectively, Sam felt the hands of the two other apprentices he had enjoyed a few hours ago rolling a condom on his cock and taking his nipples in their hands and twisting each of them with their fingers. The effect of this utterly unexpected intervention was such that Sam felt his determination not to give Arif the full extent of his tongue begin to weaken. Arif, realising that now he had the active support of the other two apprentices, tried again to use the muscles inside his arse to pull the desired wetness deeper into him. But still Sam resisted.

The other two apprentices could see this and, noting the anguished expression on the large, handsome Roman face of Sam's master, they decided to use further inducements to force

Sam to unroll his tongue into the pleasure cave of Arif's arse. Together, both apprentices lifted up their leather flaps to reveal the stiff rods of their cocks which had, for many minutes, been in a state of advanced hardness. They had been too passively witnessing the thrilling and unexpected seduction scene and now, in unison, they lifted up Sam's back leather flap and placed their flaring, hot cockheads against the sides of Sam's arse, one on the left, one on the right.

Sam was suddenly aware of their raw domes throbbing against the firm slopes of his young man's arse. In the next second he felt both those cockheads and the rigid stems beneath them gliding through the golden crop of his downy hair towards his own now partially visible rosebud. Before Sam could stop himself, he imagined the pleasure he would get when the rods of the Yorkshireman and the stocky blonde would collide just above his own portal and then together try to force themselves inside his tight arse.

The very thought of this had the effect the apprentices had planned. Sam could no longer deny himself or Arif the pleasure he had been so rebelliously keeping back. For the first time since he had been on the island Sam was going to reveal one of his best-kept secrets. His tongue. He knew, from his few other lovers, that his tongue was his secret weapon. All his lovers, however experienced, had told him that it was his tongue which was his most unexpected gift to them. And so it was again to a man who thought he knew all the best sex tricks in the book. The Turk who thought he had been pleasured by the very best men in the world.

Yet, Sam knew, he had this surprise for him, this sex-shock treatment. Slowly Sam unleashed his rough-textured, thick wet tongue into Arif's arse.

Arif was expecting and even waiting for Sam's licking tongue but what he hadn't expected at all was what Sam's tongue did to him; to every part of him.

From the moment Sam's tongue entered him, Arif felt that his arse contained zones which connected precise points directly to the sexiest parts of his outer body. This bliss Arif had not expected. It was out of his control.

In one moment Sam's luscious young tongue was caressing with a clever game of dart and retreat one tiny ridge inside Arif's arse and then, suddenly, it felt as if Sam's tongue was reaching into the hairy lushness of Arif's nipples. Then Arif felt Sam's raiding, pleasure-splashing tongue, sliding up the massive thrust of Arif's stiffening cock, riding up the sexy tunnel of his member, until Arif felt, without any stupid macho regret, Sam's tongue gently parting the tiny rim heads of his penis.

Now Sam, inside Arif's conquered arse, could be anywhere. He had the power with his tongue, inside the warm ribbed cave of Arif's super-sensual backside, to massage in one upper left curve of the arse all of Arif's outer, fleshy, muscular pectorals. Inside Arif, Sam could touch and pleasure from within Arif's hot valleys, his massive muscular and needing body.

When Sam started to lick deep inside Arif's arse, he knew, for the first time in his life, that he had the power to make any point on Arif's large and virile structure of flesh and muscle tighten and tense up with the lightest touch of his exploring, easing tongue. With one casual, six-second, upward flick, Sam could hit a spot inside Arif's arse that sent electric shudders to the very peak of Arif's aroused tits.

'Oh do that . . . do that again . . .' sighed Arif in one of his very rare returns to verbalisation as he lay under the swoon and discipline of Sam's sudden access to power over him.

Now Sam allowed his rough-sided tongue to thrust deep into the resisting caves of Arif's upper arse. Wiry hair tangled around Sam's penetrating tongue, but still Sam persisted, thrusting his swirling kissing tongue deeper into the hairy interiors of Arif's musky, hairy bottom.

Arif was deep into pleasures that he knew he should be denying. With absolute delight he let Sam's large hands grab his firm and hairy torso. He knew that Sam was using his athletic torso and nipples to hold on to and squeeze so that he was secure when he brought his stubby chin and mouth against the large circle of Arif's hairy buttocks.

As his resistance willingly collapsed, Arif felt Sam's thrusting tongue riding like a chariot into the very centre of Arif's deep cave of an arse. And, once inside, Arif was aware that Sam could arouse every part of Arif's massive external body, just by using his tongue. The sex points of his big man's body were being controlled by this apprentice's mouth.

Sam started to quickly find out, as the heat of Arif's arse breathed over Sam's lips, that if the side of his tongue touched a certain ridge deep inside Arif's arse then Arif's left nipple would tremble and Arif would let out a deep sigh.

Then Sam, certain of his new powers over Arif, allowed his under tongue's rawness to ride over Arif's broad and rough-textured lower arse waiting for the precise moment to curl his tongue, like a pagoda's tip turning back, into the already trembling arse plain and stinging it into violent convulsions so that the whole of Arif's fleshy lower body was racked with pleasure.

Arif moved suddenly. Sam did not know what was happening to him. He had seemed to be in charge until the last minute, when for some reason the passive Arif had grabbed his lean arse and, smacking it, had forced Sam's thrusting tongue to ride out of the hairy, yielding fleshiness of Arif's buttocks. At that precise moment, Sam knew what the Turk wanted. Arif no longer wanted to obey any rules, no longer wanted anything except that Sam's raging, disobedient cock would follow Sam's pleasure-blitzing tongue. He wanted to suck Sam's throbbing member into his dark Turkish cave.

Arif knew that he could not shout aloud for Sam to fuck his arse raw but that was what he wanted as he watched their coupling in the mirrors on the wall of the Roman school, whose rules he was now shamelessly breaking,

Sam, his eyes closed in bliss, wanted to stay inside Arif's arse, but, as a gesture of respect and temptation, he circled Arif's sweating rosebud with the rough textures of the side of his tongue.

Before Arif could pause after that pleasure attack and retreat,

Sam slowly lifted the hairy, twin mounts of his Turkish master's arse towards the growing red spear and throbbing dome of Sam's prick. Sam's virility and size could no longer be disguised.

Twelve inches of cockstem and another two confronting inches of flaring pink head now confronted Arif in the mirror of the massage room. Sam's leather flaps offered no restraint any more to the compulsive throbbing of his penis and, with all the arrogance of his young and beautiful lust, he tore off his apprentice's belt and flaps.

'No,' said Arif arguing with himself as he struggled to resist the magnetic pull of Sam's glowing body now so obviously at his disposal.

But Arif knew, as he took in Sam's liquid blue eyes and the throbbing manifestation of his virile lust, that the only thing that mattered in the whole world to Arif, at this moment, was that Sam's young cock pierced and corkscrewed its way into the long, hungry tunnel of Arif's lushly hairy, deeply ribbed arsehole.

For both of them it was better than either had imagined it would be.

Arif felt his heavy hairy body grabbed and lifted up from the back by Sam's wiry young torso. And then, before he could think of who was in what position, Arif felt the red-hot rod of Sam's young prick ride into his hairy arse, then slide up behind his navel and stomach and rise, thickening in the valley that divided the two halves of Arif's black tangled hairy chest.

'Soak me now with your spunk,' begged Arif bending his entire body away from Sam's lunging cock and tongue.

Sam needed no further encouragement. He felt, from inside his stomach, the hot juice of his come racing up his cock and, then, exploding against the taut and straining rubber of Sam's tightly wrapped condom. Arif could feel, as an extra pleasure, even through the rubber's denying thickness, the oven-hot splash of young man's spunk. Like a water bed's raw and teasing texture, Arif felt Sam's pushing contours of pleasure spilled out and dammed inside Sam's condom, squeezing against the intricate and delicate ridges and valleys of Arif's massive rosebud.

For a few moments which he wanted to last forever, Arif felt Sam's hot juice spilling inside Sam's condom, pressed against the many separate targets inside Arif's sensitive arse. The apprentice boy's sheath-lined stem was gliding and then forcing itself along inside the rawest edges of his master's anus.

Arif, realising that he was breaking all the taboos, forced his buttocks to clench hard on the apprentice boy's violating rod. But all that did was to bind master and apprentice, arse and cock, in an even more intense climax of sensation. Both their bodies seemed to bend at exactly the same time in the same arc of total pleasure, Sam's young-man's torso pressed with all its violent sweaty contours against the solid naked muscle of his powerful master's.

Sam was not to enjoy his swoon of pleasure for long. Almost as soon as he had finished pumping his cock juice into Arif's welcoming orifice, Sam felt a harsh rap of leather on his own exposed rump. Sam glanced over his shoulders, soaked in sex-sated sweat, and found himself immediately catapulted into the ice-blue eyes of the bald master for whom he had already developed a strong tang of desire.

The lean but steely figure of this master was now towering terrifyingly above Sam with his leather rod lifted again to swipe at him. Sam made an imploring glance which the shaven-headed master caught and understood.

'You have to be stopped and punished for leading a master of the games astray. These are the massage rooms and they are sacred to us. A proper massage is vital to our successful perform-ance in the Roman games.'

The master pushed his taut, hard face close to Sam's. Sam felt the power of his penetrating eyes and his body could already feel the first muted response of its desire to be truly mastered by this virile stranger. He could smell the other man's hot sweat as he pressed his anger closer to Sam. He smelt of something scouring and dangerous.

'You are breaking the rules of the massage house.'

As he whispered this serious reprimand, in a low and gruff voice, he flicked the leather again at Sam's firm young arse. Sam felt the blow as a streak of pain and pleasure – in equal proportions. Sam winced.

'Good,' said the other man. 'Good. And what's worse you've

led one of our best masters astray with your pretty boy, pretty tongue and pretty cock games. You need a firm hand.'

Sam saw again a flash of leather-covered rod and once more felt the same curiously mixed sensation of hurt and desire.

Arif now closed his arse against his young lover and Sam found himself roughly prised apart from Arif by the other two apprentices who, Sam suspected, would also be punished for their part in Sam's forbidden seduction of Arif.

Sam was taken to the shower and rubbed roughly down with harsh scrubbing brushes that felt like two porcupines rubbing violently over his naked flesh.

He was still recovering from the daze of his pleasure with Arif and everything that was done to him felt like a curious mix of comfort and joy. And, yet, despite the high that Sam got from possessing Arif's lush depths, Sam felt that Arif would always be bound first to Denton. What he had seen of their sex life from his hiding place led Sam to guess that he would be at best another apprentice boy in Arif's eyes.

Sam was roused from these thoughts by having two pairs of hands grab his armpits and carry him forcibly out of the shower. Once again he felt the novel feeling of being literally in the hands of other men. He could see that being powerless had a seductive charm he hadn't guessed before he came to the island.

Sam enjoyed the firm grip of the other apprentices' hands under his armpits. He also enjoyed the way that the sturdy blond apprentice gave him a secret squeeze. Sam did not look at him directly but could sense that he found even this slight contact with Sam sufficiently exciting to want to signal his feelings to Sam.

Sam was brought before the shaven-headed master who was now wearing his leather belt of office and his flaps. He had a lean and boxy body and his almost hairless stomach curved out towards what was obviously a king-sized prick, now well hidden from Sam.

'The emperor has to decide what to do with you,' the master announced, his turquoise eyes searching and raping Sam's own.

Sam had always prided himself on the purity and intensity of his own eyes but they were like cheap imitations of the colour of the eyes of the man who was now staring into Sam's pupils and without any apparent trace of desire for him.

'The master you violated against our rules is a special favourite of the emperor so I warn you that you may be in for some difficult times. Now you will be escorted out of the school. You will go back to your room. Tomorrow you will carry out your work until four o'clock when you will return here and resume your role as an apprentice to your trainer. But I warn you. By that time your transgressions here today will have been discussed and we will have decided what to do with you. If you wish to avoid this and to leave our Roman games you can take the afternoon boat tomorrow. Do you understand?'

Sam nodded. He felt that nothing was more likely to make him want to stay than what this shaved, hard man had just said to him. Sam wondered whether it was deliberate and whether he was being deliberately hotted up for his deeper involvement in their games.

He was escorted by his shaven-headed persecutor to the door of the massage room. Arif had disappeared. The door opened and Sam found himself shoved into the outer circular corridor. The door to the massage room banged shut behind him. Sam found himself facing the handsome young gatekeeper who had first let him into this strange private world. Sam had not noticed the young man's easy grin before and the way his thin covering of ginger hair emphasised the taut fitness of his body. Now Sam could appreciate more fully the details of his costume and their meaning. He saw that the gatekeeper was wearing a belt which, although wider than the apprentices' was not as wide as the belts of the masters. He was also aware that he had wrapped round his wrists two leather bands to which were attached two leather loops.

The man noticed the direction of Sam's look. 'I am Cato and I don't ask about what you're looking at. You'll know soon enough, Sam. Come. I have to escort you out.'

Sam followed Cato along the apparently endless swerving corridor lit by wall torches. Cato's thin down of ginger hair shone red in the flickering light of the torches and, as he walked,

Sam could glimpse now and again the pert firmness of the other man's solid young bum.

Cato seemed to sense what Sam was up to and gestured for him to walk alongside him. 'So, you've been a bad apprentice boy,' said Cato in the same slightly sing-song accent of the region which Sam also possessed.

Sam felt it was safest just to nod agreement.

'Arif is a special favourite and a strict upholder of the rules of the games.' Cato shot Sam a taunting grin which allowed Sam to see, for the first time, that Cato had a moustache which glowed ginger-red in the light of the flames. 'I guess,' continued Cato teasingly, 'that you must have done something quite special, quite bad, to tempt Arif to break the rules.'

'I got carried away,' replied Sam. 'He's excited me a lot since I first saw him and I had a few hours with other guys that made me too keen. And when I saw Arif's arsehole I was bursting.'

Cato gave a brief grin and Sam guessed that Cato was excited by what Sam had told him but resisted looking down at Cato's flap to see how excited he was.

Sam wondered how Cato had come to be chosen as the gatekeeper. What were his special talents? What had he done for Denton? Had Cato gone through the same violently changing range of feelings and desires as Sam had done? Sam felt an urge to bond with this man who he suspected had so much in common with him. Cato opened an outer door and suddenly they were outside again with just a few yards of open space until they reached the high wall that led back into the garden of the big house.

Both men stood in front of the heavy wooden door as Cato expertly unlocked it. Sam glanced up at the sky. On the island in the middle of the large lake there was no light pollution, so stars crowded the night sky in brilliant clusters. A light wind caressed Sam's face and at the same time he felt the hairy back of Cato's hand drift lightly across his bottom.

Cato leant close to him and, protected by the sound of the heavy lock turning, whispered. 'It's lonely being the gatekeeper. Just before dawn is my best time. Something tells me that's yours too.'

Before Sam could respond to Cato's suggestion, Cato indicated that Sam must take off his apprentice gear. Sam felt Cato's eyes travelling over his nakedness and he deliberately stretched himself in order to emphasise his muscled arms and the suppleness of his torso.

'So that's what they call a swimmer's body,' observed Cato. 'I've got almost the same shape as you and I practically never swim.'

Cato's remark gave Sam the excuse to look more closely at the gatekeeper's physique. It was remarkably like his own body even down to the large nipples and the firm but curvaceous rump. The two men looked at one another and Sam could see desire flickering in the other's eyes. Then Cato broke off their exchange.

'What do you do on the mainland?' asked Sam.

'Denton doesn't allow us to talk about that. It breaks the Roman spell, he says.' Cato gave a shrug as if he didn't believe that for a minute but Sam noticed that he didn't answer his question. Then Cato returned Sam's cleaned working clothes to him. Then, without saying anything more, he gave Sam a rough shove through the gate.

Sam found himself in the sprawling market garden which surrounded the big house. With a sudden surge of regret Sam glanced back at the gate which Cato had slammed in his face.

He was aware that maybe he had missed a chance at least for some gentle late-night caressing. He should have left a kiss on Cato's lips that would also have served as an appetiser for the ginger beauty. Sam gave a wry grin back at the blank expanse of the firmly closed door and moved on quickly through the market garden and past the empty greenhouses, lit now by the cold whiteness of the moon. After the wonderful density of desirable bodies he had been exposed to, the gardens and greenhouses now seemed particularly abandoned. Sam remembered how he had glanced at the stocky blond apprentice, plucking tomatoes, with such an air of innocence. Sam could never have guessed how much pleasure they were going to give to one another in just a few hours after their eyes first met so fleetingly.

To Sam now his silent surroundings seemed lustless and chilly. Yet his own body, by contrast, exuded a sharpened intensity of desire. For the first time in his life Sam realised that he really did now have the chance to inch closer and closer to the outermost limits of satisfaction with the bodies and the desires of other virile men like himself. He had thought, until he had come to this island, that such uninhibited physical rapture was an impossible dream, especially in the rather dull lakeland region he'd grown up in. But now, on this island, he had the chance not just to fulfil his own deepest desires but also to be taught things he had not even imagined he wanted.

Until today, for example, he would never have imagined that a leather stick, brought down hard on his muscled buttocks, could have sent delicious electric currents throughout his body creating the most intense ripples of sensation in the stem of his cock and on the very peaks of his large nipples. That had been a revelation and Sam almost hoped that his offence with Arif would lead to more such punishment.

He was starting to realise too that Denton had created a kind of brotherhood here. The hierarchy he had created of masters, trainers and apprentices actually intensified that sense of belonging to a special group. They really were as loyal, as tough and virile as the best of the ancient Romans had been. It was only now that Sam realised he had been too separate for too long, that he had held himself back from the desires of other men. It was an arrogance, perhaps. He was aware too of a certain aura he gave off, teasingly ambiguous, promising and denying. He was glad to be losing that protective shell. It had protected him from too many good things.

As he was strolling back to the big house, he had a sudden anxiety that maybe his tumultuous and very public seduction of Arif might have been an act of madness which would exile him from the new and deeper pleasures opening up to him. For a few moments he was anxious that he would not be readmitted behind the red brick wall which divided the inner from the outer island world. But as Sam stood by the open wooden door to the big house, he grinned to himself. He put his hand inside his shirt and teased his exceptionally large left nipple with his fingers. He could still detect, despite the soap and water and the harsh scrubbing by the other apprentices, Arif's musky body scent on him. It was still mixing with his own sweet and salty aroma. Sam knew that he had also left the cutting freshness of his own young body's scent in Arif's memory.

Sam also knew, after what he had done to Arif's arsehole, that there was certainly one master inside the wrestling school who would not want to send Sam back across the lake, taking his stimulating tongue and prick with him. If the Roman games were indeed about pleasure, then Sam was growing increasingly confident that he had something to give, something that even the masters of the Roman games wanted.

A plate of locally made cheese, rough-textured bread and a stone bottle of local wine were laid out on the kitchen table. Sam could not help thinking that, although some of the men inside those circular brick walls wanted to mete out punishment, others wanted to reward or, at the very least, to keep up his strength.

Five

After he had eaten alone in the empty house he had fallen gratefully on to the crisp white sheets of his bed. He had slept deeply and without dreams in his austere bedroom.

He was woken by the cool pre-dawn breezes that travelled across the lake. During the night he had thrown off his sheets and now the breezes played over his sprawled-out, naked body.

Sam automatically caressed his powerful swimmer's chest and the dark brown hair which swirled around his the fleshy islands of his nipples. As he touched himself he remembered the bodies of the other men he had encountered yesterday inside the magic walls of Denton's wrestling school. Only three days ago he would never have imagined that he would have enjoyed the bodies of so many attractive and virile men. Denton and his trainers obviously knew how to recruit the right kind of apprentices.

Sam lowered one hand towards the thin line of brown hair that ran down and encircled his navel. Almost absent-mindedly he let his hand follow the trail of hair. He loved the way his flesh sloped down into his navel, delicately brushed with wiry hair. Sam resisted lowering his hand below his navel. He reminded himself that he should save himself for his next session inside the wrestling school. He recalled how different each of the men he had encountered yesterday had been. Each of them, he thought, had offered him something unique. Their bodies, their desires, their faces, all had given him different sensations. Even the thrill of the blow on the bottom. He felt it again at this moment as he remembered the smack of the shaven-headed master's hand as it hit his rebellious arse. Until yesterday, he'd always thought that the range of men who attracted him fell into a narrow field. Yesterday had liberated him from that.

And before yesterday he had always been suspicious of sex with more than one other person. He had believed that such sex would dilute the intensity and concentration which really good one-to-one sex could achieve. Now, as he stretched out his long bronzed legs against the white sheets and remembered his recent experiences he could see how wrong he had been.

Apart from Arif who, Sam admitted to himself, was easily the man who most excited him, he found himself being drawn back to three of the men he had met: the ex-miner, the shaven-headed master who had disciplined him so forcibly and the teasing ginger-haired gatekeeper. He knew none of their names but he remembered all the details of their bodies. All that he had been able to see, that is, and he remembered the way they had each looked at him. Looked and wanted.

Sam got out of bed and went to the open window. The sun would rise very soon. The sky was already lightening. The lake looked cool and inviting and there seemed to be no living creature around at all. It was then that Sam remembered what the gatekeeper had said to him. 'Just before dawn is my best time.' He recalled the gatekeeper's thin moustache above the burnished lips and the sparkle in his hazel eyes when he had casually spoken those words. He recalled the other man's body so strangely like his own of which he had only seen tantalising glimpses.

Sam pulled on a pair of white bathing trunks which had been left in the room along with a big white towel, soap and shaving gear and moved silently through the sleeping house. He passed the imposing busts of Roman emperors and the large room dominated by the model of ancient Rome and went on to find the shower room. He showered and shaved and then decided to brave the cold waters of the lake.

He stepped out of the house and started to make his way down to the shore. Then he hesitated and looked over to the gate in the wall which surrounded the wrestling school. He recalled again what the gatekeeper had said to him. 'I'm best just before dawn and I guess you are too.'

Sam hesitated. The cool grey waters of the lake stretched before him. But what was drawing him now was the thought of the gatekeeper's body, warm with sleep, fresh and eager.

Or had he just been teasing Sam, making fun of his wildness with Arif? Sam was also afraid that if he broke any more rules they really might kick him off the island and that was the last thing he wanted to happen. So, reluctantly Sam veered from the big gate and continued his walk down to the lake.

He didn't want to be seen by anyone in the big house or by anyone who might be living in one of the cottages or even inside the wrestling school. He followed a long curve which brought him to a sheltered semicircle of pebbled beach. He saw that there was a diving board a few hundred yards out into the water so he guessed that he had, by chance, chosen the right spot.

He waded quickly into the water knowing that it would be icy at first and that he had to ignore his usual first desire to get back on to warm land. He hurled himself into the grey water and swam a vigorous breaststroke, delighting in the way the water slapped against his body as he cut a way through the lake and drove himself towards the diving board. All his muscles came into play when he was waterborne; even his buttocks were like a dynamo full of thrusting power. When he had seen videos of himself in swimming championships and had watched the way his body, especially his bum, rose and fell with such force in and out of the water he had often felt that he would have liked to fuck himself. And maybe that was why Cato's body, so much like his own, attracted him.

To keep himself in training he swam twenty big circles around the diving board, driving himself faster and faster. Eventually he swam back to the pebbled beach. He emerged from the water with a renewed sense of the vigour and power of his body. Every part of him tingled.

He started to rub himself down with the towel, then, with a shock, he realised that he was no longer alone on the beach.

A blur behind him which he had thought was a rock now came into sharp focus. It was the gatekeeper. He was also wearing white swimming trunks.

He gave Sam a lazy, provocative grin as he lay stretched out on the pebbles. 'I knew you would be best before dawn,' he said.

Sam took in the other man's body which he saw mirrored his own even more precisely than he had expected. Long and lightly muscled in the way certain swimmer's bodies were, with a powerful chest and well-developed pecs. He even had the same extra-large nipples Sam possessed. Unlike Sam the other man's body had a very light covering of golden-ginger hair. Sam guessed that like him he was in his mid-twenties.

Sam could also now see through the tight swimming costume that the gatekeeper did not lack a certain powerful and sizable manliness.

Sam remembered his name. 'Hello, Cato.' Sam threw his towel down and stretched out near him. He looked into the other man's green eyes. They still had the teasing sparkle he had seen yesterday evening. 'I remembered you saying that you were the one who was best just before dawn.'

Sam saw Cato's eyes travelling over his chest and large nipples, down over the tautness of his flat stomach to his swimming trunks where Cato's eyes lingered.

Just the contact of his eyes was making Sam's cock stiffen and swell and soon Sam was aware that his bulging member was pressing hard against the cotton trunks.

Cato broadened his grin. 'These trunks they dish out to us are not always very comfortable are they?'

Sam smiled back very well aware that his half-grin created sexy dimples in his cheeks. 'Sometimes they feel two sizes too small,' Sam responded.

'Yours look four sizes too small now. Can't I do anything to make you more comfortable?'

By now both men had locked on to one another's eyes and both read in them the heat of their desire. Their bodies were such perfect matches that both men felt that making love to the other would be very much like making love to oneself and were narcissistically excited by that thought.

'Anything you could do to make me more comfortable would be appreciated,' Sam responded.

Cato pulled himself closer to Sam so that Sam could feel the sudden warmth of the other man in the cool air.

Cato propped his head up with one hand and with the other he started to finger the top of Sam's swimming trunks. Slowly he started to roll them down. As he did this he put his mouth against Sam's and traced the outline of Sam's lips with his tongue. Then he gently placed his full lips against Sam's.

Sam shuddered at the first delicate touch of the other's moist tongue but that touch, exciting as it had been, had not prepared him for the thrill he felt when Cato placed his mouth on Sam's. Their lips made a perfect match. Only Cato's thin moustache marked a difference between them.

Before that moment Sam had never felt any attraction to men with moustaches but, maybe because Cato's moustache was so light and delicate or maybe just because it belonged to Cato, Sam found the wiry hair rubbing against the delicate arc of flesh above his lips unexpectedly exciting. Without thinking Sam had a premonition of how Cato's thin moustache might give his arsehole the same unexpected delight it was now giving his lips.

Cato whispered to Sam, 'Whatever we do now and however much you enjoy it, I want you to remember this, that I was the first one who told one of the great secrets of the Roman games . . .'

'What's that?'

'The wrestling is a way for all of us to find the men who will give us what we need most, whatever that is. You usually find that out very quickly in the wrestling ring.'

Sam was excited by what Cato said. It made sense of what had been happening to him. 'How do you know?'

Cato ran a finger across his moustache and grinned. 'You'll know.'

Sam asked the inevitable question. 'Could it be you?'

'Maybe.' Cato deliberately paused. 'Maybe not. It depends if we are matched against each other in the wrestling ring. I've learnt that's the only way of really knowing.' Cato stopped Sam's urgent questioning with another fierce invasion of Sam's mouth with his tongue.

Sam was aware that Cato had rolled down Sam's swimming trunks far enough for his firm prick to be thrusting straight up into the cool air and that Cato was expertly circling the stem with his hand, moving the loose flesh up and down in a gentle, rhythmic, teasing motion.

Sam whispered to Cato, 'I think your trunks are a bit tight on you now, too.'

Both men looked down at Cato's trunks which certainly could no longer hide the thrusting peak of Cato's cock straining hard against the taut cotton.

Sam put a hand down to them and quickly pulled them a little way down revealing Cato's cock whose size and shape, perfectly straight, uncut ten inches, was an exact mirror of Sam's own. The only difference between them was the mass of golden-ginger hair which surrounded the base of the phallus and which covered Cato's balls which, again like Sam's, were very large.

Cato seemed to have realised how physically alike they were too. He whispered to Sam, 'We could be brothers.'

The thought excited both of them.

'I wish we were,' replied Sam.

'I think we should see how much closer we match.'

'What do you mean?' asked Sam, even more excited now.

'I'll show you what I mean,' replied Cato firmly.

Quickly Cato stripped off his trunks and, lifting up Sam's lower body, pulled off Sam's as well. He made Sam stretch out fully on the towel with his arms and legs straight. Then Cato positioned himself exactly above Sam and started to slowly lower his body on to Sam's.

Sam felt first their knees and thighs meeting, then their pricks, then their flat stomachs, their chests and then their large nipples – all parts pressing against each other in a perfect match. This doubled the desire of each of them for the other.

'This is a mirror fuck,' whispered Cato as he let the flesh around his stiff stem touch and rub against the flesh around Sam's hardening penis. Gently Cato started to push their cock flesh towards their still hidden cockheads. They both emerged together and met in an explosion of sensation which both felt throughout their clenched bodies.

'Wait for my tits before you come ... wait,' commanded Cato in Sam's ear.

As he said that Cato lowered his powerful chest on to Sam's mirror image of Cato's trembling torso. Sam felt the erect tips of Cato's tits first brush against and then press triumphantly down on Sam's own large nipples as if Cato was pushing them back inside Sam.

Sam could no longer contain the violent excitement that had been building up inside his body and above all in the stem of his prick. He was fighting back against the flood which wanted to rush through his rigid member.

Sam warned Cato. 'I can't hold back any more . . .'

Even as he spoke Sam felt a powerful gush of hot liquid rising from the very base of his prick and coursing through it, spurting out over Cato's cock.

Sam's deluge acted like a trigger on Cato who had also been holding back his desperate desire to bathe Sam's torso with the heat of his own semen. Cato grabbed Sam in a vicelike grip and allowed his whole body to shudder in a raw climax of pure pleasure. His mind seemed to be sailing through a blue sky as he felt Sam's chest receiving the first full burst of his consummation. His cock squirted in violent bursts as the juice of his pleasure ran over Sam until the chest of the man under him was bathed in his spunk.

Slowly, as he came back to earth, Cato rubbed his own warm emission in circles around Sam's still-trembling nipples and chest. Sam responded by gently clenching Cato's well-muscled shoulders.

'You were right about the dawn,' said Sam.

Cato smiled and rubbed his thin moustache against Sam's upper lip. 'This is almost the only physical difference between us. Brother.'

Sam caressed Cato's spunk-soaked hairy chest which was still heaving in the aftermath of the sex they had just enjoyed together. Cato turned his body over so that the tempting hills of his buttocks were finally fully exposed to Sam's gaze. Sam pressed his mouth against the top of Cato's arse which was seared pinky gold by the rising sun. The warmth of their bodies, heated by their sex, met the warmth of the new day's sun. Sam's mouth felt the delicious protective fuzz around Cato's arsehole.

'Are you the one?' asked Sam again, as he placed one hand under Cato's stomach and lifted his lower body and arse up to Sam's waiting lips. Sam planted a lingering kiss on the furry circle of Cato's anus. Then he traced a finger along Cato's spine up to the closely shaven nape of his neck. Sam stretched out in post-coital sleepiness alongside Cato. The gatekeeper responded by very gently running his hands appreciatively over the curving slopes and dimples of Sam's arse. Sam willingly did the same to Cato. The two men's half-closed eyes met and seemed to command their mouths to meet together in a long, tender kiss.

'Whether you are the one or not,' said Sam, 'I've never enjoyed towelling down so much before.'

Cato laughed and pressed his mouth in one last hard kiss before their lips broke apart. 'You like anything that rises,' accused Cato.

Sam blushed and turned over and looked up at the already blue sky. He grinned and, tracing his finger again over the other man's pencil-thin moustache, repeated the question. 'Are you the one?'

'Why do you think there must be just one?'

'You're right. I do keep thinking that. Then are you one of the ones that's right for me?'

'I told you. You only know that in the wrestling ring. That's the lesson of the Roman games. But this was good, Sam. I almost wish we'd had an audience. I like that, when the sex is really good, to be watched and really appreciated by others.'

Sam and Cato didn't know it but they had had an audience; a very attentive and appreciative audience. There was a special reason for the attentiveness of the unseen spectator. Cato and Sam not only resembled one another they also closely resembled the body of the young man that had haunted Jack's dreams for almost ten years.

Jack always got up before the dawn. It was a habit left over from twelve years of night shift in the coal mines of Yorkshire. He wasn't a good swimmer but, after all those years underground, he was attracted to places with broad horizons and spacious skies.

He had been on the island for two weeks and it had been the best time of his life. The games and roles imposed on him, which he had thought he would hate and find ridiculous, had turned out to be techniques for letting him discover pleasures that had been locked inside his body and which he never knew existed.

He suspected that one of the sources of his attraction to many of the other men here, apprentices and masters, was that the well-defined muscles of his stocky body were the real thing. The result of hard physical labour. His muscles weren't gym muscles. They had a different feel and shape. And maybe that was linked to what, Jack suspected, was another appeal he had. For years he had denied his sexual nature even to himself.

In the pithead shower rooms, especially with some of the young miners, with their attractive mix of hard-toned bodies and rosy lips and cheeks, Jack had kept telling himself that the odd tingling he felt whenever one of them mock-wrestled him or fooled around slapping him with wet towels, was just the pleasure of being with mates; men you knew in dark and dangerous places. He had often had to hold them around their waists when they were exploring a possible new seam. That kind of physical closeness went with the job. It was buddy love.

It was the arrival of a new nineteen-year-old miner called Peter which made Jack finally stop fooling himself and wasting good years. He was preparing to go down the pit when a supervisor came in with a young man following behind.

'Hey, Jack, meet Peter. He started today. Can you show him the ropes?'

The supervisor was gone and Jack found himself facing the sexiest young man he had ever seen. Not even in his sex dreams had he ever got as close to someone who seemed almost to burn himself into Jack's body at the very first glance. He had a sturdy and agile physique with a square face that combined full and sensual lips with a perfect aquiline nose, brilliant blue eyes and tumbling curls of silky black hair. He tilted his head to one side and Jack could see his lean, muscled neck and already wanted to place a kiss on it.

'I hope I won't bother you.'

His deep and gravelly voice, with its gentle Yorkshire lilt was the final stroke for Jack. He could not hide from himself any more the nature of the magnetic pull the young stranger was having on every part of him. He realised that he was starting to tremble and quickly pulled himself together.

Jack had been able to control himself for most of the day underground. There had been only one very difficult moment. In quite a narrow tunnel Peter had asked Jack for advice about how to use the coal cutter in such an enclosed space. Jack had to stand close behind Peter. He could feel the almost perfect contours of the young man's buttocks as he pressed against him and he was instantly aware of the sheer youthful beauty of the taut neck and the wild black curls which fell around it. Jack had never before felt like kissing a man's neck and it was a shock to him. The desire to snuggle his mouth against the smooth marble of the other man's skin was almost irresistible and dangerous as he well knew.

He had thought he was safe when the two men came up from the mine shaft. Jack was so shaken by the strange heat he had felt glowing between them that he was determined not to take the risk of showering with the young miner. In the locker room he made an excuse about having to leave immediately. But then, as Peter started to undress, Jack found himself trapped by the beauty of the young man's torso with its broad chest and defined stomach muscles and the T-shape of jet black hair that ran from his honed chest down to his navel.

He guessed the lower half of Peter's body would be as perfect and compelling and Jack found he could not resist the temptation he had been trying so hard to avoid. 'I may as well take a quick shower,' he said.

As he entered the shower room other miners were leaving. He would be alone with Peter.

Jack was soaping himself when Peter entered. To Jack it seemed as if Peter's body was encased in the very last moments of his youth's dreamy innocence; still uncertain what his body wanted and what such a body could give to other men. Suddenly Jack was confronted with the unmistakable form of the man he had never been able to fully imagine but whom he knew existed. Here he was soaping his large unused prick with a delicacy and naivety that made Jack's entire body tremble. Never before in his life had he felt the temptation to rape another man. But now, for a split second, he felt that forbidden urge course through him. Jack took control of himself but he could not stop himself from taking in as many details as he could of the young man's body. At least that way he could wank himself to sleep with his ideal and impossible buddy.

A supple firm torso marked by a T-shape of dark hair that was just beginning to emerge and thicken led down a naturally muscled stomach and a cock that even as it lay semihidden among a swirling triangle of black pubic hair was obviously a king-size version of young manhood.

Peter swayed towards him with all the easy and as yet unchecked beauty and confidence of youth made more compelling for Jack by the young man's obvious awkwardness in his new surroundings. As he walked towards him Jack could see in the shower room mirror the young man's fine arse, flawless, pert, lightly covered with a down of black hair.

Jack forced himself to look into the young man's square face and his eyes sparkled with a blue intensity Jack had never seen before. Jack handed him the soap and felt a shock like static electricity as the young man's fingers briefly closed around his.

'Thanks. I think I'm lucky to have you to show me the ropes.'

Jack mumbled out a self-mocking reply. Jack was already hopelessly distracted by the way the young man, now standing inches from him, under a gushing torrent of hot water, was soaping his torso with sensually slow circular gestures. Jack forced himself to tear his eyes away from the way Peter's hands moved gracefully over his broad chest and his inverted nipple tips.

When Peter, still smiling in what Jack feared was total innocence at him, started to soap his lower stomach and then push his hands down to his prick, now more fully exposed as the water crushed his pubic hairs flat, Jack felt a sudden terror that he could no longer control himself. Neither his internal desire nor its obvious physical expression. He felt his cock start to rise and nothing he could do could stop that surge of wanting. Quickly he turned himself away from Peter and, grabbing a towel, hid his erection.

He could hear Peter soaping himself and he could not prevent the abrupt, burst dam of his desire from flooding his mind with flashbacks of the shape and texture of the body he had just been ravishing in every detail with his eyes. He saw again the supple and well-defined chest leading down to the post-adolescent rippling muscles of the stomach and then the thin down of black hair leading on to the large young-man's cock and below that the long, lightly muscled thighs and calves.

As the water splashed behind him and he could continue to hear the sound of the soap on Peter's body, Jack guessed that the raw recruit was now using both his hands to wash the hard but voluptuous curves of his arse.

Jack forced himself away from a scene too dangerously compelling for him. He quickly dried himself down in front of his locker and prayed to escape before Peter joined him in the locker room. But now Jack was in a state of after-shock. His body, which he had forced for so long to lock away his desires, was convulsed with violent and uncontrollable shudders of wanting. Jack found that he could not even hold his locker steady because his hands were trembling so badly. He managed to calm himself down but it was too late to save him from the object of his desire's reappearance.

Peter walked back in with the white towel slung loosely around his stomach, revealing his deep navel and emphasising the broadness of his chest and shoulders. The glacier of the years of self-control was melting away fast under the impact of the flawless beauty of the young man who was straying so close to him.

To stop himself revealing his feelings Jack took refuge in focusing only on Peter's face. But, immediately, Jack realised that the face did not offer his lust any respite. Its oddly square shape, the slightly angled nose, the full lips and the grin that now played on them, the vivid blue of the eyes and the way the tight mass of dark curls tumbled over Peter's high forehead and stole around the curve of his long neck. All those features, taken together as Jack stared, only poured oil on the soaring flames of Jack's infatuation and desire.

Jack felt sweat breaking out on the thick stubble of his upper lip and even trickling under his armpits and between the line of hair that ran down the middle of his chest. He realised that he had to open his locker and leave the room or risk his body revealing, in a way which would not be ambiguous, what his real feelings were for the pit's new boy. He finally managed to get the key into his locker and opened it. He turned away from Peter, dropped his towel and started to pull on his white Y-fronts. Jack hoped that his by now almost full erection could be contained by the tight material and by the jeans he was hastily pulling up. But as an extra safety precaution he kept the white towel in front of him. So disguised, he turned back to the young man who was strangely enough examining his own body with his eyes and his hands.

With one hand he was feeling the muscle of his upper arms and with the other hand he was tracing the almost square shape of one of his emerging chest muscles. He gave Jack a glance and a grin which made Jack heartily glad that he had kept his towel like a matador's cloak in front of his groin.

'It's odd how your body changes isn't it?' observed Peter in his thick yet oddly dreamy Yorkshire accent.

'Yes,' was all Jack could manage to say and prayed that Peter didn't notice how even his voice was shaking with spasms of lust which he could not get rid of, certainly not for as long as he stood next to this Adonis of the pithead.

'Are we the last ones here?'

Jack was instantly excited by the question and then thought of how ridiculous he was being. Maybe this lad was a set-up sent as a prick tease by some miners who had guessed that Jack was secretly gay.

'I reckon we are, lad. Mustn't let that happen again. Coal Board makes enough profits.'

Peter seemed suddenly absorbed with his own physique. 'My body seems to get a bit bigger and harder every day. That's normal isn't it?'

'Oh, very normal,' replied Jack hoping that Peter would stop tracing his hands so provocatively over the contours of his developing and expanding pecs.

'Did you always have such a muscular body?' asked Peter.

For the first time Jack felt that the young man had focused his attention on him. Just that alone warmed Jack and made him feel happy. Jack felt absurd. But he could not contain his satisfaction at seeing the way Peter seemed to approve of his hard, boxlike torso and his clearly defined muscles.

'Well, working down the pit, lad, has made it as hard as it is now.'

'I notice that many of the men have gone a bit to fat with beer bellies but your stomach looks as hard as a rock.'

Jack stared into Peter's shining blue eyes and wondered for a split second if Peter was trying to signal to Jack that he too was attracted to men. Jack was extra cautious just because he wanted so much for Peter to respond to Jack's own instant attraction.

'I keep myself fit and ready,' he replied.

'I see you've got some small muscles there below your chest which I think I'm starting to develop.'

'Yeah, well, those are what people call a "six pack". I started to get them when I was about your age.'

In response Peter rubbed his hands exploratively over the area beneath his chest. Jack watched with fugitive pleasure as the young man traced over his dark, silky fine flesh, for the first signs of his new muscles.

But Peter's next remark completely threw Jack. 'Could you just feel these muscles here on my body and tell me if they are going to be like yours?'

Jack's first reaction was to laugh at the request and safely leave the locker room but the temptation to touch Peter's body swept aside his caution. Keeping his protective towel in front of him, he went over to the young man. He laid one hand gently on the young man's side stomach area. Jack could feel beneath the last vestiges of the adolescent fleshiness the well-defined young-man's muscles starting to emerge.

Peter's skin was warm and silky and, standing so close, Jack was all too aware of the natural heat of the young man's strong body and the slightly bitter-sweet odour he gave off. Jack wanted desperately to lift his hand from Peter's lower stomach and to caress the broad chest. To rub his thumbs against the large inverted nipples, to make them come alive and erect for him. Jack wanted so much to loosen the towel that was slung so provokingly around the young man's waist and slide one hand around the deep navel, down towards the fleshy calm of the abdomen and then into the tangled mass of the young man's pubic hair reaching the juicy prick at the same time as Jack's other hand would be stretched caressingly across the young man's tender and yielding buttocks, feeling the silky down of his black hair.

Above all, Jack wanted to pull the young man towards him and to press his mouth against those grinning fleshy lips and to feel the young man's more than generous-sized cock swelling through his towel, pressing against Jack's own large member.

Jack's hand hesitated and was poised for a long moment on the young man's warm flesh. Jack thought that he detected through their contact of flesh on flesh stirrings below in the young miner's body. Their eyes met and, for a second or two, Jack thought he could see in Peter's unclouded, sky-blue eyes a plea for the older man to act on his desire, to simultaneously possess and free him. The two men stood unmoving, unblinking, both their bodies hot and trembling. Then Jack broke away. It was a motion he had regretted ever since. But, at that time, he had only just realised the true nature of his desires and they were too overpowering for him especially with this young man.

A few weeks later he accepted early redundancy. Mainly because the repeated sight of Peter's nakedness in the showers together with the young miner's growing affection for him made Jack realise that he would not be able to hide his real feelings for Peter. To this day he didn't know if his perfect Peter was gay or not, wanted him as a lover or a friend or both.

But that was why the sight of Sam naked and then making love had hit Jack like a blow; a blow of pleasure and pain. Pleasure at seeing a Peter lookalike in action, and pain that Jack could have enjoyed what he had seen, with Peter, if only he had been more daring then. When Jack had seen Sam arrive wearing only his swimming trunks every one of his memories of Peter came flowing back.

Sam, despite being dark blond as opposed to Peter's raven black, had a body that was uncannily like Peter's. The supple torso, the powerful chest tapering to the waist, the large cock, the tenderness of the buttocks that seemed to invite you to caress them, the long well-exercised legs, yes even the large nipples and the perfect T-shape of body hair. All were exact and disturbing echoes of Peter's body. Peter's 'lost' body.

At the very first sight of the young swimmer, Jack's ever alert member had leapt up with desire. Jack loosened his trousers and put his hand around the tightening flesh of his cockstem. Peter and Sam merged in Jack's mind as he gripped his cock and rubbed its flesh up and down pressing hard against the rim of his cockhead which quickly emerged from its fleshy protective hood. Then, just when Jack thought his luck as an accidental voyeur was complete, a second figure emerged.

Jack knew and recognised, of course, the gatekeeper to the secret wrestling complex but he had never seen Cato's body before. In an instant Jack saw that it was another replica of Peter's physique, although on this body, ginger-gold hair had been substituted for Peter's black hair.

Jack whispered to himself: 'Two Peters before breakfast. Someone up there loves me.'

Cato stood for a while watching Sam in the distance swimming in the lake. Jack was therefore free to study Cato's broad shoulders flecked with ginger-gold hairs at his leisure. To admire the deep crevice of his spine which travelled down to the ample but muscular swell of the swimmer's arse and below that the same long, lithe, lightly muscled thighs and legs. Jack imagined what it would be like to walk down towards Cato. To stand behind him and first to take hold of both sides of his chest with his hands and then to pull Cato's arse towards his own face.

Jack imagined slowly rubbing his prick against the crack between Cato's buttocks which he could see through the thin material of the swimming trunks and then watching over Cato's powerful shoulder as Cato's own cock swelled and strained against his swimming trunks. Jack imagined Cato whispering to him. 'Strip me. Take me.' But before Jack could complete his fantasy he opened his eyes and saw that Cato and Sam were lying side by side, their bodies uncannily duplicating one another's and, in Jack's mind, Peter's also. For him it was the ultimate threesome he was watching, even if one of the lovers in that tangle of identical bodies was a ghost from the past.

It had given him a special shock of pleasure then when he saw Cato and Sam take off each other's swimming trunks and then Cato's body hovering over Sam's, Cato lowering his prick down towards the stiff pillar of Sam's cock which was slowly forced down by Cato's stomach. Then he watched their two sets of large nipples meet and both their bodies convulse at the point of contact. He watched with mounting excitement as Sam clutched Cato's lightly but sexily muscled back and pulled him harder to him. He focused on Cato's arse as it started to move up and down gaining speed and momentum with every second, finally gripped hard by Sam's hands as both men yelled out their pleasure simultaneously and Jack could see rivulets of their hot spunk, trickling down both sides of Sam's torso, swirling together forming patterns on their heaving stomachs and chest, so that it looked to Jack as if their bodies were covered in warm, melting lace.

Jack had tugged off his trousers and ripped open his shirt, all the time gripping his prick and imagining being between the two replicas of his Peter: Sam's cock thrusting into Jack's hard hairy bum as Cato's cock thrust against Jack's; Sam's hot spunk pouring into the deep waiting caves of his arsehole just as Cato's hot spunk shot over Jack's cockhead and black furry stomach.

Then Jack came himself. His rigid dick was spurting jet after jet of blistering fluid across the broad, waiting expanse of his naturally hard chest. Jack fell back on to the ground and closed his eyes happily.

He knew that he had to use his trusted position with Denton

and Arif to arrange matters so that he could have a wrestling session with Cato and Sam together. Then, he knew, he would know pleasure which would go beyond even the pleasure he had come to discover on this island. As Denton had insisted: Only when you wrestle with a man do you know how much pleasure he can give you out of the ring.

'Cato and Sam and me,' Jack whispered to himself and from somewhere deep in his mind came an additional thought: And if there was Peter too . . .

But Jack knew that was an impossible dream. No man could be that lucky. Even on this island where Denton had nobly attempted to bring physical bliss and adventures to men who otherwise might have gone through their lives having only touched the edges of the pleasures this island offered.

Jack opened his eyes in time to see Sam and Cato still naked but now standing tenderly kissing one another and as they did so rolling their hands down over each other's almost identical backs and arses now lit by the rising sun. The two men seemed to be in a state of dreamy togetherness. Spunk brotherhood, thought Jack. He had to fight back a sudden jab of jealousy. In an ideal world he would go down to them and squatting above would finger fuck both their arseholes simultaneously; riding them like a charioteer would ride a pair of horses. He would make them come again without touching each other, their juice spouting against the hard pebbles as his own spunk covered both of them.

'I must have the two of you together,' said Jack to himself rubbing the pungent juice from his still-rigid phallus into the matted hair of his chest. 'Before sunset.'

Six

What Cato had called their 'mirror fuck' was still filling Sam's mind and body with memories of pleasure when he joined John in the generating room two hours later. Sam and John were both in their boiler suits, fully buttoned up against the cool morning air. Neither man made any reference to what they had done to one another the night before. And somehow this silence, which was almost like a pretence that nothing had happened, made Sam find what they had done even sexier. It was as if their voluntary, if temporary, repression of what they had done made what they had experienced more intense and new encounters more keenly anticipated.

After all, Sam thought to himself as he greased up one of the large metal cogs in a generator, I don't even know what is waiting for me this afternoon and evening. But what Sam was certain that he did know was that it was going to take him even deeper into the sensual labyrinths of other men's bodies and his own. For the time being he got on with the many tasks John had set him in his brisk and almost hostile tone. Sam wondered if John had resented the amount of pleasure he had given to and taken from the dusky Arif.

Throughout the working day, now and again, Sam had flashes of his encounter with Cato and these exploded bursts of pleasure in his mind and body. Sometimes he would suddenly recall what he had felt when Cato's exposed and yearning helmet had gently, almost imperceptibly, closed on his, like two vessels meeting in outer space. First Sam had felt the raw heat of Cato's cockhead then the first hint of its touch, so delicate that Sam had not been sure whether he was really feeling Cato's prick or just feeling the anticipation of it. Then the pleasure-drenched second of clear and unmistakable impact as Cato's silky knob had brushed against and circled the supersensitive dome of Sam's own cockhead. Sam recalled that wonderfully unexpected moment when the slit in Cato's cock came close to Sam's own weeping eye and, like a tiny mouth, seemed to kiss it, then pull back and return with another kiss and then hesitate and pull back again. And all the while Sam was receiving yet another achingly pleasurable kiss from Cato's mobile lips as Cato's mouth closed first on Sam's left and then his right nipple, first tenderly and then more harshly pulling in the nipple and the hairy chest muscle around it into what seemed to Sam to be the volcanic crater of Cato's mouth.

'I can suck spunk from your tits,' whispered Cato, as briefly he interrupted his seduction of Sam's chest to twirl his long and silky tongue into the curling, inviting ridges in Sam's ear. It was at that precise moment that Sam had thought he really had, in the sudden vortex of sensations which they had conjured up for one another, shot spunk from his tits and his cock. But thinking about his encounter with Cato, Sam thought that maybe the physical delights they had wrought on each other's body had been too easy. Because their bodies were so alike they knew the other's body too quickly. There was not enough of the danger of strangeness between them and Sam wanted more of a collision than the tender ride Cato had given him.

John seemed to read, at least, the general direction of his private thoughts. 'Don't worry, it won't be long before we have to go and train in the wrestling school and tonight there is going to be something special lined up for you.'

Sam gave an involuntary start of anticipated pleasure. 'What is it?'

John drew a thin moustache with black oil just above Sam's upper lip. 'Ah you've broken so many rules. But the worst thing you did was screwing a master without being ordered to.'

'Arif?'

'Yes. You see that broke the most basic rule of all. You imposed what he most wanted on him.'

'Will I be punished?'

John's battered face broke into a grin. 'What else?'

'What will happen to me?'

'You will find out soon enough. But don't worry. First you will have some more basic training and then comes your punishment hour.'

Sam had a sense that John was eagerly looking forward to that hour and, indeed, would play some part in it. He tried to hide the fact that he was especially excited by the prospect of John being involved in the punishment.

As they continued to work, Sam's mind was racing. In his mind he wanted his punishment to be meted out by John and the ex-miner, and by the stone-muscled, shaven-headed master who had dealt him his first punitive blows for screwing Arif so deeply and defiantly. That would provide Sam with the kind of pain which he was dimly beginning to realise could also give to him peaks of pleasure he was just starting to glimpse.

At that very moment he heard the siren which announced that all the day workers on the island were being summoned to the boats to take them back across the lake. Now the island would belong only to the Roman apprentices, trainers, masters and the emperor who, Sam imagined, might provide him with pleasure that he could not even begin to imagine yet.

John interrupted his thoughts. In his trainer's voice he spoke commandingly to Sam. 'OK, apprentice, your time has come. Prepare yourself.'

They walked together past the greenhouses to the wooden gate that led into the hidden wrestling complex. Cato opened the gate to them. He avoided looking at Sam and Sam reciprocated. John gestured for Sam to go to the door that led to the same outer room that Sam had been in yesterday.

'Trainers have a separate entrance,' John explained with a knowing grin. 'We take our daily instructions about the new apprentice wrestlers. I expect there will be a lot of instructions about you today. Sit in that room and wait for me.'

Sam's body tingled at the prospect. He entered the round brick building which he was already coming to think of as a series of Chinese boxes, each one holding a new and different man, and a new and different set of pleasure assaults on his body. His mind was immediately flooded with memories of the enjoyments he had given and had taken here just twenty-four hours before.

The afternoon sunshine was pouring in through the circular hole in the ceiling and cast a large halo of light on the raised wooden beam which spanned the room. Sam recalled, in a series of rapid flashbacks, the highlights of his encounters first with the blond and the dark wrestler apprentices of yesterday and then later the even more intense contact he had enjoyed when he had submitted to John's allotted private hour of pleasure. Sam stroked his long neck, streaked with black oil, and wondered what John was planning for him in today's private hour.

Sam leant his back against the bare brick wall which felt warm where the sun had fallen on it. In recent months he was aware of his back and upper shoulders becoming larger and more muscular as if he was shedding the very last vestiges of his tender-fleshed youth. Arif was almost the perfect partner at this stage of his evolution but Sam had a sense that however much he tried to possess Arif, Arif would always be first and foremost the partner of Denton.

What he needed was someone at his level of initiation or just beyond, someone who would be his natural equal and partner in pleasure. Sam's train of thought was interrupted by the inner door of the room slamming open. John was standing there in his leather trainer's outfit, his hairy muscles crisscrossed with leather straps.

'You've been bad, apprentice boy.'

Sam guessed immediately that his session with Cato had been seen by someone and reported.

'This is a wrestling school not a school for swimmers who want to fuck before dawn. So there will be a punishment for you later today. Do you accept that?'

Sam nodded, trying to conceal his obvious excitement at the prospect.

'Good. We will begin with a special training session in one of the rings. First, strip naked.'

Sam took off his stained suit to reveal his sweaty body and pulled down his white Y-fronts over his long legs. Sam guessed that as he was standing in the large circle of sunlight all the fine dark-blond downy hair on his body was shining, making his youthful silky flesh look even more desirable. Although he had never thought of himself as a prick teaser before, he was aware that he did take a certain fugitive enjoyment from seeing the fires of desire flame up in other men's eyes and bodies when they saw him.

John broke free of Sam's deliberately engineered spell and indicated roughly to him the black leather belt and front and back flaps which were his apprentice's uniform inside the school walls.

'The island is only a holiday remember, a lucky break. We all have to go back to the mainland in two days. And then . . .' John shrugged his shoulders as if suggesting that Sam should think about what his feelings would be about John when Sam no longer had some of the other sexy hunks available who played their roles so well at the Roman games.

As Sam dressed in silence, John contemplated the fact that, after just two days on the island, Sam had become noticeably more sexy. Before Sam had come to Skate and had started his initiation John had, of course, been attracted to the golden swimmer. Working together he had felt a pang of desire when, now and again, he had glimpsed Sam's powerful chest with his downy cover of dark blond hair through his half-undone boiler suit. But since he had come to the island, and since John had seen him in action, he had displayed a talent for giving and taking sexual pleasure which John would never have guessed possible in the shy and withdrawn swimmer he had worked with on the mainland.

John had seen many of the young men who came to the island leave liberated and happy. But a few found the outside world dull and lonely after this feast of sex and fun and companionship. John did not want that to happen to Sam and, although he was trying to resist it, he was aware of a growing attachment to Sam. The image of his body so full of tenderness and fun kept repeating itself in John's mind. John imagined them having sudden secret encounters where John could match Sam's youthful ardour with his older, foxy vitality. John was convinced that the rapid changes in Sam were not just the work of his imagination. John was certain that Sam's entire being was becoming sexually supercharged on the island.

The lazy grace of his swimmer's body, which had seemed rather passive just two days ago, now seemed full of sexual confidence. John thought that even the way that Sam was now holding his long, lightly muscled arms across his chest and bending his hands around his neck exposing and slightly thrusting forward his pelvis was a position Sam would not have taken up until this day. He would have covered his uncut dick, which already had the first hint of a certain stiffening in it, with one hand. He would not have allowed his lower body to have swelled out with such carefree and half-conscious provocativeness towards John, of all people.

Even Sam's buttocks, so obviously geared to be part of the efficient machinery of his body as a swimming dynamo, were also clearly waiting to be touched and kissed and licked. John shuddered at how much he would have liked one long night alone with Sam and his arse. He would teach him things he had not dreamt of. John thought back to his first stay here eight years ago. It was paradise found. It had changed him. It had given him the courage to see that one of the greatest things in life was to experience the vast and often hidden range of peaks of sexual satisfaction. And the island had taught him, as it was now teaching Sam, that there was an extra delight in discovering for the first time the sheer scale of this continent of pleasure with others who, like Sam, had only dimly guessed at the nirvana they were missing.

For a few moments John allowed his hunting dark eyes to enjoy contact with Sam's blue eyes, dreamy with the promise of sex that would have to be so expertly and tenderly teased from his body. John felt for a strange instant that he was almost experiencing sex through the way their eyes played a ballet of avoidance: swift glances and then the pretence that their eyes had never met.

John pulled himself together. Sam really was developing an unexpectedly charismatic sexual prowess. Just as Arif had predicted to him and to Denton. John suddenly felt too entranced by the vision before him of his young apprentice. He stormed harshly out of the room yelling at Sam as he did so.

'Follow me and don't get lost and don't break any more rules. Keep your eyes on me and don't look any trainer or master in the eye.' And, John added in his mind, don't lick a master's arse so expertly that he forgets everything except what you are doing so well and so deeply inside him.

As they jogged down the long curving corridor lit by the flickering flames of the wall lamps, John had a sudden thought. Robert. The name ricocheted in his mind. Robert, the island's best wrestler, hard, aloof and imperial. The young man both Arif and Denton had confided had been their greatest discovery in the ten years since they had started the Roman games. Robert was the only one who had been so perfect that they had not been able to bring themselves to destroy video tapes of his performances. Although all young men who came to the island were videoed in the first shower they took on the island, that was normally the only record that was ever made of them. But Robert had been so captivating that Denton had broken his own rule and now had hours of Robert on tape. Robert wrestling and, so John guessed, performing for the emperor.

What had really hit John, and which hurt too because it went against his own desire and fantasy to become Sam's perfect lover, was that Robert and Sam would make the most exciting combination as wrestlers and lovers. As Denton said: 'Hot in the ring, hotter in the sack.'

John became immediately obsessed by the threat of losing Sam. He didn't want to lose the golden boy jogging so close behind with all the lovely hot curves of his fit and proud body; a body growing in sexual power and allure hour by hour, session by session.

John felt, as he jogged along with increasing speed, his booted feet pounding on the brick floor, that even by thinking this thought, of Sam and Robert, he was renouncing any right he had of making Sam his lover. If he was going to give Sam up, John thought, at least he would give himself the consolation prize of a private hour of trainer pleasure with Sam that neither of them would ever forget for the rest of their lives.

'Yes,' John whispered to himself as he heard the naked soles of Sam's feet slapping on the raw brick floor behind him and the rhythmic smack of Sam's leather apprentice uniform as his flaps whacked alternately against his dangling cock and his warming, sweat-streaked buttocks. 'Yes, I will take my one hour of pleasure and I will make it one of the greatest hours of sex in my entire life. That will be my parting gift to Sam.'

He halted abruptly in front of a red wooden door. He could not bring himself to look into the soft blue eyes of the sexual wonder boy he intended to so completely possess after sunset. He spoke in a deliberately official trainer voice.

'Apprentice, I leave you here. For one hour you will be trained in wrestling. Bodily pick ups and throwing. Don't worry about your safety. There is a new trainer in charge who knows exactly how much your body can safely take. I will collect you in one hour.'

'I haven't showered, you know,' said Sam.

John was forced to turn to him. He took in Sam's torso, streaked with engine grease stripes. In John's eyes it made him look like a handsome and angry Apache warrior. 'The grease will help you,' he replied. He was determined that, in the hour of pleasure he was planning for Sam, the young swimmer would retain all his grease stains. John gestured commandingly towards the red door and Sam went in. John glanced at the classically well-defined, overlapping plates of muscle on his shoulders, and the provocatively active arse that helped Sam's buoyancy. John needed to remember very precisely the details of Sam's physique so that he could plot how to use his last hour with Sam for his and Sam's maximum bliss.

John decided that tomorrow Sam would meet Robert in the ring, and then, John knew with a pang of regret, Sam would be lost to him. The red door slammed shut behind Sam. He had a nose for the chemical attraction that sometimes came into play between two men and, when that happened, however unlikely their bonding seemed, it would happen at great speed and no outsider would be able to compete or come between them. John, almost in a spirit of philosophical resignation, started to run quickly to his trainer's room to prepare it for his last and best session with his lost swimmer.

Sam, for his part, had been aware as he jogged behind John's vigorous body that John seemed strange today. He was somehow more focused on Sam and yet also more distant. As if he was saying a sexual goodbye. This puzzled Sam because he realised pragmatically that when he left this island he might well need a regular and convenient good fuck. John was certainly not his ideal but he had the kind of reliable virility that some older men had in abundance. Sam might need the solid sensual mass of John's body in the months after he left this island. It would certainly be a very acceptable consolation prize and, anyway, Sam felt he owed John the use of his body for initiating him into the world of Roman games. Sometimes such a feeling of debt to someone made the sex with them better since any form of repayment pleases both he who receives and he who gives. But John said almost nothing to Sam and Sam wondered whether he had made John jealous with his escapades with Arif last night and with Cato at dawn this morning. Jealousy was not supposed to happen here on the island. Denton said there were too many cute guys for anyone to feel left out but Sam guessed that rule was more of a hope than a reality. When men desired one another there was always the possibility of desiring someone more than anyone else. So far Sam felt he had been fairly well-behaved in that, although he had felt his sharpest tangs of desire for Arif, Jack, John and Cato, he had also really wanted and enjoyed himself with all the other men he had encountered. But he felt that he had not yet reached the goal he was destined for. He had not yet come home.

Before he parted from John he glanced into the other man's dark eyes and sensed an invitation for much deeper intimacy between them but an invitation held suspended as if John was afraid of coming right out with his offer. Sam gave a pliant grin of encouragement. 'I couldn't have managed any of this without you. And afterwards I guess I'll need you even more.'

Sam felt that his words made it clear that he was not going to abandon John and he did not know how but he was sure that John was planning some unexpected and early climax to their relationship this very day.

'You can't reduce your punishment by sweet promises, Prince of the Breaststroke.' And, with that ironic response, John thrust Sam through a door.

Sam was instantly thrilled by the sight which greeted him. In a semicircular room, dominated by a slightly elevated wrestling ring, there stood Cato in one corner, dressed in exactly the same apprentice's outfit as Sam was wearing. In the other corner stood Jack, the ex-miner who Sam was surprised to see had been promoted since he'd last seen him, from apprentice to trainer. Sam thought he looked even more sexy in his trainer outfit. The crisscross of black leather straps across his chest emphasised the rugged, naturally muscled chest. Stocky and powerful, Jack's chest had a rich covering of curling jet-black hair. The big belt and leather flaps hid his cock and arse from direct view but Sam could guess, from the densely muscled thighs and the thick calves, that Jack had the kind of juicy penetrating prick that many men – even men much younger than him – dreamed of and that his arse would be as stocky, as naturally muscular and as blackly hairy as the rest of him. Sam wanted to possess and be possessed by him.

Sam caught Jack watching the way he was appraising Jack's body. There was the faintest suspicion of a grin on Jack's rough, darkly stubbled face, before he sternly shouted out to him in his thick Yorkshire accent: 'Come on lad. We've no time to waste. In the ring.'

Sam bounded into the ring. The floor felt just slightly bouncy under his naked soles.

'In this session,' declared Jack, 'the aim is for you to try to pick each other up, only using holds beneath the waist. If you walk round the ring once holding the other above your waist you win the round. Get started now.'

Sam leapt with a new-found confidence towards where Cato

was dodging in front of him. Sam did not know why it was but, ever since he had stripped himself naked in front of John, he had felt a new will to impose the smells and shapes and rhythms of his body on others, especially those compelled to be intimate with him in the wrestling ring.

He felt the whole surface of his body was tattooed with desire. He felt he was alive with fresh skills of touching, caressing, seizing, holding and possessing. He felt he could now give to other men the things they most wanted. It was in this new spirit that he faced Cato.

Sam realised in a flash that what they had done to one another that morning was only a prelude to what they would do to one another now. And, in a rapid sideways glance, Sam intuitively knew that both men would also be using Jack to add new layers of rough pleasure to their wild mating inside the ring.

Cato did not give Sam a moment to find himself. Sam sensed a spinning arc of flesh and leather and then Cato's entire body was crushed against his and he felt the strength of Cato's arms closing around his waist and lifting him high in the air.

Sam tried to resist by grabbing under Cato's exposed hairy armpits and pulling his upper arms apart but Cato was possessed with an unexpected steely strength and Sam could do nothing that way to break the lockhold Cato had on him. As Cato started to carry him in triumph around the ring, Sam knew that he had to very quickly find a way of breaking Cato's tight grip under his arms. He wrapped his legs around Cato's and tried to trip him up. But as he was doing this he become aware of a quite different sensation. Cato, taking advantage of Sam's position, was circling the downy halo that surrounded Sam's navel with his tongue. Sam had a special weakness for having his umbilicus sucked on and kissed so fiercely and he was certain that he must not allow himself to be distracted from his attempt to break Cato's wrestling grip by the sensations Cato was secretly creating on the hole in the centre of his body.

Cato's tongue pierced into his navel like a spear. Sam could almost see the blood trickling from him yet he knew that as much as he wanted those sensations he needed to ignore them in order to defeat Cato. He tried even harder to force Cato's arms to separate and so lose their grip on his waist and entire body. He concentrated more intently than he had ever done before in his life and started to feel that he was finally prising open Cato's imprisoning arms.

Cato responded in a way Sam had half-feared and half-longed for. Sam could feel Cato's tongue making narrower and narrower circles round his navel and he guessed what the target of Cato's tongue would soon be. He was right. Sam soon felt the warm tip of Cato's tongue entering the hard cave of his navel although, at first, it was just a flick which Sam could barely feel. Even so it gave him a brief shudder of delight. For Sam it was almost the same sensation as if Cato's swelling prick had prised open the pink centre of his anus.

Then Cato started to circle his tongue inside Sam's navel. First Sam could feel the silky touch of the top of Cato's tongue then the rougher leathery underside as Cato pushed himself deeper and deeper into Sam. Then Cato turned his tongue down and pushed hard against Sam's flesh and insides. Sam realised that Cato was trying to force his tongue down through Sam's navel towards Sam's inner sanctum. As Cato pressed Sam's hairy navel wall deeper into Sam using it as a kind of condom for his pressing tongue, Sam started to feel a dizzy whirl of sensations as if some carousel was suddenly spinning inside the centre of his being.

He had never before felt the sensation of being fucked from the top of his arse through his navel by another man's tongue. Suddenly he was aware under his back leather flaps of arrows of sharp sensations darting both left and right, and upwards inside the secret top chamber of his arse. Sam had no defences there. He had always expected to be penetrated from the bottom through the armed sentry of his arsehole. He had never expected another man's tongue to reach him through the closed gateway of his navel. He had never expected to be possessed like this.

It was as if Cato knew precisely, because his body was a mirror image of Sam's, just how and where he could ambush Sam.

Sam's entire body was trembling as Cato's tongue drew tiny arcs of delight through his skin. It was too intense. Sam felt that one second more and his already erect member would have to spurt out over Cato's ginger-gold chest. Sam had to force himself to escape from Cato's sensual trap and, using all the remaining force in his thighs and calves, pulled Cato's legs sufficiently far apart for the other man to topple forward.

In an instant Sam had slipped his entire upper body around Cato and, in a sharp reversal of their roles, Sam, standing square behind his opponent, encircled the other's waist and lifted him high off the floor of the ring.

Sam saw a flash of excitement in Jack's eyes as he started to carry Cato around the perimeter of the ring. He knew that Jack was also excited by the sight of Cato now in his power and Sam wondered if Jack was imagining that what he was doing to Cato now he would soon be doing to Jack also? Cato tried desperately to break Sam's grip around his waist but Sam was determined to win. He guessed that he had to succeed, to prove himself today, if he was to continue to make his way towards those men at the centre of these games, the men he was sure were the ones who were destined to take him and his body to where he had to be. Maybe Cato also guessed this and that was why he was now redoubling his efforts to break Sam's grip on him.

Already Sam had carried him around two sides of the ring. Time was running out for Cato. Cato was strong and knew the wrestling moves better than Sam who was still acting on instinct but Sam was, even in ordinary circumstances, close to the peak of his physical strength and prowess and, at this moment, when he knew so much depended on him making a convincing victory for the eyes he guessed were watching them, he found he could call on hidden reserves of power. He felt an extra surge of strength coursing through his whole body, which enabled him to fight off Cato's increasingly desperate assaults on him.

Soon Sam was halfway along the third side of the ring. Cato's back leather flap and his solid fleshy arse were crushed against the side of Sam's cheek. Cheek to cheek, thought Sam, as he struggled to keep his neck from being wrenched back by Cato high above him and aware that unless he did something soon he was being carried towards his defeat.

Sam focused all his extra strength into his neck. He imagined his veins as being made of steel. They would not yield to Cato's attacking hands, down which the sweat poured over Sam's face. Cato's sweet smell was now trickling in thin ribbons of sweat around Sam's mouth clenched tight. Sam turned and started to move along the fourth side of the ring. Cato tried one last tactic to save himself. He flung his upper body forward and down and entwined his arms around Sam's thighs in an effort to immobilise or topple him. But it was too late. Sam reached the last post of the fourth side of the ring.

He let Cato's sweating body slide through the relaxed circle of his arms and for a few seconds his defeated opponent rested the back of his body against Sam. Sam could feel the sweet smell and heat of the other man. And, now that they were both briefly freed from the pressure of the wrestling, Sam could start to appreciate the special pleasure of having pressed against his prick the first arse he had ever known which was an almost exact replica of his own. Into Sam's mind swam long-forgotten images of fantasies Sam had had, before he had ever touched another man, of the pleasure he might get from using his cock to fuck his own arse. A complete circle of sensation uninterrupted by anyone else. Sam remembered the words that had bubbled up in his mind when with this picture in his mind he had brought himself to a generous climax: Flesh of my flesh. Sam was roused from this brief daze by Cato who leant back, resting his head on Sam's shoulder.

'Can I reward the winner?' he asked. His mouth half-opened in invitation and the tip of his tongue could just be seen. Sam grinned and leant his mouth towards Cato's. Their lips met and then their tongues. As their tongues curled around each other's Sam felt the sweat that was trickling down the face of both men mingling: Sam's slightly salty-sweet sweat mixing with Cato's purely sweet flavour. And, once again, to his surprise Sam enjoyed the cropped ginger-golden hair of Cato's thin moustache tickling against the shaved area above Sam's upper lip. He enjoyed this even more at this moment because Cato's pencil-thin moustache was soaked with Cato's sweat which it laid like a tribute across Sam's shaven skin.

Their dreamy mouth sharing was broken by Jack's voice. 'That's enough of that non-wrestling stuff.'

They reluctantly withdrew their tongues from each other's mouth and parted their lips and then their sweat-drenched bodies. They both turned to face the trainer they had so obviously ignored for the last few minutes. As they confronted Jack across the white space of the wrestling ring they both knew that he was no longer going to be denied his rights over them. He would not accept his exclusion from their games.

Cato and Sam had no problems with this inevitability. The man they both faced was, although some years older than them, an exciting example of a body whose muscles were formed by many years of real hard labour. Sam could almost see the years of toiling in the depths of the earth etched on to the solid mass of Jack's torso.

Sam guessed that some of his attraction for Jack came from his frustrated attempt to appeal to John today. Yet some of the appeal also came from the obvious fact that Jack was thrilled by Sam and Cato. Sam could see it not just in the eager quivering of the shape of his big prick under his flap but also in his eyes which seemed hypnotised by the younger men's bodies. And although Jack was shorter and stockier than they were, he seemed to both of them to have the edge over them in that he exuded a raunchiness that suggested there'd be no limits to what he would give and take from them. His hard, toned body was now ready to deploy all that stored energy against their softer-edged physiques.

The aggressive way he stood with his thick hairy thighs which seemed to drill into the floor of the ring suggested that at the centre of his body was the kind of thrusting power which could take a young, less-initiated apprentice to heaven and back. Both men also realised that Jack would not have been promoted to being a trainer unless he had qualities that went beyond his wrestling skills. Sam guessed that Cato shared his impressions which meant that both men were willingly prepared to submit to his instructions. Jack stepped towards them across the ring floor still glistening with pools of their sweat.

Ever since Cato and Sam had first faced each other in the wrestling ring, Jack had felt a special excitement, an excitement which was caused both by the uncanny physical resemblance both men bore to each other and to Peter, Jack's ideal man. To have found one man who so closely resembled Peter would have been thrilling enough but to find two young men who replicated him, even down to their slightly swaying walks, was something close to a miracle and certainly sent wave after wave of raw, reawakened longing through Jack's tough and impatient body. His squat and juicy prick started to engorge as the first wafts of the men's body odours floated into his nostrils, alerting him to the fact that at this moment they were as much in heat as he was.

If he could not have Peter than at least he could have Peter's lost twins. He could get a taste of what it might have been like for Peter and him with these two young studs whose pricks and arses looked ripe for action. From the moment Cato had leapt across the ring and seized the inexperienced Sam by his waist and lifted him up and then, more discreetly, but not discreetly enough to evade Jack's notice, had plunged his tongue into the dark golden down of Sam's navel, Jack had felt his whole body tense with his desire to experience their bodies at the same time. Then, as Sam unexpectedly reversed Cato's dominance and held Cato in his tight grip, parading him around the ring with a wild half-grin on his handsome, sweat-streaked face, Jack had felt his desire for both of them mounting every second.

It was not just a matter of his famously large and thick cock starting up like a stallion's in heat. No, Jack felt his lust firing up every part of his body from his inner thighs to the raw, iron muscles of his arms and shoulders. His entire body was swaying with lust for the two young men who were now his prisoners in the ring. Their bodies too, Jack thought, were like his. Muscled by hard work. Their large shoulders, their powerful thrusting chests, their lithe, long muscular legs had all been shaped by years of proud body work in water and on the land. They were both much lighter, of course, but taken together their body weight might be just about a fair match for his and Jack certainly was planning to take them together.

Jack went closer to them and then paused. His voice fell to a whisper. 'I saw you both this morning. When they made me a trainer today and I gained the right for an hour of private pleasure with any, or all of my apprentices, I remembered you two this morning.'

With that Jack went as close as he could to them without touching them. He turned the still-sweating bodies of Sam and Cato around so that the two athletes were back to back, arse to arse.

Then, Jack took hold of one of Cato's hands and placed it just above one of Sam's large nipples around which was now gathered a halo of his gleaming sweat. Jack then took one of Sam's hands and placed it on one of Cato's large nipples which seemed to redden the ginger in Cato's swirling gold hairs.

'Sam, excite Cato with that hand. Cato, excite Sam with yours.'

As Jack commanded them, in a low husky voice, he knew that neither of the two trainee wrestlers needed much encouragement from him. Their urgent need to make contact with each other again was not hard to see.

Both men relaxed their necks on the shoulder of the other as they started to caress each other's chest. Their hands seemed to automatically mirror exactly what the other was doing. Each man seemed to need first to trace the broad half-circle shape of their pectoral muscles hardened and shaped by their athletic lives. Only gradually, when they seemed to have explored completely the broad mass of their powerful chests, did each of them move their hand towards their nipples. At first, both men's nipples, encircled by their fine body hair, were inverted. But, gradually, as both men drew narrower and firmer circles of touch around the deep pink zone of their nipples, both sets of teats rose and emerged out of the undergrowth of their hair and rapidly became hard erect peaks of flesh which needed to be squeezed between the rough skin of their fingers.

Jack watched with growing desire as both men sighed at the progress they were each making in liberating and pleasuring the body of the other. What Jack found especially exciting was the way both men's heads now rolled at ease on the pillow of the other's shoulder but that they faced away from one another. It was as if they knew that their faces, eyes and mouths could not be too near each other at this moment without them both prematurely being tempted to exchange deep-throated kisses. And after that, could even Jack control what they would want to do to one another? Jack imagined Peter doubled-up and making love to himself and almost swooned at the thought.

All day, ever since Denton and Arif had told him in the morning that he had more than earned the right to be a trainer, Jack had been planning what he would do in his first hour of pleasure and absolute command over his chosen apprentices. He had planned and replanned all day what moves, positions and words would give him and his apprentices the best time together.

'With your free hands lift the other's back flap,' he ordered quietly, now positioning himself midway between them.

Sam was the first, the keenest to obey, as Jack had guessed he would be. Jack remembered the way that, before dawn that morning, when Cato was on top of him, Sam's hands had gripped and caressed the generous curves of Cato's buttocks, with their sheen of ginger-gold hair. Jack had noticed the way Sam had glanced, at the very height of their passion, over Cato's heaving shoulders at the curves and dimples of Cato's arse. Sam's hands had then gently teased the ginger-blond down that covered the swimmer's arse and then, as both men climaxed together, Sam had dug his fingers deep into the tenderised flesh of the other man.

Now Jack, standing between them, could see both their rumps, both firm but carrying that slight layer of extra flesh which made both of their rears so tempting to grab and squeeze. Sam's looked exactly like Cato's – the only difference being that Cato's rear slopes were covered with a down of ginger gold, whilst Sam's were covered with a more dense and furry covering of dark blond. Both men's bottoms curved sharply out from their lightly but clearly muscled backs.

'Bring your arseholes together and keep making love to your tits,' commanded Jack who had longed all day for this moment.

Sam took the lead gently brushing first the left and then the right side of his cheek against the immobile mass of Cato's arse. Sam sensed Cato's reluctance. He seemed afraid to make that raw and novel contact between the pink centre of his and Sam's anus.

Sam expertly encouraged Cato by using one hand to tease Cato's buttocks into opening up for him. At the first touch, the first arse-kiss for both men, both of them shook with unexpected delight. To feel the puckered and sensitive skin of another's arsehole kissing and rubbing so tenderly and so intensely was a surprising consummation for both men of the intimacy they had forged during the day. Jack was very glad to see that both men's cocks were filling with the blood of their reawakened lust.

Jack noticed that Cato remained the more passive – happy, it seemed to Jack, to have Sam's more hairy buttocks brushing back and forth across first one and then the other of his cheeks before pressing hard against the tiny circle at the centre of his arse.

Jack watched as a trickle of sweat ran down the ravine of the spines of both men. The salty line, which had come down all the way from their broad shoulders, now spilled over from the base of their spines to the top of the deeper ravine which divided the two cheeks of their arse. Their sweat poured deep into that crack and both rivulets mingled together at the point where their bums touched. Both men had half-closed their eyes and Jack guessed that they were both enjoying the sensation of their mixed sweat circling round their rosebuds and then stinging that protected area with their body's freshly minted salt.

Jack was now ready to put his big question to his apprentices. 'Which one of your arseholes is most hungry for its trainer and which prick can I have?'

The effect of his words was instant and electric. Both men's bodies trembled again and Cato and Sam darted a glance at the solid, black-haired mass of their trainer's body as he stood so close to them that the heat and smell of all three men seemed to have formed a triangle of sharp desire.

Jack had been coming to the island for four years now and he had enough training and natural talent to know that he had Cato and Sam exactly where he wanted them. Jack guessed that what his apprentices were wanting from him was not just his body but the essential manliness of his past as a miner. Jack was sure that both men needed some older man like himself, who came with just such a virile masculine identity, to make them feel more relaxed about playing a more passive role in sex. Jack was certainly going to see to it that his novices were about to get one of their best initiations.

They had paused in their caressing of each other's chest and nipples. Jack gestured for that to continue. He knew that hard nipples meant harder cocks. They obeyed. At the same time their arseholes continued to act like the mouths of young lovers pressed in a lingering and passionate kiss of pink flesh.

Gently Jack took Sam's free hand and guided it across the solid expanse of his chest. The palm of Sam's hand pressed briefly down on Jack's left nipple teasing it into life and then Jack guided Sam's hand down the hairy line which led from his chest to his stomach, outlined with a circle of fierce black hair and then down to his trainer's thick leather belt. Cunningly, Jack held Sam's keen hand there.

Jack let Sam see that he was taking Cato's free hand with his other hand and guiding it first to the leather band that tightly bound his throat, and then across the pebbled, rippling muscles of his lower neck and upper shoulders. He then moved it down the muscular mass of his back towards the trainer's belt, that thick line of leather that, Jack knew, marked at this moment for both men the last barrier to Jack's two most prized and hidden centres of the pleasure machine that his body had become.

Jack himself felt both his prick and arse moisten with his own body sweat. He knew how very close the capable hands of both these studs were to providing him with the double sexual fix he needed. He knew they were going to give him a sex ride neither he nor they would forget in a hurry. The bodies of all three men were tensed up and covered with sweat which shone under the room's single arc light and which emphasised the well-defined lines of their torsos.

As Jack quickly fixed into his mind snapshots of their virile young manhood, he thought again of his lost Peter. He was determined that in this hour with these two strong but tender swimmers he would experience a version of some of the joys he might have known, had he been brave enough, years ago, to take Peter out of the cascading shower into his arms. He pushed his face between the slender necks of Cato and Sam and whispered to them.

'Have I made the right choice? You, Sam, need my cock and you, Cato, need my arsehole? Don't answer yet. I am about to find out in a more reliable way.'

Jack guided the hands of both men together. Sam's hand he glided over the belt and under the flap towards where Jack's stocky juicy cock was already almost completely erect. He had saved the pleasant task of coaxing his shiny dome out from his taut hood of flesh for Sam.

Sam did not need any further guidance. His hand firmly clasped around the base of Jack's cockstem, pulling into its grip some of Jack's matted black hairs. Firmly but almost shyly, just as Jack had anticipated, Sam moved his hand up and down the rigid stem of Jack's stalk only stopping just below where Jack's cockhead was still hidden by its protective hood.

Then Sam wound his surrounding hand back to the base of Jack's penis and started again with slightly increased force and speed to rub it, seeming to force all Jack's aching flesh towards the hidden circumference of his cockhead.

While Jack was more than enjoying this dose of gentle but firm expert attention he was also feeling the good effects of his other apprentice. As he was guiding Sam's willing hand towards his cock, Jack was also guiding Cato's hand towards his hidden rosebud. Jack turned Cato's hand on its side so that it was the roughest skin on Cato's hand that made first contact with the dividing crevice of Jack's arse. Like Sam, Cato seemed to know intuitively how to mix firmness and tenderness, assault and caress.

First, Cato pressed the entire side of his hand deeper into Jack's crack tugging at the dense mass of black body hairs that curled around this forbidden zone.

Jack showed his appreciation of this by squeezing hard on Cato's wrist and pressing the side of the younger man's hand deeper into him, encouraging Cato to go further than he might have dared.

It was then that Jack realised that both Cato and Sam were

taking over. They were now in control. Every now and again Sam allowed his encircling hand to travel right to the tip of Jack's cock and there give it a pleading squeeze and Cato was gradually entering into the outer zone of Jack's arsehole with his exploring finger. First it circled and then made an attempt to penetrate into the rosebud and the warm tunnel beyond waiting to be violated.

For a few minutes Jack, in his role as trainer, resisted the efforts of these two studs to make him surrender anything to them. He defied his cockhead to emerge and he clenched his buttocks together so that Cato's dangerously exciting, exploring fingers could gain no access. But it was not just their touch that Jack had to resist. In a way he had not fully realised before, he had set up a trap for himself. In front of him he had full and free gaze on two of the most beautiful bodies he had ever seen. Bodies close to that special peak of early manhood which mixed, as no time before or later would do, the last vestiges of adolescence and youth with all its teasing and doubting qualities and the first signs of later manhood's combatable toughness and pride. The wiry body hair of later manhood was starting to emerge and mingle with the last remains of youth's downy covering.

But, much more than that, was the dangerously uncontrollable excitement he felt which he had himself unleashed by putting them back to back, neck to neck, shoulder to shoulder and arse to dimpled arse. And then he had recklessly added to all this the mutual sultry caressing of their broad chests and unusually large nipples. Jack had to confront all this, the sex show he had set in motion, on top of which he had to cope with the actual touch of these two men. He had not expected their hands and fingers to be so strong and yet so tender, so accurate in the targeting of what would give him the deepest physical bliss.

Against what he thought his wishes had been, Jack found himself having to surrender to the circles of pressure of Sam's hand on his cockstem and caresses to his cockhead, now no longer able to resist emerging, desperate for direct contact by Sam's naturally expert fingers. Nor could Jack resist any longer, now that he was so unavoidably confronted both by the physical touch of these two men and by the sight of their sex-soaked bodies pressed hard back to back, Cato's young fingers eager to seduce his arsehole.

Jack felt his back arch violently back as Cato's longest finger slid deeper into him, twisting back and forth inside the gulleys and valleys of his anus. Jack wanted more of Cato's fingers and hand deep inside him and, more than that, needed the raw fullness and hardness of Cato's young wild member plunging into the very centre of him.

'I was right,' breathed Jack as he undid the belts of both men. He slipped himself between their bodies as their belts and flaps fell to the canvas floor of the wrestling ring.

Jack knew that there was no point in telling them how they were to serve him. He realised that both his young men, his ideal apprentice team, knew better even than he did what would take him to the peaks of ecstasy.

This certainty was confirmed when Jack had both Sam and Cato's bodies revolved against his, until he was face to face with Sam's subtle blue eyes and grin and when the young man's first act was to use his pulsing cock to lift Jack's leather flap and to place his prick against the older man's thick stem.

Cato's slow turn had brought that young man's pressing penis hard against Jack's back flap which Cato deftly lifted, wasting no precious time in pressing his throbbing erection against the dense hairy surface of Jack's rock-solid arse of pure muscle.

Cato lightly touched his nipple peaks against Jack's rugged back muscles. They were like two points of bliss teasing him to flinch from their delicate and unexpected caress. Cato then moved his upper torso in a gentle swirling motion so that his nipples drew a series of circles on Jack's hairy back, which Jack knew were copies of the rosebud that Cato's finger's had so recently discovered.

Jack knew he was even closer than he had imagined he could be to one of the best sex sessions of his life. He had done exactly what he had dreamed of doing that morning when he had seen these two young athletes topple on one another. He had put his body between them and he knew that both of them now would be channelling the pleasure they wanted to give each other through his densely and honestly muscled body. He was about to receive from both of them all the pleasure they had so carelessly thrown at each other on the edge of the lake just a few hours ago.

The moment when Jack forgot that it was Peter who had inspired all this was when Sam's fleshy young lips touched his and the tip of Sam's tongue curled under them. At the same time the thin line of Cato's moustache pressed against the nape of Jack's thick and hairy neck and Cato's tongue just touched for a second the tip of the V shape of Jack's haircut on his neck. Tip to tip. And then Jack was aware of both men's mouths opening dangerously wider.

Both of his apprentices now had lowered their warm, spittle-moist lips to the left and right side of his lower neck. Gently at first and then more harshly and insistently their teeth bit into his dark flesh. The entire taut frame of his powerful and stocky body shook under this double-impact love bite which Jack had not planned or expected but which he now knew was the contact he had most wanted to be given by them. He was very close to coming over Sam's tight stomach as he felt both sets of teeth pull part of the flesh of his neck together into a loose oval shape and half bite into the dark skin with their animal mouths.

He felt he was riding on some of the highest sensations of his life. He felt not just the two men's mouths closing on him but all the steely yet tender contours of their bodies too. He had come between them but in the act of denying them their pleasure together they had found through him a new and even more intense way of reaching one another. They were reaching to each other through his body.

Sam did not know why but from the moment Jack placed him back to back against Cato and stood between them, Sam had known that Jack would create a new way for them to find bliss in each other's mirror image even if, or even because, Jack needed, for reasons of his own, to deny him and Cato direct contact.

Jack's forcing their arseholes together had been for Sam an inspired position. In a brief moment of fantasy which Jack's actual orders had prevented, Sam had anticipated the pleasure he would feel if Jack had ordered them to open their tightly held arse cracks to each other and then with a brief beating with his thick trainer's belt on both their raw butts had forced their rosebuds into the open and then ordered their anuses to meet and kiss like their lips had done on the cold beach before dawn.

Sam had never before wanted to rub his arsehole deep against another man's, but Cato, maybe just because he was so close to being Sam's double, had inspired this wild desire for the ultimate forbidden kiss. And his trainer, Jack, had given Sam the chance to try out this latest desire with Cato.

Sam had enjoyed this arse to arse contact a lot with his physical twin. He had enjoyed brushing his own rocking arse against the resistant, firm, fleshy curves of Cato's arse. But the deeper pleasure had only started when Jack took Sam and Cato's hands and allowed them to play with him.

Sam had often thought in the last few days what Jack's cock would be like. He had guessed that, as Jack resembled John in many ways, like John, Jack's prick would resemble the rest of his sturdy, stocky body. It would be uncut, longish and thick with a well-hidden cockhead which might be difficult to tease out but when teased out would be difficult to stop thrusting and juicing. And he had been right. Now Jack was pulling Sam towards him and Sam loved the brutal contact.

Jack's chest muscles, covered by a thick layer of twirling wiry black hair, had been as hard as Sam had anticipated. It felt like a granite cliff against Sam's upper back and the ex-miner's stomach was solid too. Below the thick leather frontier of his belt, Sam could make out the outline of Jack's cock itself, thicker than Sam had expected. And then Sam felt Jack lift up his leather flap to free his cock for direct contact. Jack gently urged his meaty prick against Sam's buttocks. Trembling, in response, Sam pressed his bum harder against Jack's vibrant member teasing open his crack to make entry easier and more welcoming.

What made this contact even more pleasurable for Sam was that he knew that on the other side of the solid hairy mass of Jack's body, Cato's supple fingers were sliding over Jack's hairy buttocks and fondling his moist rosebud, ready to prise their way into the tight tunnel of Jack's arsehole. Sam hoped that Cato's prick would penetrate Jack's arse just at the moment when Jack would sink his bulging member into Sam's smooth anus. His only anxiety was how much of that thick stem he could take without pain up his longing, but tight passage.

But to Sam's surprise Jack withdrew his prick and its promises and started to slowly turn Sam round to face him. Sam looked disappointed.

'Do you know what most excited me about what I saw this morning?' whispered Jack.

Sam shook his head. He was trying to avoid looking down towards where he knew that thick throbbing tool of Jack's was pressing itself against the black leather flap, straining to touch Sam's own rigid manhood.

'What excited me most,' continued Jack, 'was the sight of your two great young pricks pressed against each other, swirling around each other, stem on stem, cockhead on cockhead. And what really made my dick fill to bursting was that cock-to-cock combat this morning and the thought I had of me putting my body between your two penises, stopping your two dicks from mating . . . both of them struggling to meet through my body.' Jack started to caress Sam's broad chest muscles. His own words were exciting him. 'So that's what I want from you two now. I want to feel both your hot cocks struggling through me to find the other's prick. I want to feel at the same time what it's like to have a Sam dick and a Cato dick thrusting against me and through me.'

As he said this Jack gently rocked his solid body back and forth, rocking his penis against Sam's, and rocking his arse against Cato's cock.

Sam could sense that Cato was as excited as Jack was. And Sam knew that Jack had certainly been right about one thing: Sam really did want at this moment, more than anything else, to feel the long stem and thick bulbous head of his 'double's' cock against his. By denying the two men the contact they craved, Jack was succeeding in increasing their longing for one another. And he knew he could feel this in the zeal of both their pricks trying to reach each other: one plunging headlong through his arse the other spearing him through his navel. Jack knew it would feel like two rockets being launched at and coursing through him.

'Strip your trainer naked,' Jack ordered.

Sam and Cato both started to undo the buckle on Jack's thick trainer's belt. They did not hurry, but undressed Jack slowly and seductively, so that they could enjoy this brief moment of physical contact between themselves, their fingers hungrily touching one another reminding them both how much they longed for their 'twin' cocks to be together again.

Then the leather belt and the thick flaps fell to the floor and Sam was confronted by Jack in all his glory, his long, thick-stemmed prick backed up by two powerfully muscled thighs thickly covered in black hair. It was a body that reeked of raw, powerful masculinity. And Sam sensed that Cato was equally pleased by the sight he now had of Jack's solid, square-shaped arse with his anus well hidden and protected from him.

Gently Jack rocked his stolid nakedness against first Sam's and then Cato's hungry cock. Both men's members quickly stiffened and reached their maximum size with both moist cockheads emerging simultaneously from the sweet fleshy flaps of their foreskins. Both helmets, it seemed, wanted to have no barrier between them and Jack's cock, navel and anus. Jack soaked up the joy of being so fiercely admired by his raunchy apprentices' pricks.

'The two of you,' he growled. 'The two of you, that's what I need.'

'You are going to get us both, hard and hot,' Cato said. 'Nothing can stop us now.'

As Sam pressed his yearning penis deep into Jack's navel, he brushed aside Jack's prick's attempt to block him. Over the rippling muscles of Jack's shoulder he could see Cato withdraw his cock from Jack's arsehole and then press the full length of his massively erect prick between Jack's square, hard buttocks.

'Take me again,' begged Jack, his body arching back towards Cato's sweating, handsome face.

Sam could see the swelling purple dome of Cato's cockhead,

which he knew had the power to touch with electric force, pressing against the small triangle of black hair that pointed down into the silently resisting valley of Jack's crease.

Automatically, Sam rested his chin on Jack's right shoulder and Cato on Jack's left shoulder. Both men were using the stubble on their chins to ride roughly over Jack's dark leathery flesh. Jack's rocking motion started to get faster and faster as Sam guessed he could feel the full force of their cocks, striving to reach one another through the solid mass of Jack's own body. Jack was being speared now in his puckered arsehole and through his navel. He felt that his lads' pricks were about to meet inside him, prevented from touching only by the rugged flesh of his body.

'Come together like you did this morning,' Jack commanded, desperate to reach a climax.

Sam did not need any encouragement for, just as Jack spoke to them, his voice thick with desire, Sam could feel the first signs of Cato's cock pushing deep into Jack's arse and towards Sam's own cock. Both of his apprentices knew by Jack's moans and by his hectic rocking motion, slapping his body alternately against both of them, that he could feel what he most wanted: Sam's and Cato's pricks pressed close, striving to reach each other through him, and inside him. Sam just knew he had reached the exact moment when he could no longer stop his spunk flowing out of him. He could feel Cato's steady pumping motion inside Jack's anus and with a shout of release, they came.

Together they were drenching Jack with the warm white liquid of their rapture.

'Oh yes! Yes! Yes!' yelled Jack as his most precious fantasy was at last fulfilled and, in a frenzied pitch of passion, Jack released a cascade of come over Sam's cock and taut stomach. Cato put his hands around Jack's stomach and bathed them in the miner's liquid virility. Then both men simultaneously planted a tender love bite on Jack's neck, a mark of pleasure and thanks for letting them unite in such an exquisite way.

★

Sam found himself alone back in the circular room with the wooden beam and the circle of open sky high above his head. He had showered with the others and then been ordered back here. He stretched out on the sandy floor dressed once again in the leather belt and flaps of an apprentice. Sam brooded on his latest threesome. He certainly didn't regret it. Indeed the obvious excitement Jack caused him made him wonder if he was wrong to be so often on the lookout for men of his own age. Maybe he was the type of man who needed an older brother figure to teach and control him. Maybe his dream of an absolute equality in every respect between him and his lovers was a false ideal. On this island, Sam realised, he was fortunate enough to be giving a crash course in all possible variations of physical and personality types. Perhaps he needed both an equal and a master. He stroked his freshly shaved cheeks and considered the third option too, a younger man or men with whom he could play the controller, teacher and liberator. That last possibility he had not yet directly met on the island.

Sam looked down dreamily at his own body bound in its leather trappings. It seemed to him that his entire body had become freer, more relaxed and open, less inward looking. He no longer admired the long firm curves of his swimmer's physique in the same way. Now he was coming much more to think of his body in terms of others, of how his body could complement others either through mirroring them or being their opposite. Quite different sets of enjoyment and sensation flowed from those two basic options, as he was coming to see more clearly. Did he want to concentrate on one set of pleasures or did he want to flit from one to another? And which of those two options would yield the most enduring and searing physical and emotional contentment? In a few years he would be thirty. He was now acutely aware that his present status, halfway from youth to full manhood, was not going to last for much longer. At the moment, of course, he was perhaps in the most physically privileged position of all; desired by almost everyone, even desired by himself! He grinned at his own smug arrogance. 'Pride before a fall,' he cautioned himself.

He brooded on Denton's claim that you could tell if you had

found a near-perfect fit with another man only by meeting in the wrestling ring. But surely Cato and he had passed that test with flying colours? Yet Sam's body seemed to ache for something more. Was it something rougher or more tender? Sam could not say. All he did know, as he stretched out on the sandy floor warmed by the halo of sunlight, was that he was certain that this crazy place, presided over by the benign tyrant Denton, had not yet revealed to him all its secrets and possibilities. He sat and hunched his knees to his chest, resolving to be open to all the experiences that were ahead of him and also to be more vigilant about the ones that he really wanted and needed most of all in his real life outside this temporary erotic Utopia.

Struggling with these difficult thoughts, Sam half-dreaded yet half-wanted his punishment hour to arrive. What would the punishment consist of and who would be the punishers? Would this be another fresh set of options he and his body would need to absorb and decide about? Sam allowed his hands to play over his rising and falling swimmer's chest which seemed to him, at this moment, to resemble the sea's own regular swelling and dipping motion. Absent-mindedly he gently teased both his large nipples into needle-sharp points and then, leaning forward, gave himself one of his favourite private pleasures. With the tip of his tongue he licked the lower foothills of hard pink flesh and then the peaks of his nipples, resting the rough underside of his tongue on each of them for long enough to feel his own sexiness surge through his stomach and spine and fill his lower body's most sensitive parts with a renewed and recharged sense of his sexual being. Three days on the island and already Sam felt that he was transformed, that he could give and take much that had been beyond him before his island stay.

'Robert.' The name rose spontaneously to his lips and sounded in the still and sunny afternoon like a promise.

He remembered what John had told him about Robert. Robert was the favourite of Denton and Arif. Robert was the most ingenious, original and virile young wrestler who had ever performed on this island in the last ten years. Robert was credited with being, in some way which Sam did not yet understand, the

most 'Roman' of all those men who had been enticed here to
play Denton's serious games. Sam did not usually believe in fate,
he was too much of a lakes man for such nonsense, but somehow
he had a feeling that when John had mentioned Robert to Sam
for the first time John was right to have a premonition that the
two men might have a special link. Maybe Robert would just be
the last stepping stone to the solution that Sam was looking for,
the right combination of sex and love, of lust and comradeship
which he felt a reawakened hunger for.

Although Sam still felt very much a novice as a wrestler he
was starting to realise that he was not a novice at sex any longer.
His island encounters had convinced him that he had a natural
talent for diving deep into the pools of Cupid, giving and taking
good quality satisfaction. He was not a star stud yet but he felt it
was not too immodest to think that he had at least gained
candidate status. As Sam curled his body on the warm red sand
he was sure, yet again, that there was still another level of
sensation and intimacy to be reached. There was another higher
wave for him and his body to ride. There was a squall of pleasure
gathering in distant oceans, gathering and rising and surging
towards him.

'Robert,' he said again as the inner wooden door burst open
and Sam found his thoughts shattered and his body roughly
assaulted.

It all happened so quickly that Sam did not realise, for a few
minutes, what was happening to him. At one moment he was
stretched out on the warm sand, safely alone with his hazy
speculations and his self-pleasing body. The next he found his
body wrenched up by two men in the outfits of trainers and
armed with leather rods. He felt himself lifted up from the
ground and carried to the room with the wooden beam where
his wrists were inserted into metal rings and his ankles tied with
leather thongs to metal rings in the floor which he had not seen
before.

Before he could focus on who his assailants were he was
blindfolded with a leather strap. Too late he tried to resist. Sam
found himself completely immobilised and discovered that all he

could do was to swing his body a little way backwards and forwards.

'Obey and don't resist, apprentice boy.'

The voice came out of the darkness like the lash of a whip. Sam had heard the voice before. He struggled to recall who it belonged to. Then it came to him in a flash; it was the shaven-headed master who had so violently interrupted Sam's forbidden session with Arif in the massage room. Sam was torn between trepidation and expectation. He remembered the man's fine torso with its well-defined, rounded chest muscles, and the thin line of black hair which led down to a stomach where every muscle could be seen tensing under the thin layer of taut dark flesh. He remembered too the man's handsome, if battered, oval face and the big shaved dome of his head. He felt the man's breath as he moved his face very close to Sam's ear.

'Apprentice, we have had enough disobedience from you. Do you understand?'

The voice rasped loudly in Sam's ear. 'Yes I do.'

'Do you?' The man was yelling now, the sound reverberating in Sam's ear like a drum roll.

'Yes.'

Sam felt the harsh stubble of the master's bony cheek brush against the dark blond down on his softer, fleshier face.

'I don't think you do yet. I don't think you know what obedience means.'

Sam said nothing. The air was full of the aroma of the sweat of unseen men and Sam knew something was about to happen to him but he couldn't imagine what it would be. He was aware that both men seemed to be positioning themselves on either side of him.

The silence seemed to last forever and then, finally, the shaven-headed master spoke again. 'Trainer, begin the punishment. I will take over when we get to stage two.'

Sam automatically clenched his arse tight. He could feel the deep ovals of the dimples in his backside forming under his leather flap.

'Begin.'

Sam heard a strange buzz in the air and then he felt the harsh rap of a leather rod full across his buttocks. A stinging sensation filled his entire rump.

'Ten more, trainer!' commanded the master.

Once again Sam heard the whoosh of the rod as it travelled from some height down in a great arc to his tingling arse. Leather smacked hard against leather and, despite the protective covering of his apprentice's leather back flap, Sam again felt the stinging impact of the blow on his buttocks.

Yet, as it was repeated again and again, Sam grasped at last that the sensations of pain he was undoubtedly feeling were now starting to give him a strange and unexpected feeling of pleasure too. The idea of his young arse being flayed, and of him being under the complete control of the unknown trainer and the shaven-headed master; the idea that these two virile wrestling men could do anything to their young apprentice boy gave Sam a sharp tingle of pleasure which ran up his spine and which met in a triangle of sensations in his loins. The blows seemed to create both zones of pain on his flesh and yet also each blow seemed to send a jolt of satisfaction to Sam's mind. He came quickly to see that he was getting a kind of emotional satisfaction from the concept of being so utterly in the power of another man so that he had no way of knowing or controlling what would happen to him next.

Every time the rod hit his still-clenched and dimpled buttocks, his front leather flap was thrown outwards and came back with a gentle slap against his cock. This quiet rhythmic contact, Sam became aware, was urging his prick back into life. Against his will he felt his member stiffen in response to the slapping contact of the leather flap over which he had no control. No control, Sam thought. That was the real reason he was finding such an odd maze of pleasure in the pain of his beating. In all his encounters so far on the island, and in his life, he had always kept some measure of control. Often he had been the one who set the agenda and he was, he guessed, starting to feel the enjoyment that came from not having to worry about what to do because everything was done to him. It was the unexpected joy of surrender and submission; of being as passive as putty.

Eventually, and almost too soon for Sam's fresh appetite for them, the ten lashes came to an end.

'Are you more ready to obey now?' yelled the shaven-headed master.

'Yes I am,' replied Sam in a penitent voice.

'I'm not convinced yet, are you trainer?'

'No,' came the reply. Sam at once knew the trainer's identity. It was John. And now that John was starting to sweat in his role as Sam's punisher, Sam could again smell the exciting, foxy scent of his body. So maybe the older-man option was the one that he should seriously consider. His rigid prick thrusting out far in front of his softly curving stomach clearly supported Sam's giving serious consideration to that option.

'Lift his back flap,' the master ordered. 'We will see if his famous arse is as sensitive to punishment as Arif's arsehole was to pleasure.'

Sam felt the master's face coming closer again to his. The other man rubbed his bony, stubbled cheek against Sam's tender flesh which instinctively flinched from such sudden roughness.

'You've just enough spare flesh there to take our blows, flesh on flesh,' he whispered. 'And for them to vibrate through you.'

Sam felt his cock stiffen at the very thought of their bare hands in punishing contact with his curvaceous bottom.

'The one-two method?' asked John.

'Yes. The best way to deal with someone as disobedient as him.'

Sam tensed himself up yet more and could feel the dimples on both of his buttocks deepen into hollows covered by the light down of his hair. There was a moment of absolute silence when Sam did not know what was going to happen to him. Then he sensed some movement and the left cheek of his arse received a mighty blow from the fully outstretched palm of John's hand. So harsh was the blow that it propelled Sam's body as far forward as it could go before the metal rings and the wooden bar across his chest held him in check. Before he could recover from this blow the shaven-headed master's hand smacked the right cheek of his arse.

Once more Sam felt his body being hurled forward by the

force of the blow. It was a few seconds before Sam became aware of the burning and stinging sensations that now radiated out from both cheeks of his rear. He was given no time to recover. Another blow from John struck him and it was quickly followed by another blow from the other master. Sam imagined what these two manly figures must look like with their solidly muscular arms rising and falling in tandem and their eyes focused on Sam's tender, seared buttocks. The two men were getting themselves into a rhythm and the spanking started to come faster and faster until to Sam it felt as if there was not even a split second's pause between his punisher's blows.

Yet the rhythm of their slapping started to affect Sam in a way he had not expected. Although he was feeling real stinging pain in his arse he also started to become aware that somewhere within him the very rhythms of the punishment, by making him feel so vulnerable to anything they wanted to do to him, was causing him to feel a warm glow. He was no longer having to do anything and could surrender to the subtle and, for most men, forbidden joys of total passivity. He felt himself falling through barriers of inhibition, falling deeper into a state where even the prospect of being violently raped by both his punishers seemed more and more desirable. He felt his buttocks relax so much that his rosebud was now peeping out at his masters, inviting them to take the final step. This new-found delight in passive submission intensified as Sam could feel the heat and smell the raw stench of their bodies as they pummelled his disobedient bum.

Sam felt as though he was rising higher and higher into a dreamy state of slavelike pleasure. The more blows that rained on his dimpled arse the more excited he became until his cock finally burst out round the side of his front flap and stood erect for both of his punishers to see and admire – and seize and also punish if they so wanted.

As if reading his mind, Sam suddenly became aware of the masters repositioning themselves on either side of him. The heavy weight of John's prick suddenly thwacked down on Sam's cockstem and, before Sam could recover from that, the shaven-headed master's dick whacked down on another part of Sam's rigid member. Sam almost came on the spot. Then, just before Sam could reach the climax of his pleasure, at what must have been a silent signal the blows stopped.

In the silence that followed all that could be heard was the heavy breathing of all three men. It was the unmistakable heavy breathing of excitement at what had happened and at what was about to happen next.

'Get him ready for me, trainer,' ordered the shaven-headed master.

Sam, who had relaxed his arse, allowing his dimples to fill out with his down-covered flesh, tensed his body up again. He could smell once more the acrid, foxy scent of John as he moved close behind Sam. If he knew anything now it was that he wanted John to use his dick as a punishing rod on his erect member at the first opportunity. It was a discovery Sam sensed he would quickly want to get addicted to and he knew intuitively that there were many more subtle variations in that act of cock beating that he could derive hours of delight from. That led Sam on to imagine John's boxy, hairy physique protected by his leather trainer's outfit standing behind his newly passive rear. He was certain John's cock was as stiff as his and he dreamt now of a beautifully rough act of violation by John. Surely this is what John had been wanting to do to Sam for months and now he had got Sam into wanting the same thing. Surely he would not let this golden chance slip from his hands and prick? John's hands did then fall on Sam's naked shoulders.

'Submit,' said John as he started to massage the muscles and flesh of Sam's broad upper back and shoulders. 'Relax, the worst is over and the best is yet to come.'

Sam was not at all sure that he wanted the worst to be over. It was the worst he wanted. But once again he found John's manipulating hands difficult to resist, especially as, to tease him now and again, John would brush his front flap against Sam's naked arse. Every time he did so, Sam could feel John's stiff, thick member throbbing and full-blown under the thin leather flap. Even the touch of the cock's leather-covered outline shook Sam to the core of his body; his stomach shook with longing to be violated. And Sam suspected that if John had been alone with him nothing could have stopped John from giving in to his desire to penetrate Sam's long silky tunnel with his thick and hungry phallus.

Sam was equally certain that, if they had been alone, John would have grabbed Sam's chest and nipples and used them as leverage and a hold for him as he lifted his shorter body up to Sam's reluctant rosebud to thrust his cockhead deep into Sam's furry slopes. But the presence of the shaven-headed master held him back. The rules of the games were for the first time acting against what Sam's body was crying out for, what it needed and deserved.

Sam could hear some whispered words of command pass between the masters. Through his blindfold he was aware of their bodies moving around him. He tensed himself up for what was going to happen to him next. He had no idea what was being planned and did not want to guess it. He kept his mind blank, ready to receive whatever he was going to be given. He was aware that both men seemed to have taken up kneeling positions. From the distinctive body smells he knew that John was in front of him and the other master behind. Then Sam was aware of his upper thighs being grabbed by John's firm hands and his front flap lifted high.

John used his grip on Sam's thighs to push Sam's entire body, especially his long erect prick, forward towards the oval of John's warm, hungry mouth. In the darkness Sam felt the heat of John's firm lips moments before he felt their actual touch.

It occurred to Sam that he had not been sucked off on the island as much as he would have liked. Now, it seemed that was going to be remedied by someone who, Sam guessed, was no amateur at giving that kind of pleasure to another man's prick, particularly if it belonged to the blond swimmer he had, for so long, wanted to possess in every way he could.

So it was with great expectation that Sam felt John's lips finally close softly around the flesh at the top of his penis and, with tiny motions, make their way towards the lip of the circumference of his cockhead which had burst forth at the very first hint that Jack's mouth would be taking his prick into its welcoming depths. This was not the anal violation that Sam had most hoped for but it was going to be a very acceptable second best.

John's lip, mouth and tongue skills were all that Sam had anticipated. His lips seemed to know exactly where to land on Sam with every part of his mouth's repertoire of pleasure. Sam felt as if his knob was now entirely encircled by Jack's eager luscious lips which had started with the most gentle motion imaginable to pull Sam's cock deeper into the cave of promise that John's entire mouth had become for him.

Sam did not thrust himself forward deeper into the other man's mouth. He just knew that such an action would be seen as another act of unforgivable disobedience. He knew that he had to allow the other men to do whatever they wanted to him and that he had to find new pleasures in his passiveness and defencelessness before them. He had to surrender his will and his body to theirs.

Anything else would have been taken as an act of rebellion not just against their present desires but against their whole world, here on the island, which Sam wanted, more than he had ever wanted anything else, to remain a part of.

With these thoughts dominant in his mind it was much easier for him to resist his natural inclination to make his cockhead glide around John's large and welcoming mouth and with every completed circle of that mouth to push his aching penis gradually further and further down into John's waiting throat. This was a technique which had always made his first lover, Paul, come within minutes. But Sam knew that every man had a different action which was closest of all to the mysterious trigger of the male orgasm.

So, relinquishing his own skills, Sam allowed John instead to slowly tug Sam's glans deeper into his mouth without Sam allowing his prick any movement of its own at all – except for the slight vibration it made as Sam's desire to rape John's throat had to be kept under tight control. Then John did something that was both unexpected and wonderful. In one motion he released his teeth so that they very slightly started to move as if they were biting into the base of Sam's cockstem whilst at the same instant John's long tongue started to patrol around Sam's cockhead.

Sam was aware of feeling at one moment the rough textures of John's under-tongue on this, the most sensitive part of his being, and then that was swiftly followed by the smoother textures of the top of John's tongue as it glided under the lower half of Sam's pounding cockhead. Against his will, Sam let out a small groan of pleasure. He hadn't wanted to do this. He knew it might anger his masters but when John started to use his teeth to pull Sam's cock deeper into his mouth, and when, at the same time, a great wave of the sexy, foxy stench of John's hairy torso rose up and filled Sam's nose with its chemical sting of lust, Sam could no longer hide his pleasure. Sam's groan inevitably prompted the master who had been strangely inactive behind him to speak.

'I think you are enjoying yourself too much, apprentice boy. I will have to see about that.'

As he spoke, the master swiftly placed the palms of his hands in each of the deep dimples in the sides of Sam's arse, dimples made ever deeper by the shocks of pleasure he was getting now from his prick's manipulation by John's mouth, teeth and tongue, all acting together on his gently vibrating manhood.

The next thing Sam knew was that the bony shell of the master's shaved head was forcing its way between his thighs where the covering of downy hair was now so soaked with sweat that it clung to the muscular surface of his flesh in tangled curls. Sam felt the shaved head's stubble harsh and prickly against the smooth pillars of his inner thighs and, shaking himself out of the daze of the passivity that had been subtly imposed on him, resisted out of sheer terror the prospect of being fucked by the vast dome of a shaved head.

Sam clenched his arse and his thighs in an act of what he knew was a dangerous defiance. But he felt he had to defend himself against this violent attack on him. He did not know where such a strange assault might lead. Then he felt the fingers of the master digging painfully hard into his clenched buttocks and dimples. Suddenly Sam found the pain taking over from pleasure and he felt the nails of the shaven-headed master piercing the tenderness of his flesh.

'Stop resisting and obey,' shouted the master from below Sam's body.

Sam did not reply and still fought hard against this assault. But it was no use, his resistance came too late to save him. Somehow the master beneath him knew exactly what points inside Sam's still-inexperienced arsehole to target, with all the concentrated force of his thumbs, in order to compel Sam's body, against his will, to part his thighs and to let the master's shaved head force an entry between them.

Sam felt real pain as his legs were forced very far apart and the shaved hair seemed to thrust into Sam's tender skin like he imagined a porcupine's needles might feel.

'Don't resist,' ordered the master in an even firmer voice than he had used before. 'This is not a full head fuck yet. This is just a rubbing job. A visiting job. It's lesson one for you . . . you lucky brat. You must learn to want what *we* want, not what *you* want,' he said. 'And then maybe you will be allowed to find out what you really want.'

While he spoke, the master, whose head was now firmly wedged between Sam's inner thighs, was rubbing hard against the thin ridge of flesh at the base of Sam's arse. He skilfully started to lift Sam's entire body up and, in doing this, he also tipped Sam's cock deeper into John's mouth. John responded, as if on cue, by letting the tiny slit at the very top of Sam's cockhead encounter his tongue for the first time which he now eased almost inside Sam's cock as his lips closed hard on it. Then, with a great sucking motion, Sam felt his entire member travelling down into the deepest depths of John's throat. Suddenly Sam felt his arsehole filled with the bony, stubbly surface of the other master's head and every part of his rosebud's surface, after the initial shock of pain of the needles of stubble, eased into shudders of enjoyment. The hardest and the most sensitive parts of a man's body met and, after an initial hurt and struggle, had found a rare pleasure in the contact.

As his mind struggled to take this in, Sam felt the master lowering his body and he thought for a foolish moment that this meant that the master was retiring to allow Sam to concentrate on John's irresistible cock sucking. For a few moments Sam was distracted by the delight he was getting from feeling how deep into John's long throat his cock was travelling. Deeper and deeper until, in Sam's mind, he imagined that his prick could go so deep that it would emerge from the bottom of John's throat so that when Sam came his spunk would splash against the inner walls of John's hairy chest.

But the shaven-headed master, Sam soon discovered, had not the slightest wish to stop giving Sam his full attention. Between Sam's thighs he was using his hands to again prise open Sam's clenched arse. Sam was really afraid about what the master's shaved head was planning to do down there now. But the master had obviously developed a very strong grip in his time on the island and even all the youthful strength Sam could summon to resist the assault was not enough to prevent him achieving his goal. Sam knew that after the first onslaught his resistance was understandably now weakened. To refuse pleasure was always a mistake. To resist undreamt of pleasure would be a sin.

Within moments Sam started to feel for the second time the heat of the shaven head approaching the exposed bud of his anus. Sam knew he had only seconds in which to try to summon up superhuman strength and deny the master access. Sam resisted with most of his will but it was to no avail. Sam knew once pleasure was planted in him he sought it out again.

The next thing Sam was aware of was the prickly stubble of the master's shaved head starting to press against the outer pink frontier of his rosebud again. Once more he experienced the sensation of his arse being apparently penetrated by the domed top of the shaved head. This time it felt to Sam as if he were being entered by a huge bone prick. And, because he was blindfolded and could not see what was being done to him, this seemed to make every sensation even more intense and vivid.

Against his will Sam's rear body arched back in a violent spasm of pleasure as he felt the full force of the master's violating head fill his entire arsehole with its steely curves and prickly surface. Once again, after the first spasms of pain, the entire crater of his anus seemed to be dancing with hundreds of tiny explosions of pleasure.

It was at this same moment that John, tugging with his lips

and tongue, finally pulled Sam's cock down deeper into another man's throat than Sam would ever have dared go before. Sam's mind exploded with white flashes of uncontrolled enjoyment under the impact of the joint climax of the double assault against him. All he knew was that at one particular second his entire arsehole was being fucked by the great dome of his shaven-headed master's skull and that his own cock was reaching down into unimaginable hot depths inside the welcoming tunnel of John's clenching and unclenching throat. Sam was so far gone in a daze of physical joy and release that he had no awareness even of coming or where he came.

All Sam knew was that after what seemed like an endless series of explosions of pure sensual bliss in his mind and body he felt himself clinging to the beam he had been chained to as if shipwrecked. Gradually, as his normal consciousness returned, he heard the sound of Jack and the shaven-headed master splashing water over themselves. Without warning, one of them tossed a bucket of ice-cold water over Sam. His body convulsed with shock but Sam knew better than to yell out. He could sense the shaven-headed master walking up to him.

'I think you are starting to learn to be a bit more obedient. But you still have a long way to go, apprentice boy. I hope we taught you one good lesson. Don't ever presume to think you know what your body really wants. What we really want and need most we often don't tell ourselves. That's one of the benefits of the Roman games. It speeds up the time it takes for a man to know what he really wants and how much he really wants. Not everyone wants to have so much pleasure in their lives. It can be too unsettling for some.'

With that the master delivered a blow to Sam's naked buttocks which resounded through the whole of Sam's body. Despite the stinging, he felt it was a blow that he would not have minded receiving just once more. There was the sound of a door slamming then Sam's blindfold was removed.

John gave him a snaggletoothed grin. 'I think that's the kind of punishment you won't swim away from too fast,' he said knowingly. 'Get dressed. You have been summoned to see the emperor. A rare honour. Make sure there's none of your disobedient dried spunk on you when you enter his presence. At least not today.'

Sam hadn't had time to absorb this latest wave of experience before he found himself being bundled out of the room he now associated with happy discoveries. He felt he was on a carousel which was starting to spin faster and faster. He had to find the inner strength not to fall off.

Dazed, and half-blinded by even the modest disc of sunlight in the room, he followed John out into the inner curving corridor and trotted after him around its permanently flame-lit walls and mysterious doors. Sam wondered whether the different colours they were painted had any meaning and whether he would soon know what it was.

As they moved swiftly along the corridors Sam could some-times get a passing glimpse through a few of the doors that were partly open. In one he caught sight of the delicately sensual Thai who had so gently moulded his body in the shower. Now the Thai was in a ring with another very much burlier and rougher redhead. Sam watched with surprise as the much smaller Thai effortlessly tripped the giant redhead over one leg and then, in a seamless gesture, threw the larger man to the floor and in a second had his brawny arm pressed high against the back of his neck.

As this tempting sight passed from view Sam could hear the redhead's hoarse voice yell, 'I submit. I submit.'

Sam wondered what rights that would now give the Thai over the giant figure sprawled in defeat on the canvas of the ring. The Thai was much younger than Sam – maybe just over twenty. Sam recalled the mixture of delicacy and strength the Thai had used to wash him down. The Thai might be the best opportunity that Sam would have for his third option, the younger man who he could teach and protect. But Sam realised that this would be a difficult role to play without seeming patronising or exploitative. And yet, as the scene he had just witnessed seemed to confirm, this particular younger man seemed endowed with the kind of self-confidence, pride and style which would make it much easier to play the role Sam was tempted by. Sam sensed that his own body and desires would take on a different meaning with such a man. Sam would have to learn how to use his body to guide without dominating. And, equally, he would have to learn how to avoid becoming intoxicated and enslaved by the deadly power of the other's extreme youth and arrogant beauty. Sam was driven on through the complex of many rooms within rooms, pleasures within pleasures.

Through yet another half-opened door Sam could see the stocky, very English blond, whose open-hearted appetite for a good time he had enjoyed the day before. That was another option thought Sam. Simple, robust, uncomplicated fucking. He was naked and was sitting on the shoulders of a slim young man whose leather flap had been lifted by the slightly curved pillar of his erection. The stocky blond seemed to be about to lean forward as if to reach down and, from that unlikely position, scoop up the young man's flared cock into his mouth. But before Sam could confirm his guess about what was about to happen he had to move on. He had to keep up with his trainer; after all he too was an option he had to keep available.

Finally, John halted before a double pair of massive wooden doors painted purple. They were flanked by statues of Roman youths with pouting expressions holding up laurel wreaths of victory out of which a circle of green-coloured flames danced. Denton's secret world had not been created cheaply, Sam thought.

John rapped on the door three times.

'Enter,' boomed a husky voice that Sam knew belonged to Arif.

Sam was amazed by what he saw as he passed through the double wooden gates. Sam found himself facing an exact replica of an oval Roman amphitheatre.

Five tiers of brick steps which, he guessed, functioned as seats, looked on to an oval area of red sand which was at least twenty metres wide. The whole interior was dotted with bronze braziers which Sam assumed lit the amphitheatre when it was used at night. The bare brick walls rose to a ceiling which was half-open to the sky. What held Sam's eye most was a marble sculpture, raised on a stone plinth, showing two life-size Roman wrestlers locked in battle with each other with one imitating, almost exactly, the victorious position which Sam had just seen the Thai take up over his defeated redhead. One of the wrestlers was carved in black marble, the other in white. For some reason Sam felt a prickly sensation in the nape of his neck as if the sculpted figures, so intensely bound up in one another, were offering him some kind of premonition. Sam shook himself and told himself to stop having such crazy thoughts.

It was only now that he was able to focus on Arif and Denton who was, as Sam had suspected, the emperor. Sam glanced nervously away from Denton to Arif. Arif exuded that blend of virile forcefulness and deeply ingrained, uninhibited sensuality which Sam thought of as being especially Eastern. Sam tried hard not to remember how wonderful the hidden rear of Arif's body was and how many sensations Sam had recklessly awakened in the gulleys and ridges of his arse. It was so deep and wide and he had been so arrogantly sure that the invitation it offered could not be resisted. For a few moments Sam wondered if he had been wrong to dismiss Arif from his options list. Maybe it was Arif who was his perfect partner. He had broken the rules for Sam and Sam had taken advantage and would do it all over again just to have given and taken so much.

Denton, like everyone else on the island, was wearing a Roman wrestling uniform. But unlike his minions' costumes, Denton's covered most of his body except for his midriff, thighs and arms. Even so, the leather uniform, which had obviously been stitched to fit the contours of his body, revealed that Denton really did have the proportions of a Roman athlete. His wide shoulders tapered to a narrow waist which then gave way to thighs whose bulging muscles gleamed under their coating of the brilliant blond hair. The entire uniform was decorated with wrestling scenes cut in metal and studded on to the leather surface.

Denton looked a man at the absolute peak of his physical powers. And Sam could not forget the first evening on the island when he had spied on their sexual games and had seen the enormous size and thrusting power of Denton's cock. Sam felt that he could certainly rule out Denton as an option. He was sure that he could never match the demands of such a man. Sam wondered what apprentices who were given the honour of submitting to Denton's manhood felt after he withdrew from them. Relief or sadness or both? Anyway Denton seemed to Sam to be in every sense too large and overpowering a figure to ever be a possible long-term sexual partner.

'Come here Sam.' Denton's voice was low in the way certain voices are which are so used to command that they almost never rise above a whisper.

Sam approached with some trepidation. If he was going to be told he had broken too many rules, especially in his forbidden sessions with Cato and Arif, he would be devastated. He desperately needed a little more time on the island to help him crystallise which of the erotic options open to him he should pursue when this island was no more than a distant memory.

He considered for the first time whether his seduction of the sensual Aladdin's cave of Arif's arse, which had been so unexpectedly intense for both men, had made Denton jealous. But Sam assumed this was not likely on this island where Denton ruled so many studs so completely. Sam opted for recklessness. He looked directly into Denton's piercing eyes which had a steady hypnotic violet-blue light inside them that Sam had not noticed before. It took all his strength not to allow his eyes to be defeated by the gaze of the emperor.

'You have broken our rules. The guest has abused his hosts,' said Denton in a cold flat voice.

Sam's heart thumped. He really did fear now that he was going to be banished from the island and from the last essential stages of the experiments he needed so desperately to complete. Could his life-long, swimmer's luck be deserting him? Sam nodded. Defiance was probably a mistake. Then Sam noticed just the slightest play of a smirk over the emperor's features.

'But Caesar forgives you.'

Arif flashed Sam a brief and secret smile, his teeth like a brilliant crescent moon against his dark coffee-coloured skin.

'In fact Sam, you have proved to be rather more of a success than we had anticipated. We had decided to recruit you because we didn't have many men with swimmer's physiques and, as you have realised, I like to have a variety of bodies and types attending my wrestling school. And, as you must know, you are in that very special point of transition between the last touches of youth and the first firming grasps of complete manhood. That makes your body a very desirable cocktail and maybe cock tease, too. No accusations though as yet. Anyway we have a custom here that if an apprentice shows that he has special talents with all or any part of a male body –' here Denton gave Arif a reproachful glance '– then we give him the chance to work with one of our star performers.'

Sam felt a lump of hope in his throat and he glanced over at the marble statues.

Denton caught his glance. 'Do you see an omen for you in those stone wrestlers?' he asked.

'I've been told that they were lovers as well as wrestling partners over two thousand years ago. Can you imagine being able to hold a position as full of possibilities as theirs for so long? Don't answer that question. I wouldn't want to encourage your vanity any more.'

Sam shrugged his shoulders defensively. He saw Arif take in his gesture with an appreciative smirk. So Arif at least remained interested in him.

Denton spoke again. 'We will show you how your star partner performs before you meet him in the flesh. But be careful about dreams of possessing anyone here. The men I have chosen are not the kind who enjoy possessiveness. Even the ones who take their deepest pleasure in being as roughly taken as you have not-yet been, still most of them don't want to be possessed. They want to be taken but not to feel owned, you understand? So be careful.'

Denton came down from his dais and walked slowly up to the apprentice. Sam often judged other men by the tang of the sweat they gave off but, as he had suspected, Denton defeated him here too. His body odour was unclassifiable: a mixture of hot steel and lavender. Dangerous to know too closely, however tempting the excitement of making love with such a charismatic figure might be. Denton came very close to Sam. He stood at least three inches above him and close up he was a much broader and statuesque figure than Sam had realised. Without an expression on his eerily Roman face, Denton ran two of his fingers down from Sam's eyebrows down the sides of his nose. He squeezed Sam's nostrils so tight Sam felt his eyes bulge. It was a bizarre unexpected contact. Then swiftly Denton withdrew his fingers leaving Sam feeling oddly assaulted and excited.

'There are more pleasures here than you have dreamed of in your agenda, Sam,' said Denton in his ice-cold, clipped voice. 'Remember, we are not all here for your use, however pretty-pretty you are or think you are.'

Denton gave Sam a nod of dismissal. Arif jumped down from the pedestal and joined Sam and Denton in the sandy ring.

'I will take you,' he said in his lilting Turkish voice.

Arif led Sam back out into the corridor slamming the great doors behind them.

Sam had to fight back his desire to nuzzle himself again inside Arif's rosebud where he had planted so many pleasures.

Arif slapped Sam on the back. 'Don't be too intimidated by Denton. He's been watching your action with me on video and I can tell you it made him very hot and a bit angry too.' Arif gestured at his rolling muscular rump. 'That's where a lot of his anger ended up. It was torture.' Arif roared with laughter and Sam grinned gratefully back at his kindly intended words.

Sam had to fight down the excitement he felt as the gentle nature revealed by his remarks mixed with Arif's musky odour. And the giant's whole consoling nature seeped into Sam again bringing with it precise memories of the contours of his body, his vast chest and that heavy prick with its especially thick and velvety layer of protective flesh. That too gave off a rich aromatic tang which Sam could taste in his memory.

'When is the amphitheatre used?' asked Sam hoping his semi-erection was not visible under his front flap.

Arif gave him a smouldering smile. 'When all the apprentices are ready for the great game,' he answered.

'And when will that be?'

Arif pushed a hand through his tumble of jet black curls. 'Maybe when you are ready,' he replied.

'Why me?'

'Because every year there is only one apprentice at most who has the potential to become another master here. Maybe you are that one? Or maybe there is another and stronger contender?' Arif lowered his voice. 'Remember, "ruler of the waves", it is in the wrestling ring that you'll find the most certain answer to the question I know you have been asking yourself.'

'Do you watch me on video too?' asked Sam brazenly.

Arif gave an ambiguous smile. 'Not enough.'

Arif gestured for Sam to be silent from now on and led him through a blue wooden door. It was a tiny cupboard of a room and Sam realised that in fact it was really just an observation box. Arif slid back a wooden flap in the brick wall and invited Sam to peer through. Sam instantly recognised the room they were overlooking. It was the one with the large wrestling ring, whose walls were lined from ceiling to floor by scarlet strips of cloth which rippled and rustled in the breezes which came from the hole in the roof. Leaning against the ropes of the ring was the Thai that Sam had just seen scoring a victory over the redheaded giant.

'That is Sen,' whispered Arif. 'He also has great potential.'

Sam was able to admire the compact steely beauty of the young man's body. As he flipped his body along the ropes in a series of vertical somersaults, Sam could see how agile he was and how, although apparently only lightly muscled, he seemed able to propel himself through the air as if his body weighed nothing at all. Sen's smooth, glistening and boyish slenderness, Sam suspected, was a kind of trap hiding the steely toughness and agile power he held tautly inside that apparently lightweight frame.

Sam caught his eyes. They were alive with light and energy. His face looked like that of a high-cheeked courtier from some vanished kingdom but Sam suspected that underneath all this brazen confidence was a much more vulnerable youth.

Arif seemed to read Sam's thoughts and encircled Sam's waist with his gentle arms. He let his large butterfly-shaped lips lightly kiss Sam's nipple, which hardened in response. Arif spoke to Sam in a low and lilting voice. 'Some men are still too lost in the mirror of their own youth and beauty to give any lover the attention he needs.'

'Do you think I'm like that?'

Arif replied by standing behind Sam and pulling him against the warmth and immensity of his body. Sam felt the pleasure of being enveloped by the other's man's tender power and protectiveness and let Arif caress the nape of his neck with his mouth and gently nibble on his ear with his glacier-white teeth. All the time Sam was aware of the other man's body growing and warming as he seemed to be pulling Sam into him.

As Arif offered up the temptation of his body again, Sam was also aware of movement in the wrestling ring. Sen performed a series of somersaults around the four sides of the ring and, as he spun himself along one side of the ring, Sam caught occasional glimpses of the soft curling shapes of Sen's hairless buttocks on which there was not one spare ounce of flesh. Sam marvelled at the youth's fearless agility which, Sam suspected, was not confined to the wrestling ring.

The whole surface of Sen's elegant flesh seemed to be waiting to be set alight by the touch of another. In his body the feminine and the masculine seemed to be blended together into a dazzling harmony of toughness and tenderness. Boy, youth, man, all seemed to be held in a delicate balance in the frame of the young Thai wrestler. Just as Arif, by virtue of his age, size and experience, exerted a special control and fascination over Sam, Sam could imagine him creating the same guiding relationship with Sen.

'Watch the ring,' whispered Arif.

Sen had stopped moving and his eyes focused with an almost animal alertness on where some of the scarlet banners seemed to billow out like sails, almost threatening him.

Arif laid his hand on Sam's shoulder giving Sam a small electric convulsion. Even in the man's arms he could feel the sensual charge he contained inside his giant frame.

'Soon the moment you, perhaps, have been waiting for,' whispered Arif.

Sam sensed something too and fixed his eyes alertly on the billowing red cloth opposite their spy hole. Then, without warning, one of the banners was snatched back and there, emerging as if out of nowhere, stood a figure Sam would never have been able to conjure up even after months here, even in his most satisfying fantasies.

The man who now stood exactly opposite the concealed pair had the kind of body Sam associated more with Greek gods than Roman wrestlers. A large stern head, of perfectly proportioned features, topped a torso so flawless in every muscle shape and tone that it surpassed even the physiques of the finest athletes Sam had seen. He could have been one of Denton's statues except for the fine lines of black hair which seemed only to underline the sculpted nature of his body. He did not, it seemed to Sam, lost in a haze of admiration, move towards the wrestling ring so much as bound towards it in a few arcs of virile grace.

Closer up the man's extraordinary beauty became transformed into a more sexy reality by tiny details that Sam was now able to pick out, such as the small island of black hair in the centre of his chest, the dimple in his chin, the slight kink in the fine profile of his nose. Sam was captivated too by the way the muscles in his body seemed to suddenly emerge when needed and then fade back into the apparently soft and yielding flesh. But what was most important for Sam was that this compelling figure seemed not to correspond to the types of men that Sam had been considering as his options. This man who was now climbing into the wrestling ring was a type unique to himself. Sam had not seen in magazines or the movies, and much less in life, anyone who could rival him. Sam literally could not take his eyes off him.

Arif obviously sensed Sam's instant and total attraction to the new wrestler.

'So you like our black star?' he asked, lightly licking Sam's neck.

'I've never seen anyone like him. Never.' Sam felt Arif's hand slip under his back leather flap and caress the furry slopes of his arse.

'For me your swimmer's golden buns are even sexier,' declared Arif gently but firmly starting to explore all parts of that region of Sam's body.

Sam did not object. Yet even that hot contact could not distract him much from his concentrated gaze into the room below them. 'What's his name?' asked Sam.

'Robert,' replied Arif. 'But he is soon to be honoured with an island name; a Roman name which Denton only gives to very specially talented young men.'

'What will his new name be?'

'Marcus,' responded Arif, gently kissing Sam on his cheek. 'I think he has already marked you.'

Sam could not tear his eyes away from the ring.

Robert was circling Sen who, although looking very boyish next to the athletic sturdiness of Robert, yet had all the advantage of his speed. In a flash of flesh Sen had whipped behind Robert and had now got him in a firm arm lock. Sen's clenched hands were pressing down hard on the nape of Robert's neck.

Then, to Sam's surprise, the acrobatic Sen was being lifted in the air and somersaulted over Robert's head. He landed with a loud thud on the floor of the ring and, before he could recover, Robert was on top of him lifting one of his arms high behind his back.

Arif was now circling Sam's arsehole with the tip of his large tongue. 'You feel very furry today,' he said.

Normally Sam would have responded immediately to Arif's tender approach but Sam simply could not take his eyes off Robert.

As Robert was forcing Sen's body to the floor of the ring, Sam took in the pads of muscle on the huge shoulder blades, glistening now under the arc lamp with ribbons of his sweat. Sam looked at Robert's thighs, their athletic bulk seeming to gleam in the arc lights. Sam also absorbed the deep ravine of Robert's spine, revealing on either side of it an expanse of shimmering rich-black flesh.

Sen, by some adroit ploy, slipped from out of Robert's grasp and was now on top of Robert gripping him in an arm lock that forced the other man down towards the canvas ring and defeat. But once again Robert showed his qualities as a wrestler. He wrapped one of his muscular thighs around Sen's more slender one and flipped him off his back. Sen had barely hit the ring before he bounced upright. But Robert had anticipated his move. He flung himself at Sen and the two men leant their bodies towards one another, their arms gripped in a titanic struggle. Although they were wrestling, Sam imagined that making love to either of the two men would also involve almost identical moves, grips and postures.

As they fought, Sam caught glimpses of Robert's cock which, even in its resting position, Sam could see was generously large and, it seemed to Sam, would be generous in what it could give too.

Sam caught more glimpses of Robert's arse as the two wrestlers struggled. Seen closer its steely sculptured hardness was softened by a thin fuzz of black hair and a certain inviting fleshiness near to Robert's arsehole which, Sam imagined, would certainly be as rewarding as Arif's.

Arif, for his part, was very excited by Sam's arousal. He had stopped tipping up Sam's anus with his tongue and had now resumed his earlier position pressing his large body behind Sam's. He lifted up Sam's back flap and pressed his already large, although only half-grown, prick into the deep crevice between Sam's buttocks. Sam felt the warmth of the rippled flesh of Arif's cock squeezing deeper into the crevice that divided Sam's buttocks. It was a touch that Sam found doubly exciting as he watched Sen and Robert's tussle with each other.

Sam could feel his cock rising and not just because of Arif's growing pressure to penetrate him. Robert now achieved victory by arm wrestling Sen to the ground and defeat and, as Robert forced Sen's shoulders to the canvas ring, Sam could see the hidden muscles in Robert's shoulders suddenly emerge from the apparent softness of his flesh. This confirmation of muscularity hidden under a layer of sensual silky flesh was part of what drew him so compulsively towards Robert.

The two wrestlers stood upright and Sen slapped Robert's outstretched palm in a gesture indicating that there were no hard feelings between the two of them.

'Now it's your turn,' announced Arif with a grin. Arif bent his head down and surrounding Sam's large nipple with the flesh of his lips sucked it deep into his mouth. Then he let Sam free.

'My turn?' Sam could not believe his luck.

'Yes. Your turn. We planned this match after your great performance especially with me and then Cato. We think you deserve it.'

Sam felt butterflies in his stomach. He glanced back into the room where Robert was splashing water over the casual perfection of his body. He was gripped with anxiety about what Robert would feel about him when he saw him.

Sam was instantly conscious of what he saw as his body flaws. His chest, although admired by others and certainly powerful, was not as big as he wanted it to be. One of his nipples was larger than the other and his stomach and buttocks were maybe just a bit too curvaceous. He wasn't an Adonis. These anxieties gripped him as Arif opened a hidden door that led into the red-bannered room. As Sam went to leave the room Arif held him back by his arm.

'But there is one thing I have to tell you. Robert has taken a vow of celibacy for three years so that he can concentrate entirely on his skills as a wrestler. If you make him break that rule you and he will have to leave this island forever. Do you understand?'

Sam had to work hard to stop the groan of disappointment from leaving his mouth. He nodded curtly at Arif and stepped out into the room. Just as Robert had done, Sam had to throw back one of the red banners to get into the room and that, Sam knew, made for a dramatic entrance. He pulled himself to his full height and walked as confidently as he could towards the ring and Robert.

He feared his own shape might seem too soft and adolescent for someone whose muscles were so flawlessly sculptured but he saw Robert carefully but casually assessing him as he came closer. He started to think that Robert was not so disappointed in the physique and bearing of his new wrestling partner and, as Sam got nearer, he focused his vivid blue eyes on Robert's, not allowing any of his self-doubts to flicker there. He was more aware than he felt safe to be of Robert's own eyes. There was something so tender and seductive about them. For a few moments Sam could not work out why, then he realised it was that they were pale grey and seemed to glisten as if all the power of his flawless body were concentrated into them.

With deliberate, agile speed, Sam climbed over the ropes into the ring and saw Robert appraising his upper and then his lower body. Sam became acutely aware that Robert was one of those rare men who become more, not less, attractive the closer you get to them. There were so many features of the other man that Sam wanted to immediately caress. He had firm high cheek bones which framed an aquiline nose, slightly askew, and two straight ridges which led down to lips that seemed to wear a permanent and fascinating broken smile. Underneath that smile was a dimpled chin – marine, square and virile. But what impressed itself on Sam, now that he was this close, was how Robert's body seemed to combine a classical well-defined physique with a sleek and graceful mobility. Sam felt it was as if one of Denton's most idealised statues had been given a panther's sheen of black flesh. The combination was overwhelming.

When Robert stepped forward and grasped Sam's hand in his own and let his cool grey eyes play over Sam's more ordinary pools of blue, Sam could feel the immediate and irresistible charge between them. Indeed Sam had to work hard to hide the convulsion his body felt. Sam could see in the way Robert's eyes became, for an instant, hooded from him and his broad shoulders seemed to rock a little that Robert was starting to share at least some of Sam's attraction to his wrestling partner.

'They don't like us to waste any time,' said Robert quickly, bending his fine torso towards Sam's and holding his clenched hands up before him in the approved first position of their Roman wrestling game.

As Sam bent into the same position a few feet away from Robert his ears were still buzzing with the sound of Robert's voice. It was deep but warm and seemed, in these first moments of their meeting, to further confirm Sam's certainty that, of all the men he had met on the island and before, it was Robert who was the one most likely to offer him the best option of all; the one he had never expected.

Sam's entire body was tensed in a way it had rarely been before. He wanted very badly to impress on Robert that he too had skills in the ring, or at least could put up a good fight even if he was to be defeated. He remembered the island's hypothesis that it was in the ring that you knew how good your partner would be in the sack.

Sam could barely disguise the yearning he felt to make contact with Robert's awe-inspiring physique and the panther sheen and suppleness of his flesh. And he thought he could read almost the same level of desire for Sam in Robert's grey eyes. Robert's gaze travelled quickly over the swimmer's pouting stomach and deep navel, bisected and cut off from his sight by the tight leather apprentice's belt.

Sam did not even see Robert's first move. All he knew was that at one moment Robert was crouching before him, and the next, Robert's head was leaning on Sam's shoulder and his hands were bending Sam's arms up behind his back towards his neck.

Sam could sense every well-defined muscle on Robert's straining torso pressed against his softer muscles. Only Sam's chest, which was as broad and as granite-hard as Robert's, and only Sam's large nipples, now instantly erect, could outmatch and smother Robert's own hard peaks now pressed deeply into Sam's. Sam tingled with delight as he felt the raw peaks of Robert's nipples piercing into his. In a blur of images Sam immediately guessed what it would be like to have Robert's prick throbbing into his nipples where so much of Sam's sex pleasure was concentrated.

Every part of Robert's body seemed, when touched, to give off a subtle vibration of sex knowledge and skills. When Sam grabbed his upper arm and felt the velvety warmth of his flesh, it was as if Sam was instantly travelling to all parts of the other man. Almost everywhere there was a possible site of pleasure waiting for Sam. Sam felt certain that in deeper contact with Robert there would be none of the usual physical or emotional boundaries at all. Indeed, Sam had a sense that Robert, in that first wild leap, had himself had an abrupt intuition that they were destined to be very strong meat for one another. For that very reason he had held back his lower body and his prick from touching Sam even through the protective leather flaps.

Sam hoped that Robert had guessed, as he hurled himself

against the young swimmer, that he was launching himself into a new realm of erotic exploration and intensity. He was leaping into the fire of a bonding he had never anticipated or experienced before. The sweat poured down Robert's neck as he struggled to lift Sam's imprisoned hands higher and higher up his neck. Robert's distinct body scent wafted to Sam's nostrils and Sam noted that he always associated his sex partners with the distinctive odours of their bodies and their body's sweat.

But Sam could find no words for Robert's subtle aroma. It was how he imagined black roses might smell. Sam knew he was instantly addicted to it. Even his cock, distracted by what he needed to do to break free of Robert's wrestling hold, started to stiffen quickly as the sweat carrying that arresting odour started to trickle over Sam's chest, curling around his nipples and stinging them with it's invasive saltiness.

It took Sam all his willpower to resist being overwhelmed immediately by this single feature of Robert's. He knew that he had to fight back. He knew that he had to show that Robert and he were destined to be equals in the wrestling ring as they were destined to be in the secret, naked tussling Sam had already planned for them in the woods under that night's full moon.

Sam, shaking himself free of his first wave of intoxication with Robert, managed to place one of his long legs between the other man's smooth but steely thighs and, by willing all his strength into that one leg, Sam was able to trip Robert backwards. Robert tried to hold his grip behind Sam's back and pull Sam down on top of him but Sam prevented this by twisting Robert's wrists violently to one side just before they hit the floor. Sam had broken free for just long enough to slide himself under his opponent. Now it was Sam who had Robert in a lock. He could feel the other man's heart. It was beating with a strangely serene rhythm suggesting to Sam that maybe Robert was playing with him, allowing him a few token victories in order to save his face. That suggested a generosity which further attracted Sam to him.

Sam's mouth had become buried by chance against the nape of Robert's neck, at just that point where his hair ended in a precise V shape. Sam knew he should not, and that it was against all the rules, but he could not resist placing the warmth of his mouth there. Then, pulling a little of Robert's neck into his mouth, he used his teeth to leave a mark on just a tiny fragment of that flesh which Sam already knew he needed more of and quickly. Robert's neck gave a sudden jerk away from Sam but he did not betray Sam.

Sam guessed that Robert was both shocked and intrigued by Sam's unexpected addition to their wrestling routine, and, although Robert redoubled his efforts to escape from Sam's grip, Sam suspected that he had broken Robert's normally pure concentration on his wrestling technique by his dramatic daring and by the strange intensity that their first physical contact had aroused in each of them. Robert could not break free and Sam, to his own surprise, found that he was able to pin Robert's shoulder for long enough to the canvas floor for the other man to be forced to spill out the words, 'I submit.'

Sam and Robert stood up in the silence of the room, a silence broken only by the rustle of the scarlet banners on the wall.

Robert looked at Sam with new respect. 'You took me by surprise. I thought you would be easy. They told me you were more of a swimmer than a wrestler.'

'I didn't play by the rules,' responded Sam.

'The important thing,' said Robert without a smile, 'is to know when to obey the rules and when to break them. We have to shower now. That's a rule we can't break.'

Robert leapt from the ring and was immediately swallowed up by the swirling red banners on the walls. For a second Sam was thrown into a panic. Did Robert exist? Then he saw the still-wet sweat stains on the ring and bent down to smell them. His own salty sweetness mixed with the sweat he now could only think of as black rose. As he climbed out of the ring he glanced up at Arif's secret spy hole. Sam knew he was too excited to follow Robert directly into the showers. He would be too tempted to lunge at him. He had to find some other more immediate and less dangerous relief. He glanced up again at the peep hole.

Barely a few moments later Sam had positioned himself so that

Arif could obtain maximum thrust as his adoring prick parted the flesh of Sam's buttocks and plunged deeply into the young swimmer repaying him for all the joy he had brought to Arif the day before.

Seven

Robert wondered why the hauntingly attractive young swimmer hadn't followed him to the shower room. Yet Robert was glad. It gave him a chance to think about the bizarre intensity of the feelings the swimmer had caused to flare up within him.

Robert was used to feeling the sharp pangs of desire and, in his time, he had had many lovers. Indeed he had carefully chosen his lovers so that by the time he had reached his twenty-ninth year he had been intimate with as many types of men as possible. His lovers included boxers, magicians, army officers, painters, bricklayers and actors. He had wanted to taste as much of mankind as possible. He had had many physical and emotional types: twosomes, threesomes, even intense onesomes. Sex in water. Sex with pain. Sex in the street. Sex in the forest. Sex on a trapeze. Even sex in bed. And Robert knew that he had had many high-quality encounters. But he was the one who was in control. Always. And his obvious physical beauty had always meant that it was he who set the rules and enforced them.

It was he who always made the break with his lovers, usually after he had given them the kind of lovemaking which made his parting even more traumatic for them, even though he had always honestly told them that being his lover could never be forever or a full-time role. But Sam was already unsettling him

189

in ways he had never experienced before. He had been told to expect a sexy young swimmer who was becoming the island's unexpected sex bomb. That was the gossip in the apprentices' and trainers' showers.

Robert had heard it all before and had seen many sexy and handsome men dressed in the exciting livery of the games come and go. There was a new arrival this year named Peter, who Robert had found very exciting. Indeed, until this encounter with Sam, Robert had decided he was the one new apprentice he was going to see after he left the island. Against the rules of course. Then came this Sam, and he was already changing everything in Robert's mind and body.

After Robert had defeated Sen, his excellent if much younger wrestling rival, Robert had expected an average Joe to march into the wrestling arena. A hunk – but an average kind of hunk, the kind Robert wrestled with every day and could have had every day if he'd wanted. He had not been prepared for what happened next.

He should have been warned by a strange tension he felt as he surveyed the billowing scarlet banners, wondering which of the hidden entrances Sam would use. It was not like him to feel such a knot in his stomach. Automatically he started to caress his stomach's furry surface while his eyes patrolled the rising and falling motion of the banners.

If Sam came from one direction it meant that he had been giving an hour of pleasure to his trainer. If he came from another it meant that he had been mud wrestling. If he came from another it meant that he had been with Arif watching from Arif's secret observation place. When they came from that direction Robert felt the most excitement. Perhaps it was the memory of what he had done to Arif in there two days ago, whilst Arif watched Denton open up to the charms of Peter, who undoubtedly had the largest cock even this island had ever seen.

Now, as Robert turned on the hot cascades of water, he struggled to figure out why Sam had made such an almost scary impact on him. Robert had seen many more conventionally handsome apprentices. The swimmer had a good physique but it was far from flawless. Sam's neck was a bit too long and his stomach, although firm, pouted out a little too much and his buttocks had just a little too much flesh on them. His face was charming with its fine mouth and those vivid dancing blue eyes. And his nipples were big, with one higher than the other.

Robert looked down at his own lathered, flawless athlete's body and smiled. In a flash he saw that it was precisely Sam's 'flaws', which he was so busy listing in his mind's eye, that were part of what were making him invoke again and again the images of the seminaked body of the swimmer apprentice.

By the time Sam entered the shower room, Robert knew he had to avoid looking at Sam's body as he stripped down. It was the face that Robert wanted to glance at. In the ring Sam's face had been just a golden blur but now, as Robert turned on a shower tap for him, he was able to look at Sam more closely. His face was a perfect oval with brilliant cornflower-blue eyes that just faintly turned upwards. Robert thought that those eyes, together with the tiny hint of a pointedness in Sam's ears, gave his whole face the appearance of a dangerous faun. That impression was increased a hundred times by the hesitant, shy grin Sam flashed at Robert. Robert felt his heart thud and it was not the only part of his anatomy that felt a surge of desire. He discreetly turned away from Sam so that he would not see his excitement. He soaped himself with his eyes closed and tried to drive out the images of Sam so that his body would cool down.

Robert recalled, with a wry grin, that he had one month of chastity to go. If he gave way to the kind of desire Sam had ignited in him he would risk losing the wrestling prize. Only total concentration guaranteed victory as Denton always said. Already, today in the ring, he had lost concentration when Sam had given him that love bite. That was definitely against the rules. Yet now the rules Robert had lived by seemed endangered by this swimmer, this dangerous faun.

He could no longer resist the temptation to gaze again at Sam's nakedness. When he opened his eyes, Sam had his back to Robert. This allowed Robert welcome time to explore those parts of the other man which had been hidden from him until now.

His head's dark gold mass of curling hair led down to a long neck and then to the broad shoulders and the broad upper back, the muscles of which were clearly quickly growing in size and strength. The whole mass of his back seemed both strong and delicate, full of willpower but also boyishly supple. His spine was a deep ravine lined with two frontiers of dark blond hair. His back tapered sharply to his thin waist. His body hair then expanded a little to form a triangle at the base of his spine which led down to the more fleshy curves of his buttocks framed by two faint dimples in his cheeks. After all the promise contained in those dimples came the thighs, stern and hard, firmly shaped like most swimmers, with particularly well-sculpted calves. But more than any physical feature was the way Sam's entire body seemed to be suffused with a chemical sexiness that was both intense and playful. He gave off for Robert all the phallic power and teasing sensuality of a faun. Denton had often described the power of fauns to Robert.

Sam slowly turned towards the wrestler he had just unexpectedly defeated. Robert sensed that Sam was as reluctant as he was to confront their tempting nakedness. His head was modestly turned away so that Robert had a few seconds in which he could drink in again the promise of Sam's chest broadened and hardened by years of pushing back the cold waters of the lakes and the more fleshy stomach leading down, by a trail of dark gold hair, to Sam's prick which looked as strong and agile and eager as the rest of him.

Then Sam looked up, straight into Robert's grey eyes. Robert could not resist returning the full force of the other's gaze. For a moment Robert felt that he was almost sailing through the blue sky of Sam's eyes. It was an instant when his whole body seemed to have departed from him and flown into the dangerous intimacies of the world Sam's eyes were offering. Robert had to force himself to pull back from the younger man's magnetic blue eyes.

Then he noticed again the slight, almost imperceptible slant of Sam's eyes and the way his lips, hovering between a scowl and a grin, seemed to be inviting Robert's mouth close to his. Robert paused, taking in the dimples which now appeared in Sam's

tanned gold cheeks and which were echoes of the dimples
Robert had just intently observed on Sam's beautiful backside.
They were the same. Robert could feel their bodies moving
closer. It was as if neither of them were moving of their
own accord but were being moved by some invisible puppet
master closer and closer together, against their own instinct for
safety.

Sam's eyes were now swimming inside Robert's owl-grey eyes
which had seduced so many other men, without a word being
spoken.

Robert could no longer obey his mind's commands. He
suddenly felt the dam of desire, which he had held back in the
wrestling ring, burst and surge through his body. He felt his
nipples swell up and his cock start to unfold itself to its full
proud, conquering extent. Robert saw Sam's curled prick start
to unwind from the golden nest of his pubic hairs and begin its
journey up and out towards him.

The warm water cascaded over both men as if uniting them
under one waterfall. But at that moment, when it seemed their
magnetic bonding had to drive them together into their first
purely sexual embrace, Robert pulled back. He was confused by
the rawness of his lust; he had never felt such an uncontrollable
pull towards another man before. To Sam's obvious surprise
Robert put his hands on Sam's shoulders and gently pressed him
away.

'It wouldn't be fair to you the day before the final wrestling
competition to waste your strength.'

'It wouldn't be a waste,' replied Sam, his voice choked with
longing.

Robert grinned sadly and spoke consolingly. 'Let's just wish
each other well in the final games tomorrow.'

Turning to one side, so that his erect cock did not even brush
against Sam's tempting body, shaking as it was with frustrated
desire for him, Robert placed the dark oval of his Roman lips
against Sam's puckered, brooding mouth. With his tongue he
prised Sam's blocking teeth apart. Robert had never entered a
mouth so sweet and hungry for him before. Sam's tongue lay
waiting and Robert held back for a few precious seconds and

then tenderly slipped his own tongue under Sam's. Then the tip of his tongue slowly explored the rough surface of Sam's curled up tongue. It seemed as if Sam was trying to punish Robert by pulling his tongue back from the touch he longed for so Robert closed his eyes and imagined, as his tongue traced the subtle ridges there, that his tongue was in another deeper place inside Sam's imploring body. Robert could feel that Sam understood what Robert's tongue was doing in their imaginations, to that other sacred place inside Sam's body. His tongue went deeper into Sam's mouth. Then, in a motion which had thrilled and surprised so many of his past lovers, he slid his sinuous tongue around the base of Sam's tongue and binding tongues together rode them both into the innermost depths of Sam's throat. Robert could not stop himself relishing the shock of pleasure he saw in Sam's vivid blue eyes and even more in Sam's buttocks. They gave a violent clench and the luscious dimples trembled with what Robert had just done to Sam.

Part of Robert wanted Sam to know that, however much he could exert his pull on Robert, it was Robert who could still call the hottest shots between them. Sam had thrown aside his restraint and now, in his excitement, he reached desperately out for Robert's hard prick but Robert seized Sam's hand and held it an inch above his pulsing member. Sam struggled to bring Robert's cock alongside his own but Robert didn't yield. Then Sam struggled to hold Robert's tongue in his mouth. But Robert could not be forced. Robert withdrew his tongue and parted with one last chaste kiss on Sam's mouth. Still Sam resisted their separation. Sam, startled, then tried to push his tongue back into Robert's mouth but the shape of Robert's lips made them perfect Roman sentries and they barred entry to Sam's tongue. Perplexed, Sam withdrew.

By way of consolation, Robert put his hands firmly around Sam's neck and pulled the other man's head and mouth to his. With all his power Robert crushed his mouth against Sam's. As they separated, the brutality of that embrace was softened by the simultaneous embrace of their eyes. For a few sweet moments Robert soared again into the endless blue promise of Sam's eyes. Then Robert finally pushed Sam from him.

'Where on earth did you come from?' He threw the question over his shoulder as he swiftly left the room.

Racing back to his room Robert kept asking himself: What is happening to me today of all days? He half-suspected Denton of having plotted their meeting to tempt Robert away from tomorrow's final test of his wrestling skills and the emperor had nearly succeeded.

Sam stood forlorn, his wet body at a loss under the silent shower heads. He had been so sure that Robert and he were just starting a great adventure when he was gone. And if he had wanted to break from Sam why had he given him a glimpse of his sexual powers before he vanished? One thing Sam was certain of was that even in their brief and interrupted encounter Sam knew that Robert was the one Sam wanted to spend his last night on the island with. And yet it seemed as if Robert was going to deny him that night. Sam's mind was filled with all the positions, the roles, the caresses, they could act out together.

'Fuck the wrestling!' Sam shouted with rage and smashed his fist against the wall tiles.

It was then that Sam was aware of another man in the echoing shower room.

Sen was wearing the standard uniform of the apprentices. A thin leather belt around his narrow waist and leather flaps hiding what Sam knew to be the firm and compact contours of his bum. Excitingly, Sen's unexpectedly large prick was half-aroused. Tonight Sen looked different to Sam.

Sam had never met any men from Thailand before though he had heard that they combined a highly formal society with a free and open sensuality. He had always assumed they would be rather passive although this was not how Sen looked tonight. The steely compactness of his body gave off the aura of a real stud. There was not an ounce of needless flesh on Sen's body and he had the pared down look of a winning jockey.

But besides that Sen reminded Sam of his own younger self; the man he had been five years ago. Sen seemed to be lit from within by his natural innocence, charm and confidence, the confidence that came with beauty in its first virile flush.

'Robert obeys the rules of the Roman games,' said Sen giving Sam a flash of his military-style black eyes. Sen thrust his loins covered in the leather flaps towards Sam who was rubbing his body down with a towel.

Sam had always imagined that if he ever met someone like Sen, so sleek and beautiful that he, Sam, would call the macho shots. But Sam was starting to realise that pleasure had a life of its own. Sam could feel the steely strength of the discreetly but powerfully muscled young man blocking his exit from the shower room.

'I will lead you to where Robert is although he does not know he is waiting and needing you,' declared Sen in a sudden burst of speech. His voice was much deeper than Sam had remembered.

Sam wanted to hear what Sen had said more than he had wanted to hear anything in his life. In a blazing moment of spontaneous gratitude Sam spoke to Sen. 'You don't know what that means to me. Is there something I can do for you?'

Sen's agile, muscled hand traced the square features on Sam's face and then Sen, in an almost prayer-like motion, put his two hands together and started to undo the clumsy knot Sam had made in his towel below his navel.

'Yes Sam,' said Sen in a hushed, confident tone. 'I am going to prepare you for Robert. I am the essential link between you and Robert. Now get back into the shower room and do exactly what I demand of you. I will begin the Robert initiation ceremony.'

Sam, pleased that Sen had reversed the roles he had at first imagined for them and so made their games more unpredictably exciting, walked back into the empty shower cubicle. Sen seemed to transmit his own confident optimism to Sam and Sam felt all his doubts disappear. He was going to see Robert again tonight and, despite everything, Sam knew that the two of them would discover in each other more than they had known or dreamed of before, wrestling final or not. 'Tonight will be ours,' Sam whispered to himself.

Sam decided that he would do whatever Sen asked of him and, as Sen started to unbuckle his leather belt, Sam studied him.

It began to occur to him what so many of the men he had met so far on the island had in common. Whatever their age, regional or race differences they could all have been Roman statues. Whether solid and earthy types like Jack, or delicate and steely like Sen, they all had Roman features. Sen himself could have been an adolescent Roman boy with the almost feminine curves of his arse, naked now before Sam, and his pouting lips and teasing eyes.

Sen had dropped his apprentice leather flaps to the marble floor and Sam watched with a grin of admiration as Sen's cock rose freely from the silky delicacy of his flesh. Sam was shaken as the younger man's prick grew bigger and bigger, longer and longer. Sam had not expected such a nimble body to have such a massive and heavy cock. Yet he had noticed before that it was often men who had the most adolescent and lithe bodies who arrived in bed armed with the biggest pricks of all. Sen advanced towards Sam. He could feel his own cock responding to the approach of Sen's monster. Sen traced a finger around Sam's moist lips then put a finger inside Sam's mouth and swirled it round Sam's tongue.

'You wanted me to be your toy boy didn't you?' declared Sen with a smile. 'But you are going to be mine. On your knees,' he ordered, 'I want to fuck your mouth.'

Sam did not need any more encouragement than that. He fell on his knees, the marble floor pressing cold against his kneecaps.

'This will get you in the right mood for Robert,' whispered Sen as he grabbed Sam by his ears and positioned his mouth close to Sen's now fully exposed prick. 'I will control you now,' said Sen as, using Sam's ears like rudders he guided his head and mouth towards his eager member.

Sam could see Sen's penis approaching his mouth. The glans was vivid red and the slit seemed like a dark slash in the middle of its domed surface. Sam imagined how sweet the juice that would soon pour through that hole would taste. Even if he was denied the right to drink it Sam hoped that he would at least be able to feel it splashing over his face or body. But that was for later. For now Sam was only aware of the sheer heat of Sen's cock as it made its first contact with Sam's lips. Although Sen was still holding firmly on to Sam's ears he was agile enough to precisely control the position and movement of his penis which he now directed from his deceptively boyish loins.

First Sam felt Sen's glans tracing the shape of his lips, slowly allowing the smooth head to glide over the oval of Sam's mouth. Sen repeated this movement until he knew Sam was eager to take the silky dome inside his mouth. But Sam held back. Glancing up, Sam could see how much Sen was enjoying the touch of Sam's mouth on his cock and wanted to delay moving beyond that first delicate contact for a few more moments. Sen then took his prick and whipped it back and forth across the emerging stubble on Sam's upper lip causing Sen's entire body to shudder at that meeting of prick flesh and golden bristles.

'Is the hair in your arse as spiky?' asked Sen.

'Yes,' replied Sam. 'More.'

Sen nodded and grinned at the delights to come. He spoke again to Sam. 'Cradle my arse with your hands and slowly start to rock my cock into your mouth. I will decide how much of me enters and fucks your mouth.'

Sam liked the precise and formal way Sen had set out what he intended to do and how he planned to use Sam to fulfil his desires. Sam did as he was told. All his plans about training up this Thai youth had been blown to the winds. He placed his hands around the boyish-shaped but solidly muscular slopes of Sen's arse. Sen's buttocks clenched at Sam's touch and Sam used the broad spread of his hands to cradle Sen's bottom and to ease it backwards and forwards.

Sen started to beat his cockhead against Sam's closed lips. The rocking motion Sam had created had converted Sen's entire cock into a battering ram smashing again and again against the fleshy barrier of Sam's denying lips. Finally, Sam carefully allowed Sen's penis to prise them open. He knew exactly what Sen needed next. Opening his teeth just enough to let the tip of his tongue slip through, Sam touched the slit in Sen's glans. At that first touch, Sen's whole body trembled and Sam could feel the effect of his tongue whip through Sen's entire body, even his arse cradled in Sam's hands gave a slight judder of pleasure.

Sam closed his eyes and imagined that his tongue was trying

to prise apart the crack in Sen's anus. Imagining forcing his way inside that furry valley made Sam's cock spring straight up so that he knew it was now pointing directly towards Sen's arse. Sam was tempted to use his hands to force the youthful rump down towards his cock but what held him back was the sheer enjoyment he was now getting from probing his tongue into the slit in Sen's penis which became combined in Sam's mind with Sen's arse crack.

Sam had so stimulated Sen with his tongue that Sen's prick had pushed through Sam's half-clenched teeth into his mouth. Sam gratefully opened his mouth until it was filled with the smooth sensitive flesh of Sen's large member. It seemed to be rubbing simultaneously against Sam's now passive tongue and the bony roof of his mouth. His mouth had never felt so completely filled by another man and it was only then that Sam realised, as Sen began to pull Sam's head close to his compact body, that Sen had just begun.

'Now I am going to really fuck your mouth,' announced Sen.

With a deep sigh he took control of Sam's head and forced it towards his triumphant cock. Sam wanted the deepest recesses of his throat to be filled with Sen's hard young prick and felt his mouth filling with the flesh of Sen's cockstem. He could feel the steel-hard structure beneath the smooth skin. It was like the barrel of a revolver covered in silk.

Before his mouth was completely filled, Sam was able to gasp a few words.

'Yes, I want you to fuck my mouth as hard as you want. Go on, fuck it. I am your slave swimmer now.'

Sam's words achieved their desired effect and Sen abandoned Sam's ears and grabbed his neck, forcing his entire head hard on to Sen's hungry cock.

Sam felt the dome of Sen's glans sliding deeper down his throat followed by the gun barrel of Sen's cockstem. His throat felt so wonderfully full of Sen's commanding prick. To further increase the physical delight he was taking in the young man's invading dick, Sam started to help Sen's journey into him by sucking with all his might, pulling the angry red dome and the thick trunk behind it deeper and deeper into him. Sam was also using his grip on Sen's smooth buttocks to rock his body so that his cock moved back and forth inside Sam's mouth and throat which were now swimming with the lubrication of his enjoyment.

Sam loved the way he could make Sen's cock enter and withdraw from him. And with each return Sam made sure that Sen's cock went just that extra bit deeper into his throat. The rhythm of this wet withdrawal and returning grew faster and faster as Sen's desire to fuck Sam's mouth and Sam's desire for his mouth to be fucked merged together in a frenzy of pleasure.

Sen now began to use the well-defined muscles and the supple flesh of his upper thighs to rub hard against Sam's sensitive nipples until Sam had the sensation that his hard peaks were almost penetrating Sen's slim inner thighs. Sam had daringly started to caress Sen's hidden rosebud with one finger and Sen quickly allowed Sam's exploring finger to circle the moistening entrance to his arse. After only a few moments of resistance he allowed Sam's long finger to enter into him. Sam made his finger echo the movements of Sen's cock in his mouth so that everything that Sen's penis did in Sam's throat, Sam copied exactly inside Sen's compact arse. This was almost too much for both men.

As the tip of Sen's cockhead touched the very last frontier of Sam's throat, Sam felt his own prick surge with his semen and he was certain he could feel Sen's cockstem swell out even more and heat up. Gorged with Sen's penis, Sam could sense Sen's semen starting to course through his thickened and thrilling prick.

Sen must have reached the same high plateau of satisfaction because, with a wild cry, he withdrew his entire cock and pointing it at Sam's broad chest and nipples started to pour out his spunk over them. The hot white lava cascaded over Sam. Instantaneously Sam's own cock shot its load high up over Sen's body and the violent spasms of Sam's complete physical relief hit Sen's chest and nipples.

For a while the two men held their positions without moving. Sam suspected that neither of them had expected their encounter to have given them such a high of mutual satisfaction. Sam struggled to his feet and pressed his grateful body against Sen's. The warm spunk of both men now met and merged on their sweat-soaked bodies. Sam was only then aware that his finger was still plunged deep inside Sen.

He withdrew his finger with infinite care slowly rotating it as he did so. Sen let out a small groan of delight.

Sam rested his mouth on Sen's neck. He could taste the sweetness of the other man's skin and they lay for a while with their cocks pressed against one another, drenched in their mixed spunk.

'Why didn't you give my mouth and throat what they wanted?' asked Sam.

Sen sighed. 'I wanted to. But there are some things which you are destined to do only with one other man.'

Sam kissed Sen's ear. 'You mean Robert?'

Sen sighed. 'He is very lucky. If you had not seen him tonight I might have really fucked your mouth and . . .'

'Where will I find him?' asked Sam.

Sen broke away. 'There must be no more delays for you two,' declared Sen generously. 'I will show you where to find him. It is a secret place. It's where you can make your own rules.'

Sen led Sam through the woods down to the shore. He pointed to a distant speck on the grey surface of the lake.

'Fall Island. That's where he is.' Sen gave him a lingering kiss and held Sam's face between his hands. He gazed for a moment into Sam's pure blue eyes. 'You won't need me again after tonight,' said Sen his face flushed with a youthful melancholy.

'Don't bank on it,' yelled Sam as he plunged into the icy waters of the lake. He felt at once that he was swimming not just towards an island but towards his destiny.

The sun was starting to set as Sam put his first wet foot on the red earth of the shore. He heard the sound of water cascading and he followed the sound. As he made his way through the woods, shivering, he started to warm himself up by thinking of the men he had most enjoyed in the last few days. Images of Arif, Jack, John, Cato, Sen and even the brief encounter with the stocky blond spun through his mind. He remembered how they looked; what they had done to him and he to them; the distinctive aromas of their bodies; how their faces had looked at the moment of climax. He had enjoyed them all and wanted them again. But Robert was in a different league for him. Robert was the real surprise, the Joker in the pack. In his many fantasies in his lakeside cottage he had never anticipated anyone like Robert. The Roman features, the black flesh, the super-athlete's body, the grey eyes and above all that eerie mixture of coldness and tenderness. All those things and so much more that lay beyond the level of words and thoughts pulled Sam violently towards Robert. Sam's greatest anxiety now, as he approached the falling water, was that Robert would feel their sudden sense of belonging to one another was too strong and strange to be surrendered to. Hadn't that been the message of his withdrawal from Sam in the shower? And then there were the wrestling finals. Robert was so determined to win, would he really give up his rest the crucial night before? Sam pressed on through the tangled undergrowth more determined than ever that nothing would stand between him and Robert, not even Robert himself.

Then, straight ahead of him the woods gave way to an unexpected sight: an artificial grotto over the front of which poured a man-made waterfall. It formed a curtain of moving water which was now blood-coloured in the light of the setting sun. This was Sam's sexiest time and always had been. He slowly traced his hand over the waking islands of both his nipples and then let his other hand fall over his furry stomach down to the outer surface of his underpants. Gently he pushed the palm of his hand against the bulge of his dormant prick. At the first pressure from his palm he could feel his manhood start to rise.

It was at that moment, when he thought he was on the edge of great pleasure and happiness in his life, that he saw a sight which made his blood run cold. To one side of the grotto stood Robert wearing a white T-shirt and swimming trunks. He looked even better than Sam remembered. But he was not alone. A strikingly handsome man in his late twenties, wearing only tight white jeans, was moving towards Robert.

Sam froze. He felt as if he had been hit in the stomach and his heart thumped with misery. The young man before him had a well-defined chest and a brooding dark face which now wore a lopsided smile which made Sam wince. The striking young man advanced towards Robert and, putting his arms around Robert's neck, pulled him down to his waiting lips. They kissed long and hard.

Sam felt his world crash about him. Anger, disappointment and jealousy all combined to force tears into his eyes and he was about to turn and flee the island when he saw the young man break from Robert and walk away. He waved back at him before disappearing down some steps. Robert turned away and sat on a fallen tree trunk in front of the waterfall. He took up a wild flower and looked at it for a long time. Then he kissed it and tossed it melancholically into the waterfall.

Sam decided he had nothing to lose now by revealing both himself and his desires. It was all or nothing. He prayed that his luck would not desert him. Before he entered the clearing Sam tore some ivy from a tree and wound it into a crown which he put round his head. With that he stepped out into the sunlight.

Robert tensed up and, for a moment, his grey eyes and clenched fists flashed a warning at the intruder. Then he saw who it was and abandoned his desire to leap at him, pantherlike, and bring him to earth. Instead, Robert gave Sam the very faintest glimmer of a welcoming smile. Sam guessed he was also uneasy and although he tried to resist, Sam could tell that Robert's grey eyes were clearly eager to revisit all the features of Sam's body. Sam watched Robert's eyes travelling slowly down the lean and sculptured shape of his long legs. Even Sam's toes smeared with wet earth were the object of Robert's reluctant and yet devouring scrutiny.

Robert spoke. His voice was gravelly and low. 'Fauns aren't allowed on this island,' he warned. 'Especially swimming ones. Especially you.'

'Why especially me?'

Robert shook his large head reproachfully. 'You know why. Too much.'

Sam moved cautiously closer to his accuser. 'Can too much ever be bad?'

Robert leant back revealing the generous half-circles of his torso under his T-shirt. Sam noticed that his nipples were still inverted, denying Sam.

Sam spoke again. 'How can you think too much is bad? I just saw you with that cute guy. You have a man on every island?'

Robert said nothing but stood up and walked to the edge of the steps where the young man had disappeared. Robert gestured with his head for Sam to join him. Sam did just that. Looking over Robert's shoulder Sam saw the steps that led down to a tiny version of the amphitheatre on the big island. Approaching each other Sam saw the young man and Jack. Both were wearing only the leather wrestling flaps and belts. They circled each other with an electric intensity Sam could feel even at this distance. Abruptly the young man lunged at Jack and instantly both men were grappling with each other. Then, out of the blue, this classic wrestling grip slowly transformed itself into something quite different. Their clenched hands relaxed and, instead of struggling to use their arms to keep their bodies apart, their arms and hands seemed to be drawing them closer. Their lips met very slowly as if they had been waiting for a long time for this moment of intimacy. Sam's view was suddenly blocked by Robert who blindfolded Sam with his hand. He turned Sam around and they walked back to the tree trunk. Robert sat on it again and looked up at Sam who was now baffled.

'That was Peter. Jack's lost love. I brought them together today. So you see I'm not the sex machine you think I am or want me to be. Tomorrow is the final test. I have taken a vow of celibacy. I can't break it.'

A voice inside Sam told him that the right thing to do, if he really cared for Robert at this point, would be to swim from this island. There would be other nights and other opportunities and, if the worst came to the worst, other men. But that was not the voice Sam listened to.

Imitating Sen, Sam broke into a series of cartwheels which he executed in a semicircle in front of a startled Robert. He returned to a position just a few feet away. The curtain of spilling water behind Robert was now turning a vivid scarlet in the light of the setting sun and memories of Sam's cottage, and the pleasures he had prepared himself for, flooded back to him. He took this as a sign that he was right to press on.

Sam could see by Robert's troubled face that he too was torn between his obsession to become the champion of the Roman games tomorrow and his potent but repressed desire to make love with Sam. Sam found the wrinkled evidence on his noble forehead, that he found this dilemma provoking, almost the sexiest thing he had ever seen. Sam felt that the way their eyes avoided one another's was more provocative than any amount of direct gazing could be.

The whole of the island around them seemed to be sharing in this tense, momentous pause between them. The birds had fallen quiet. The leaves seemed to be rustling in slow motion. Even the waterfall behind Robert seemed at this moment to be frozen, resembling the red banners out of which Robert had first emerged into Sam's life. All that broke this tension was the sound of Peter's pleasure from the amphitheatre beneath. Sam hoped that those sounds of ecstasy would be the final argument for Robert to choose Sam and only Sam.

Without a word Robert bent towards Sam. He lifted Sam's foot towards his mouth and, with the tip of his tongue, Robert started to lick the red earth off his toes. Then he took Sam's big toe into his mouth and started to circle it with his tongue. Sam only gradually started to lift his toe inside Robert's mouth and he knew that neither of them could say exactly when it was that Sam's toe became Sam's cock. Sam could barely remember how or when it was that Robert used the commanding pillar of his prick to push down the elastic band around Sam's underpants. The moments he did remember afterwards were when Robert, recovering Sam's crown of ivy from the grass, placed it around the quivering rigidity of Sam's cock just before Sam felt his entire member travelling as if on a roller coaster down the curves and depths of Robert's apparently endlessly spacious and attentive throat.

Under the blood-coloured cascade of the waterfall at sunset, Sam used his tongue to tug Robert's T-shirt free from his bathing trunks and then, pulling the T-shirt with his teeth, had revealed the nipples that crowned the peak of Robert's mountainous pecs. When Sam first reached there, Robert's left nipple was still half-inverted. Sam encircled the nipple and the wider area of muscle around it and, with gradually increasing pressure, sucked it into his mouth. When finally he felt the nipple rise up he closed his mouth on the emerging peak and sucked it as hard as if it had been the glory of Robert's own cockhead. Soon the nipple was as hard as an arrow's head between Sam's seductive lips as the last site of resistance to his lovemaking was conquered.

In the middle of the waterfall Robert showed him an immensely powerful spout of water. A Denton touch for sure. Sam didn't know exactly how it worked, but, in a haze of delight, both their bodies rode on these spouts of water in such a way that their arses opened gladly. In quick, rhythmic succession, first Sam's prick rode through the many ridges and valleys into the very centre of Robert's body and then Sam would suddenly feel the jets of water parting his own buttocks to make them ready for the mighty and not entirely painless pillar of Robert's conquering prick. Sam was lifted up higher physically by Robert and, more memorably, sexually as he was brought to new peaks through being so roughly taken by his real master.

Sometimes it seemed to Sam that his entire arse was chock full of Robert's demanding, possessive dick that night. Sam recalled that, at times, under that constant, roaring cascade of blood-red water, he had felt as if Robert's penis had expanded to fill the entire hungry cave of Sam's anus. And Sam relished every moment of Robert's prick's pumping and caressing motions inside him. At one point Sam felt Robert's inspired lovemaking was so violent that the great column of his prick would burst from his arse through his navel. There was one glorious second Sam was later to remember when he thought Robert's cock was thrusting so hard up into him that he would be both fucking Sam and demanding a blow job from him in the depths of his throat.

There were so many climaxes and they did so much to each other that it was only days later that Sam realised that, at some point in that mad sunset and even wilder night, Jack and Peter had also been involved in Robert and Sam's pleasure. Sam could recall a moment when Jack, Sam and Robert had fulfilled a fantasy for the youngest man, Peter. All three of their cocks had entered his youthful, carelessly inviting hairiness in one combined motion and Sam shuddered at the memory of how the different flavours of their three sets of spunk mingled inside his delighted arse. After that they did something even more unexpected and wonderful to each other. It involved a delicate ballet of pricks caressing the chest and nipples and then the entry of tongues and cockheads into the hottest, most needy rosebuds. But so intense had been that round of pleasure that Sam's mind could not recover it.

As Sam had feared sun broke too soon on the happy ruins of their ecstasy. Sam found the body of a perfect Roman athlete wrapped with an infinitely tender protectiveness around his shoulders and waist. As his eyes adjusted to the light Sam could see that the waterfall was splashing on Jack and Peter who, despite being fast asleep, had their mouths pressed against one another's.

Sam slipped from Robert's curled sentry guard position round him and faced the rising sun. They had been true at least to the real spirit of the Roman games. They had let the pleasure their manly bodies gave and took be their only gods.

They travelled back to Skate in silence. Their arms were around each other, on the small motorboat Jack used to ferry them. They arrived back on the main island just as they could see the last of the daytime staff, in their boats, fading into the distance. The island seemed to be waiting for their arrival. They could see no one. At Jack's suggestion they made their way towards the wrestling school building.

Unusually, Cato was not at his post. The wooden entrance door was open and unguarded and they made their way around the curved brick corridor towards the main amphitheatre. They arrived at the large wooden doors flanked by the statues with their ivy crowns of green flames. Bonded now, as they would be forever, Robert and Sam glanced at each other and with a nod pushed open the doors.

Sam gasped at the spectacle that greeted him. The entire amphitheatre was filled by men in meagre leather flaps and belts. Sam was aware of a great variety of physical types, colourings and races but he was delighted to realise that what they all had in common were Roman features. If you took away the colour of their skin, their body hair, their obvious talent for sex, they could all have been Roman statues. Sam glimpsed Sen and his sturdy blond, and was Paul there too? Sam did not dare look in that direction again. Denton stood in the centre of the amphitheatre and gestured for them to join him.

As they moved defiantly towards him, arm in arm, like true comrades, a giant video screen started to descend from the ceiling. Sam stared at it with a look of obvious curiosity.

Denton flashed a smile at him. 'Yes, Sam. On this screen we are all about to see what you and Robert, Jack and Peter did last night. It will inspire the wrestling that will soon take place here. When we have finished watching you champions, we will let the real Roman games begin. But only with your permission. That is an absolute rule here and one which even our golden swimmers aren't allowed to break.'

Sam put his arm around Robert's proud neck and nodded assent. He did not feel anything except pride and joy in what they had given to one another last night under the approving pagan brilliance of the full moon. Sam had found the one he had always been looking for but would never have guessed at and, indeed, would never have met but for this crazy island. Sam, now that his body was so full of Robert and Robert so full of him, had the confidence to feel that it could only be an honour to share his new life and love with so many handsome, sexy and loving comrades and brothers, united through the Roman games.

IDOL NEW BOOKS

Also published:

THE KING'S MEN
Christian Fall

Ned Medcombe, spoilt son of an Oxfordshire landowner, has always remembered his first love: the beautiful, golden-haired Lewis. But seventeenth-century England forbids such a love and Ned is content to indulge his domineering passions with the willing members of the local community, including the submissive parish cleric. Until the Civil War changes his world, and he is forced to pursue his desires as a soldier in Cromwell's army – while his long-lost lover fights as one of the King's men.

ISBN 0 352 33207 7

THE VELVET WEB
Christopher Summerisle

The year is 1889. Daniel McGaw arrives at Calverdale, a centre of academic excellence buried deep in the English countryside. But this is like no other college. As Daniel explores, he discovers secret passages in the grounds and forbidden texts in the library. The young male students, isolated from the outside world, share a darkly bizarre brotherhood based on the most extreme forms of erotic expression. It isn't long before Daniel is initiated into the rites that bind together the youths of Calverdale in a web of desire.

ISBN 0 352 33208 5

CHAINS OF DECEIT
Paul C. Alexander

Journalist Nathan Dexter's life is turned around when he meets a young student called Scott – someone who offers him the relationship for which he's been searching. Then Nathan's best friend goes missing, and Nathan uncovers evidence that he has become the victim of a slavery ring which is rumoured to be operating out of London's leather scene. To rescue their friend and expose the perverted slave trade, Nathan and Scott must go undercover, risking detection and betrayal at every turn.

ISBN 0 352 33206 9

DARK RIDER
Jack Gordon

While the rulers of a remote Scottish island play bizarre games of sexual dominance with the Argentinian Angelo, his friend Robert – consumed with jealous longing for his coffee-skinned companion – assuages his desires with the willing locals.

ISBN 0 352 33243 3

CONQUISTADOR
Jeff Hunter

It is the dying days of the Aztec empire. Axaten and Quetzel are members of the Stable, servants of the Sun Prince chosen for their bravery and beauty. But it is not just an honour and a duty to join this society, it is also the ultimate sexual achievement. Until the arrival of Juan, a young Spanish conquistador, sets the men of the Stable on an adventure of bondage, lust and deception.

ISBN 0 352 33244 1

TO SERVE TWO MASTERS
Gordon Neale

In the isolated land of Ilyria men are bought and sold as slaves. Rock, brought up to expect to be treated as mere 'livestock', yearns to be sold to the beautiful youth Dorian. But Dorian's brother is as cruel as he is handsome, and if Rock is bought by one brother he will be owned by both.

ISBN 0 352 33245 X

CUSTOMS OF THE COUNTRY
Rupert Thomas

James Cardell has left school and is looking forward to going to Oxford. That summer of 1924, however, he will spend with his cousins in a tiny village in rural Kent. There he finds he can pursue his love of painting – and begin to explore his obsession with the male physique.

ISBN 0 352 33246 8

DOCTOR REYNARD'S EXPERIMENT
Robert Black

A dark world of secret brothels, dungeons and sexual cabarets exists behind the respectable facade of Victorian London. The degenerate Lord Spearman introduces Dr Richard Reynard, dashing bachelor, to this hidden world. And Walter Starling, the doctor's new footman, finds himself torn between affection for his master and the attractions of London's underworld.

ISBN 0 352 33252 2

CODE OF SUBMISSION
Paul C. Alexander

Having uncovered and defeated a slave ring operating in London's leather scene, journalist Nathan Dexter had hoped to enjoy a peaceful life with his boyfriend Scott. But when it becomes clear that the perverted slave trade has started again, Nathan has no choice but to travel across Europe and America in his bid to stop it.

ISBN 0 352 33272 7

SLAVES OF TARNE
Gordon Neale

Pascal willingly follows the mysterious and alluring Casper to Tarne, a community of men enslaved to men. Tarne is everything that Pascal has ever fantasised about, but he begins to sense a sinister aspect to Casper's magnetism. Pascal has to choose between the pleasures of submission and acting to save the people he loves.

ISBN 0 352 33273 5

ROUGH WITH THE SMOOTH
Dominic Arrow

Amid the crime, violence and unemployment of North London, the young men who attend Jonathan Carey's drop-in centre have few choices. One of the young men, Stewart, finds himself torn between the increasingly intimate horseplay of his fellows and the perverse allure of the criminal underworld. Can Jonathan save Stewart from the bullies on the streets and behind bars?

ISBN 0 352 33292 1

CONVICT CHAINS
Philip Markham

Peter Warren, printer's apprentice in the London of the 1830s, discovers his sexuality and taste for submission at the hands of Richard Barkworth. Thus begins a downward spiral of degradation, of which transportation to the Australian colonies is only the beginning.

ISBN 0 352 33300 6

SHAME
Raydon Pelham

On holiday in West Hollywood, Briton Martyn Townsend meets and falls in love with the daredevil Scott. When Scott is murdered, Martyn's hunt for the truth and for the mysterious Peter, Scott's ex-lover, leads him to the clubs of London and Ibiza.

ISBN 0 352 33302 2

HMS SUBMISSION
Jack Gordon

Under the command of Josiah Rock, a man of cruel passions, HMS *Impregnable* sails to the colonies. Christopher, Viscount Fitzgibbons is a reluctant officer; Mick Savage part of the wretched cargo. They are on a voyage to a shared destiny.

ISBN 0 352 33301 4

THE FINAL RESTRAINT
Paul C. Alexander
January 1999

The trilogy that began with *Chains of Deceit* and continued in *Code of Submission* concludes in this powerfully erotic novel. The evil Adrian Delancey has finally outwitted journalist Nathan Dexter in his deathly game of cat-and-mouse – destroying Nathan's relationship with student Scott in the bargain. From the dungeons and saunas of London to the deepest jungles of South America, Nathan Dexter is forced to play the ultimate chess game, with people as sexual pawns.

ISBN 0 352 33303 0

HARD TIME
Robert Black
February 1999

HMP Cairncrow prison is a corrupt and cruel institution, run by sadistic officers and bullying hard-cases. It's also a sexual minefield – the old-timers prey on the newcomers and the guards prey on everybody. Three new inmates must find their niche in this brutish environment – as sexual victims or lovers, predators or protectors. This is the story of how they find love, sex and redemption behind prison walls.

ISBN 0 352 33304 9

ROMAN GAMES
Tasker Dean
February 1999

When Sam visits the island of Skate, he is taught how to submit to other men; acting out an elaborate fantasy in which young men become wrestling slaves – just as in ancient Rome.

ISBN 0 352 33322 7

WE NEED YOUR HELP . . .
to plan the future of Idol books –

Yours are the only opinions that matter. Idol is a new and exciting venture: the first British series of books devoted to homoerotic fiction for men.

We're going to do our best to provide the sexiest, best-written books you can buy. And we'd like you to help in these early stages. Tell us what you want to read. There's a freepost address for your filled-in questionnaires, so you won't even need to buy a stamp.

THE IDOL QUESTIONNAIRE

SECTION ONE: ABOUT YOU

1.1   Sex (*we presume you are male, but just in case*)
    Are you?
        Male   ☐
        Female   ☐

1.2   Age
        under 21   ☐   21–30   ☐
        31–40   ☐   41–50   ☐
        51–60   ☐   over 60   ☐

1.3   At what age did you leave full-time education?
        still in education   ☐   16 or younger   ☐
        17–19   ☐   20 or older   ☐

1.4   Occupation _____

1.5   Annual household income _____

1.6   We are perfectly happy for you to remain anonymous; but if you would
      like us to send you a free booklist of Idol books, please insert your name
      and address

      _____

      _____

      _____

      _____

SECTION TWO: ABOUT BUYING IDOL BOOKS

2.1   Where did you get this copy of *Roman Games*?
      Bought at chain book shop   ☐
      Bought at independent book shop   ☐
      Bought at supermarket   ☐
      Bought at book exchange or used book shop   ☐
      I borrowed it/found it   ☐
      My partner bought it   ☐

2.2   How did you find out about Idol books?
      I saw them in a shop   ☐
      I saw them advertised in a magazine   ☐
      I read about them in _____
      Other _____

2.3   Please tick the following statements you agree with:
      I would be less embarrassed about buying Idol
      books if the cover pictures were less explicit   ☐
      I think that in general the pictures on Idol
      books are about right   ☐
      I think Idol cover pictures should be as
      explicit as possible   ☐

2.4   Would you read an Idol book in a public place – on a train for instance?
      Yes   ☐   No   ☐

SECTION THREE: ABOUT THIS IDOL BOOK

3.1   Do you think the sex content in this book is:
      Too much   ☐   About right   ☐
      Not enough   ☐

3.2 Do you think the writing style in this book is:
       Too unreal/escapist   ☐   About right   ☐
       Too down to earth   ☐

3.3 Do you think the story in this book is:
       Too complicated   ☐   About right   ☐
       Too boring/simple   ☐

3.4 Do you think the cover of this book is:
       Too explicit   ☐   About right   ☐
       Not explicit enough   ☐
Here's a space for any other comments:

SECTION FOUR: ABOUT OTHER IDOL BOOKS

4.1 How many Idol books have you read?

4.2 If more than one, which one did you prefer?

       _____

4.3 Why?

SECTION FIVE: ABOUT YOUR IDEAL EROTIC NOVEL

We want to publish the books you want to read – so this is your chance to tell
us exactly what your ideal erotic novel would be like.

5.1 Using a scale of 1 to 5 (1 = no interest at all, 5 = your ideal), please rate
       the following possible settings for an erotic novel:
                Roman / Ancient World   ☐
                Medieval / barbarian / sword 'n' sorcery   ☐
                Renaissance / Elizabethan / Restoration   ☐
                Victorian / Edwardian   ☐
                1920s & 1930s   ☐
                Present day   ☐
                Future / Science Fiction   ☐

5.2 Using the same scale of 1 to 5, please rate the following themes you may find in an erotic novel:

Bondage / fetishism ☐
Romantic love ☐
SM / corporal punishment ☐
Bisexuality ☐
Group sex ☐
Watersports ☐
Rent / sex for money ☐

5.3 Using the same scale of 1 to 5, please rate the following styles in which an erotic novel could be written:

Gritty realism, down to earth ☐
Set in real life but ignoring its more unpleasant aspects ☐
Escapist fantasy, but just about believable ☐
Complete escapism, totally unrealistic ☐

5.4 In a book that features power differentials or sexual initiation, would you prefer the writing to be from the viewpoint of the dominant / experienced or submissive / inexperienced characters:

Dominant / Experienced ☐
Submissive / Inexperienced ☐
Both ☐

5.5 We'd like to include characters close to your ideal lover. What characteristics would your ideal lover have? Tick as many as you want:

Dominant	☐	Caring	☐
Slim	☐	Rugged	☐
Extroverted	☐	Romantic	☐
Bisexual	☐	Old	☐
Working Class	☐	Intellectual	☐
Introverted	☐	Professional	☐
Submissive	☐	Pervy	☐
Cruel	☐	Ordinary	☐
Young	☐	Muscular	☐
Naïve	☐		

Anything else? _____

5.6 Is there one particular setting or subject matter that your ideal erotic novel would contain:

_____

5.7 As you'll have seen, we include safe-sex guidelines in every book. However, while our policy is always to show safe sex in stories with contemporary settings, we don't insist on safe-sex practices in stories with historical settings because it would be anachronistic. What, if anything, would you change about this policy?

_____

_____

SECTION SIX: LAST WORDS

6.1 What do you like best about Idol books?

_____

6.2 What do you most dislike about Idol books?

_____

6.3 In what way, if any, would you like to change Idol covers?

_____

6.4 Here's a space for any other comments:

_____

_____

_____

_____

Thanks for completing this questionnaire. Now either tear it out, or photocopy it, then put it in an envelope and send it to:

Idol
FREEPOST
London
W10 5BR

You don't need a stamp if you're in the UK, but you'll need one if you're posting from overseas.